Picnic in Venice

Konnie Ellis

Rocket Science Press

SHIPWRECKT BOOKS PUBLISHING COMPANY

IN®
DIE

Minnesota

Cover art and interior design by
Shipwreckt Books

take your heart
and toss it into the sea of life
let it join the eternal unity of this universe

from SEA by Abbas Khajeaian

Picnic in Venice

Contents

Part One   1

  Adamant   1

Part Two   5

  1. Insomnia   5

  2. The Pope of Tomatoes   11

  3. Venice   19

  4. Giovanni's Studio   25

  5. The Fortune Teller   33

  6. At the Inn   47

  7. Giovanni the Baptist   53

  8. Marble Dust   57

  9. Orazio's Mural   63

  10. Mario's Pipe   87

  11. Friends and Enemies   109

  12. Lint   117

  13. Livia   121

  14. The Luau   129

  15. Last of the Mohicans   141

  16. Dr. Giovanni   161

  17. On the Road   171

Part Three   199

  Gold   199

Acknowledgments   201

About the author   203

Part One

Adamant

KINDERGARTEN—Gina is sitting inside her cardboard box reading *Lolita*. Her dad is ringing her doorbell, which is the bell she found in the yard, part of a hanging contraption that fell apart and is now attached to the front door of the cardboard box with a wire. She can see her father's big nose at her cut-out window as he tells her that dinner is in five minutes. Probably enough time to finish the chapter she's on.

The Windhams believe their child should have access to any and all reading material in the house. Both products of a commune they lived on, they now reside in a suburban home and have traditional means of employment. The remnants of their past are directed to an inspired free-form parenting, a large vegetable garden, and a serious interest in native plant cultivation and foraging.

"I'm going to have a lover in the woods," Gina says, coming to the dinner table. "We'll live in a tree and have a moss carpet." Mrs. Windham pours wine, smiling to herself. Gina has said the same thing each day since reading *Lady Chatterly's Lover*. She pours grape juice in Gina's wine glass.

Mr. Windham has them laughing as he describes his childhood golf course on the prairie. They had a good acre of useless land, quite flat, as their designated course. They saved old soup cans, made perforations in the bottoms with nails and hammer, and dug holes in the ground for the cans set in a row at the back of the course. A slightly bent golf club worked just fine. He liked to come to the table with a story, and like his father before him, had a knack for it. It makes him a popular principal at the private high school where the kids are friendly and open, especially around him. He wants everyone to be happy and successful, in their own way.

Gina wants to have black potatoes tomorrow night, the ones they cook in the embers of the backyard fire pit. She and her mom work as an architectural team when they pile branches for a fire. She loves sitting by a fire, watching the beautiful flames. "Just butter and pepper," Gina says. "Black potatoes are the best."

Her parents have decided not to make a big deal of her truancy. She has been running home during Kindergarten recess for the last three weeks. She dashes off, too quick for the teachers. Mrs. Windham thinks when the cold weather moves in she'll stop all that so they're really not that concerned as they live so near school, with only one quiet residential street to cross. The first time Gina left school they found her asleep in the backyard sandbox, unable to get into the house, with neither parent scheduled to be home before five o'clock. Now they leave the side door open and she works on her cardboard box house, cutting pictures from magazines and pasting them to the interior walls. They are strict about her calling to let them know she's run home, and other than that, they're waiting out the situation, and she's either asleep in the house or reading in the box when they get home.

CR

THIRD GRADE—and a third school. They're hopeful this will be the right one, but Gina continues to lie. Her dad says it's because she is such a good storyteller and likes to embellish. Mrs. Windham says, no, she just lies, it's the simple truth. She can tell. It's her business to tell a lie from the truth. He says that's for lawyers, isn't it? not school counselors. The Windhams are losing their sense of humor.

Tobacco. They smell it on her hands, her breath. And last week the empty bottle of rum in the backyard. It's just a phase, he says, but it's been keeping him awake. Mrs. Windham has been researching counselors, seeking out someone Gina can see twice a week instead of just Saturdays after her dance class, which thank heavens, she still likes.

FIFTH GRADE—Gina, who is now ten years old, looked so small when they saw her sitting in that row of chairs at the police station. Theft. Why? She has an allowance for miscellaneous purchases. Stealing candy bars. Why is this happening to them?

CR

SIXTH GRADE—The bottom is falling out. Finding her in the garage with those boys, laughing their heads off, the air filled with marijuana smoke and the music blaring so loud the neighbors call the cops. Just lucky Mrs. Windham left work early that day before the police arrived. The week afterwards they have to pick her up at the train depot. Wouldn't explain where she got the money, just rambled on about moving to Italy and living in a cathedral with her twin. On drugs, going on and on about her twin as they drive home, the one she had when she was little. So far back, when she was three or four she had that invisible twin, and cut holes in her pocket so he could breathe.

So where had the money come from? Turns out she was a runner for a drug gang; all of them grade school age with an older supplier. Someone named Tommy Booker. They hire a well-respected psychiatrist, Dr. Mario L. O'Reilly.

CR

TIME OUT—The facility is nearby and luckily their insurance covers much of it. They can't tell if she's really doing so much better because she's off drugs and alcohol, but she seems happy and reads a lot, and loves the art room with easels and paints and the print making room. Is she pretending to be perfectly normal and ready to move home again and go back to school, the new school?

CR

Boys—Too much makeup. Tight jeans and T-shirts with sparkles. Loud music behind a closed door. Dancing at all hours, yet doing well in school. She loves art class, adores her teacher. So happy, but then goes back to the lies. Sneaking out on summer nights. The last straw, again.

CR

Almost Sweet Sixteen—She will not, she will not, she will not give up the baby. Gina is adamant.

She gets that stubbornness from you, Mrs. Windham says. Me? Hah, he says, slamming the door. Late that night with Gina asleep, they decide to sit at the table until they have a solution. The art teacher moved to New Zealand, so that's out. She doesn't want him to know anyway.

Mr. Windham has confided their troubles to his good friend Charles, unbeknownst to Mrs. Windham. Out of the blue, Charles had proposed a solution. Gina can live with him and his sister, Francesca. Gina knows him, as he has been the family dentist for over ten years, and she has always gotten on well with Charles. They have a similar dry sense of humor, he tells James. And they would be in the same neighborhood.

That's ridiculous, Mrs. Windham says. She can stay at home. You know she won't, he says. She's screamed that at us. If we force her she'll just run off. You know that. We both know that.

They sit at the table, their tea gone cold. Well, we could propose it. See what she'd say, Mrs. Windham says. Surprised at her readiness, he agrees, thinking they've probably all half-lost their minds.

Part Two

1. Insomnia

I t's 2:17 a.m. by the kitchen clock, mountain standard time, and Gina hasn't turned on the light. She is studying the burner of the stove, which glows red-orange in the dark kitchen. It seems like a red-hot snake, nicely coiled and behaving itself; if she doesn't look away it won't strike. It slithers into a river of fiery lava – the blood of the earth on top of the stove. Oh great Vesuvius, Mount St. Helen of the sleepless night! In her weary madness, she clicks on the other three burners, turning them all on high, a good and hot quartet. With all four blazing, she calms down from their warmth and the pleasant glow in the silent kitchen. Clicking off the final burner, she remembers the night coffee which she had intended to heat. Still cold, she pours the murky left-over coffee down the drain. Good riddance. She yawns and heads back to bed.

CR

IN THE AIR—"We forgot the 'Fruit of the Month Club,'" Charles says, looking up from his dental journal.

Gina shrugs her shoulders.

"We'll just have to miss three months. I think cherries are next. Then pears."

"What's after pears?" she asks, to see if he knows, quite sure he's memorized the selection of all twelve months.

"Peaches," he tells her, turning his attention back to the magazine.

Gina hears the boys goofing off behind her. She turns and Chris waves. Waving back, a finger at her lips to quiet them even though she's pleased at how lively and happy they are. Danny has the window seat but he and Chris plan on trading places later on, Danny tells her, using his authoritarian voice, making him seem older than his 9 years. But they are both old enough for this long trip, even with Chris barely 6 years old. She adjusts her seat a notch, leans back, catching a glimpse of a raw tooth stump in Charles's glossy journal before she closes her eyes.

ITALY—Six weeks have passed under the Mediterranean sun. Gina and the boys are golden; Charles's complexion is the same ruddy red as on the day they arrived. He takes an occasional dip in the sea, but prefers to work in the cool of the study on the north side of the house. He fell in love with the house after seeing photos on a vacationing site one cold day last February. It didn't hurt that he had met the owner while standing in a museum ticket line in London the previous fall. A coincidence of luck and it turned out the timing was perfect for both parties, and now the Italian acquaintance is on sabbatical in Boulder, Colorado and Charles is here in Italy.

Scanning through the computer images of gum tissue in various inflamed, blistery stages of disease and the return to a healthy shining pink, he's satisfied with the presentation, the before and after using his new treatment. Yes, Vienna will be the best session, for sure. His thoughts have solidified over the past three weekends while lecturing at dental schools across Europe.

He leans back in his comfort chair, confident and ready for Vienna, one of his favorite cities. And now with his sister resettled in the old town, it makes taking the family along convenient. And the boys love their Aunt Cesca. She's one of those warm people, outgoing, optimistic, always with some new big adventure just around the corner. He sips his tepid coffee, pondering whether it really is a good idea for Gina to stay at the beach house. She wants to work, to paint, and he gets that. She seems nearly back to her old self. She's humming in the mornings again, something she started when Danny was a baby. Back then he would come up behind her and hum along in his monotone bass, making them both laugh. Funny, but that was the beginning of a real love between them.

After that, they would just laugh at any old thing. How good it was. How simple and good.

Charles sighs, stretches and steps out onto the deck. He loves this view of the sea, close enough so you hear the waves. He listens to the sound of the waves and the laughter of the boys just inside the glass door.

☙

Gina is helping the boys pack. They're getting good at rolling up their shirts as she showed them back in Colorado. Finishing up, Danny rolls up his PJs and Chris squishes his into a corner. Both have questions about what it'll be like in Vienna, staying at their Aunt Cesca's house, instead of a hotel. Charles's sister laughs more than anyone alive, she's sure. She loves Cesca, and the boys think she is their coolest relative ever. Gina would like to go along and yet feels a need to stay behind and paint. Charles thinks she is doing well with her de-stressing, and that the time to herself will do her good. It's true she has been sleeping well, and painting, and she knows the boys will be fine, and Cesca or Charles will call as soon as they arrive. Small toy cars are tucked into the sides of both suitcases yet they zip up easily, leaving room for any souvenirs they may bring back.

☙

In the morning Gina drives Charles and the boys to the station where they'll board the train to Rome and then on to Vienna by plane. They should have left earlier, but made it to the train just in time, just the same. Good thing for the rail passes, enabling them to bypass the ticket line. She watches until she sees them at a window looking back at her. How far away they seem through the glass of the train car. Chris looks so small. She waves until they're out of sight.

7

On her way home in the empty van, Gina pulls over to the side of the road and opens the glove compartment. She finds the sunglasses she was looking for and pulls out a postcard she received last week from Mario, her shrink. It's from Florence. She can't remember sending him the address, yet she must have.

She was forgetful those last weeks in Colorado. It was before she discovered the burner that she wrote letters, sitting at the dining room table late at night writing long letters to everyone she knew. Her mother had called to tell her she had received a letter from her that began *Dear Uncle Ted*. She had mixed up the letters and the envelopes, though she had thrown most of those letters in the trash, well down under the coffee grounds and old newspapers. She looks again at the postcard, the statue of the Medici Venus, and turns it over to read the address and note written in his half-printed and half-written stylized hand.

> Dear Gina and Charles,
> Just bought a new bike. Italian, of course.
> Great country isn't it! Gina, keep up your
> journaling.
> Ciao,
> Mario

He travels so much, on his biking trips. Last year he biked through China, and before that, from village to village in Peru, high in the Andes. She shouldn't be surprised. She puts the card back, slamming the small door of the glove compartment harder than necessary. She doesn't want to think of him, her head doctor of many years, the renowned Dr. Mario Lanza O'Reilly. She's better now. Mostly she is. She pulls back onto the road, looking forward to the empty house and the easy routine of the days ahead, with no need for meal planning or the huge washings from twice daily swims and the mountains of soggy towels.

Back at the beach house Gina walks through the quiet rooms. She slips into her bathing suit and walks barefoot down the cool stone steps of the hill to the beach. Standing ankle deep in the sea, the cool water swishes against her legs. She swims a fair distance along the shoreline rather than straight out into the bay where she would swim if Charles was home. Best to be safe. Back on shore she walks along the beach, scavenging shells and bits of driftwood. The warm sand is clean, never any broken glass, and her steps are firm and confident. As a child she spent hours in her backyard sandbox, making trails and mountains topped with dandelions and twig trees. That was before she started school. Back when she was still herself. Back in those early years of wonder, those days of endless time so near to when her world began.

Filled with vague sandy memories, she climbs the hill to the house and changes into shorts and a T-shirt. Hungry after the drive and the swim, she heads to the kitchen and spoons out a large dish of hazelnut gelato.

After cleaning up in the kitchen, including the breakfast dishes, she walks from empty room to empty room before heading to her studio where she picks up where she left off on a large blue painting. As usual, after she begins, she loses track of time, and it's dark by the time she is cleaning the brushes. Too tired to fix more than toast, she eats standing out on the porch watching the sea and the sky. Climbing into bed and unaware of the hour, she falls asleep with the scent of turpentine in her hair

2. The Pope of Tomatoes

Gina opens her eyes and blinks at the wall, momentarily disoriented. The profile of the man in the wall is always there. Each morning she studies the sienna tones of the old fresco, and the man in profile who never moves. She sits up and slides out of bed onto the cool tiled floor, basking in the Mediterranean sun turning the room a warm pale orange.

Walking from room to room in her nightgown, she almost expects Chris or Danny, or Charles, or someone. She is not yet accustomed to the emptiness of the house in the morning, the most comfortable family time, especially breakfast, when the boys are still sleepy in pajamas, still just a step away from their dreams. Sliding the patio door open, she steps outside and looks down at the deserted beach. Surprised to see the sun so high, she checks her watch. It's already nearing noon when she is to meet Rosa. Better hurry.

That first week in Italy she met Rosa beside the tomatoes at the outdoor market in town. Gina was leaning against the tomato bin with her nose in an Italian phrase book when Rosa came up beside her and offered assistance. Rosa helped her pick out good tomatoes, rejecting several that Gina had thought looked fine. Rosa scrutinized the bin as though searching out ones filled with rubies and emeralds, winking at Gina. Smell them, she had said. Turn them around. She laughed and said her husband called her the Pope of Tomatoes, but he was dead now. Her husband had taught her English. Learning they were neighbors, Rosa had given her a live crab, which she took home in a net sack, trying not to watch its slow scissoring claws next to her on the passenger seat as she drove. Rosa told her to drop it into boiling water and leave it to cook for fifteen minutes, but instead she had brought it over to their next door neighbor, Rinaldo.

Now on her way to Rosa's house, she sees Rinaldo out digging in his garden. His goat, Mussolini, is on guard at the top of his rock pile behind the fence. "*Bon Giorno,*" she calls out to him as she drives past. Rinaldo waves with a spade and smiles from his work to watch her drive along until the van vanishes in road dust at the top of the hill. She drives past the long vineyard that ends just before Rosa's narrow driveway and pulls into her usual parking spot in the shade of the umbrella pine.

Rosa opens the door before Gina knocks, and greets her with a hearty laugh.

"Mmm, what's cooking? It smells so good," she says, walking into the cozy, cluttered kitchen.

"Minestrone," Rosa tells her and turns to the stove to ladle out two large bowls for their lunch. Gina pours two coffees. They sit at the small kitchen table and Rosa slices fresh herb bread, her nails encrusted with hardened bits of dough. Sipping soup, Rosa says she's been baking up a blizzard, and she also has spaghetti sauce simmering on the back burner. Gina eyes the enormous black pot on the stove. How good it is to be in this friendly little kitchen, with white lace curtains framing the two tall windows above the sink, their deep ledges filled with clay pots of herbs and geraniums.

As usual, Rosa does most of the talking, and stops mainly to eat and take little gulps of air, while Gina listens. Rosa tells stories about the olden days, when her children were little and at home and her husband, Giuseppe, was still alive. She talks about the food she used to cook for her large family more than she talks about her family. She looks about the room for prying eyes or ears before telling the most ordinary culinary details, as though they are great secrets she really shouldn't be telling, or is telling at great risk. Gina accepts Rosa's confidences with genuine appreciation because she likes Rosa, and she too likes to cook. After lunch, Rosa continues her monologue as Gina takes her leave. They say good-bye at the door, and as she backs down the driveway, she watches Rosa wave with one hand and shake her apron of flour with the other.

CR

Gina takes the long way home, along the gravel road above the sea cliffs. Rinaldo is out working on his fence next to his second pasture across the road from the cliffs. She inhales the freshness of sea air and the piney scent of this neighborhood she's come to love.

Back home, she does the work pages in her Italian phrase book, saying the phrases aloud as suggested at the end of each chapter, with more gusto now that she is alone in the house. She reads a few chapters of a novel, does a little cleaning, and the day passes by. Later, it's out to the terrace with a glass of iced tea to watch the sunset. On the patio, watching the sea, she feels like someone in a brochure advertising the Italian Riviera, except there is always a couple in those ads, never a lone person. And the sunset does seem too big for just one, a silent opera with an audience of only one. It feels both pleasant and a little spooky being alone. The sky above the beach is a pale red, and she watches the flaming colors turn to brilliant red streaks as she sips her tea. It's silent, except for the waves below and the wind rustling in the cypress trees.

When they first arrived in Italy, she had told the boys the seagulls went under the sea when the sun set, and they made the night waves by jumping and snapping at the surface as they tried to get out. They didn't want to go to bed under the sea. Danny laughed at her story; she kept it silly. But then one night she found Chris sitting outside in his pajamas, patiently looking for birds. He told her it's true; there aren't any birds at night, and they sat outside talking on the patio swing until he fell asleep against her shoulder.

Back in the house she wanders around her studio before gathering up canvases. She carries them outside to the patio, one under each arm, leaning them against the railing, the wet ones face to face. It takes three trips to get them to the beach, carrying them two by two. A master fire maker, she leans pieces of driftwood together and tucks in kindling. There is little wind and the fire starts quickly and within minutes there is a good fire. She coughs from the smoke as she tips the canvases onto the fire. The flames burn holes in the canvases and the smoke darkens the colored and bare sections of canvas.

Walking around the fire, her hands behind her back, she concentrates on the black tattered remains of the paintings, poking at them with a stick. Finally, she sits down to watch the last of the canvases burn, until there are just embers, just right for potatoes. Next time she'll bring potatoes. She loves black potatoes. After dousing the fire she climbs the hill to the house. From the top, she notes a night fishing boat move slowly offshore from the south.

She opens the patio door to the ringing of the phone.

"Hi," Charles says. "I was getting worried. I called several times. You should keep your cell phone with you."

"I was at the beach. I burned some canvases."

"I thought you were over that."

"Well, I have something else in mind so I need a fresh start. I'm thinking of a collage, a big one," she tells him. "How are the boys?"

"Fine. Just fine," Charles replies. "Always hungry. Cesca keeps them busy, and well fed, for sure. She's a great tour guide, taking them all over on the tram, which they think is very cool. Oh, they'll have lots to tell you."

"Are they speaking German?"

"You should hear them. Perfectly fluent ordering streusel in the bakery."

"Are they up?"

"Sound asleep."

"Well, tell them I love them. Are you ready for the convention?"

"All set," Charles answers through a yawn that Gina can hear over the phone. She tells him she might drive up to Venice in a day or so to go to the museums and galleries, and to take photographs. Charles reminds her that she would have to leave the van outside of Venice and take the train in, so she might as well take the train right from the start; it runs twice a day from their town. He tells her not to go out after dark in Venice, says everyone gets lost in Venice after dark. She assures him she'll be careful, says goodnight and hangs up.

Gina changes into her robe and fixes a cup of cocoa to drink in bed. All tucked in, she sets the alarm so she can get up early in order to get to the cove to collect stuff for the collage she's planning. The cove is the best place to find things like papers and corks, odds and ends that drift in from the boats. There is an old board in the garage perfect for a base, and that strong quick-drying glue, if it hasn't dried out. She'll use acrylic instead of oil. Closing her eyes and almost asleep, the steady rhythm of her own breath puts her to sleep to the dying image of the fire's last embers and thoughts of streusel.

CR

The next morning Gina drives to the cove and pulls in at the parking spot near the steep rocky ledge. With backpack and a net scoop over her shoulder, she makes her way down the winding trail, stepping with care over ancient cedar roots and scruffy shrubbery. Just as she approaches the small protected bay at the bottom of the hill, a blue heron lifts off, tucking its long legs beneath its body as it rises above the water, moving in great wing flaps down the coast.

Now to work. She scans the bay for collage material, spotting an array of papers washed up at the water's edge. She shakes off the water as she gathers up papers, noting the faded lettering in various languages, some she recognizes, others not. A couple of torn photos and old envelopes add to the mix. An old cigar box lid flops in the waves beside a dead fish jiggling among pastel colored mini-marshmallows. She scoops out a long blue feather, a few corks and a shoelace. A sandal bobs near the shore. Rapping the water off the shoe on a boulder, she notes its primitive craftsmanship, the leather and twine. She spreads delicate water-logged papers, some intact and others in bits and pieces, upon an old board to dry; the rest, including feathers, string and reeds, she organizes like a botanical display on a large flat rock.

Enough. Gina plunks down on a log and stretches out her legs and takes off her hat to soak up the sun. An old broken cart bobs in the center of the bay, and her mind drifts. In the open water the nose of a boat appears. Gina watches the boat move along in boat time and before long her loot has dried enough to be gathered up. Back up the hill, she loads it all into the van. Before pulling out, another boat moves up the coast.

On the way home, her neighbor Rinaldo is out walking his fence line with a shovel over his shoulder. He waves. By the time she turns into the drive she is cheerful and slightly giddy with her bits and pieces from the cove. In her studio she leans the wooden board from the garage on her makeshift prop and sets to work. The collage grows piece by piece. She's been collecting tea bags and metallic candy wrappers for the past few weeks, so with the addition of the findings from the cove, she has a nice variety to choose from. She slathers on glue and smoothes the papers with precision, rolling out wrinkles with the small brayer she found in a garage drawer. She dabs gold paint here and there, shapes bits of rice paper into circles and bird-like shapes, adds string, some reeds, and then paints lines and curves with sumi ink. The hours pass like minutes and the sky darkens into evening.

Smoothing out the last piece of faded newspaper, she stands back. The colors are soft seashore colors, accented by the Renaissance gold and rice papers, and a pale green of the East. She signs her name and dates the collage. She'll take it to the contemporary gallery in Venice she's read about. While contemplating the collage, the phone rings. Answering, she assumes it'll be either Rosa or Charles.

"Hi Gina. How you doing?" She doesn't answer for a moment. It's her shrink.

"Mario, where are you?"

"I'm in the village, right here in Cecci. I'm with Anita, and some others. We're on a tour," he says, and laughs. "Eight of us. I'd like to stop out tomorrow. Do you want company? Do you mind? We could bike out in the morning, maybe have a swim. I want you to meet Anita."

"I leave for Venice tonight," Gina says, making a quick decision to leave immediately, telling him that he should feel free to come out anyway, and have a swim tomorrow. She gives him directions to the beach house, tells him where to find the key. She explains that Charles and the boys are in Vienna for a few days. Hearing her own voice as she speaks, she listens to herself as if to a stranger. Has she always sounded like a bird? Has Mario always sounded like a bear?

She twists a strand of her hair until it hurts, startling herself. She asks about the biking tour and he tells her he got in on it at the last minute, that Anita took a preparatory class called *Exploratory Walking and Biking for Peace of Mind* from the tour guide, who's also the bike mechanic, and they needed two more people for the tour so they joined up. He asks when she'll be back from Venice. Gina hears a knock at the door and pauses.

"Mario?" She doesn't know what she wants to ask him. Who is this Anita anyway?

"When do you get back?" he asks again.

"I don't know, a day or so. Really, I've got to go – someone's at the door. Just come out tomorrow and enjoy yourself. I have to run. Ciao." She ends the call and shudders. Mario's disembodied voice follows her as she heads toward the door. Calm down, breathe. Like he taught me. Good deep breaths.

It's Rinaldo and he's brought a box of tomatoes from his garden. He says they're already cleaned as he heads straight to the kitchen where he sets them on the counter. She thanks him, and he is in and out in a quick minute. She hears his old truck rattle off down the road. Now what to do with this huge amount of tomatoes? She dumps the entire box into her largest pot and adds water, turning the heat on low. As an afterthought, she adds a few stems of rosemary, then, pacing around restlessly, she decides to iron. She irons a dress for the trip and folds it neatly into her bag. Tomorrow she'll wear a dress. Tonight, her jeans and the *You've Gotta Have Art* T-shirt will do. She calls and makes a reservation at a hotel she's found in her guidebook. According to the little map it appears to be close to a museum and the gallery she's interested in. She should just be able to make the evening train.

Sliding the collage into the largest bubble wrap envelope, she hopes it will fit in the van. She carries it out and slides it in the back door. It just fits at an angle. She uses an old throw rug around the edges for extra protection and wedges it in securely. Back in the house she pours the half-cooked tomatoes into plastic cartons and snaps the lids on the steaming tomatoes. The containers fill the freezer. After a last check around the house to turn off the lights, she leaves with her bag, hoping the tomatoes won't explode in the freezer after she leaves.

There's no traffic on the road and it's a bright starry night. She is wide awake and surprised at how quickly the day has gone by. When did she lose track of time? She sails over the hills and decides to drive through town before leaving the van at the depot lot. There's still time; maybe she'll see the biking group.

Coming into town, she drives slowly down the narrow curve of the main street and sees the lights of the movie theater. It's the same western the boys saw before they left. She slows before she gets to the Fizz, her usual stop for cappuccino, and pulls in at the road's bend beside an arbor of cascading vines. Mario and his group are sitting at the outdoor tables of the Fizz. Something smells delicious, and she realizes she hasn't eaten since breakfast. They've pulled three of the little tables together and it looks like a scene from a Van Gogh painting, with umbrellas and strings of yellow lights. The woman sitting in one of the chairs must be Anita with the red hair, she's sure of it, and she's wearing a white dress. She should join them or at least introduce herself. But no, she slinks down and drives off. How could Anita look so refreshed and fashionable after a day of biking? She drives faster than usual, angry that she saw what she came to see. Of course he should be with someone. I'm not jealous. I'm not.

3. Venice

Gina has left her collage at the gallery near the museum and is having coffee at a nearby café. She has an hour to kill before ten o'clock when someone from the gallery will meet with her. She sips coffee and thinks about smoking, of how it helps pass the time and gives a person something to do. This morning, without a cigarette, the coffee seems to lack meaning, substance, and she feels lonely. She watches a large woman smoke by the window, a woman who pecks at her cigarette as though she doesn't actually want her lips to touch the cigarette. Gina suspects she isn't even inhaling, and it irritates her and makes her want to stride over there, a la Bette Davis, and show the woman how to smoke.

A man comes into the café and sits down at the table near Gina. He slowly, intentionally, lights up a cigarette and exhales through his nose. Gina sighs. She has always been afraid to try that. He turns toward her and looks at her kindly, but so unflinchingly that she turns her attention to her coffee. She studies her coffee cup as if there is something of particular interest deep at the bottom. She's embarrassed and knows she had been staring at him too, and that's why he was staring back.

Then, there he is, standing beside her. Still, she doesn't look up. He stands above her, blocking the sun from the window and she notes this as a darkening across the surface of her coffee. He says something in Italian that she doesn't follow. He pulls out the chair across from her and sits down and asks if she speaks English. She looks up. He nods, grins, says in English that he saw her at the gallery earlier; that he works at the museum next door.

"You called me," he says.

"No, I don't think so," she says, on the verge of getting up to leave. He doesn't say anything, but just looks at her.

"Tell me about your collage. I saw it at the gallery."

Though he's from the museum, she's not sure she wants to keep talking to him. She tells him he was quite mistaken, she was only admiring his style of smoking, she didn't call him. He watches her fingers drumming on the table and has the distinct feeling that he wants to hold her hand, calm her down. He offers her a cigarette but she shakes her head, says she doesn't smoke, anymore. He's tall and pale, with thick, curly blond hair. His face is almost pretty, almost too perfect. Probably in his early 30s, he makes her think of a reclusive athlete without a sport. He's wearing a hand-knit sweater of rust, blue and gray, with leather buttons.

"I love it," he says. "Your collage; it's beautiful. I do mosaics."

She looks at him with surprise. Although she knows people still do mosaics, it seems most odd to actually meet someone who does that. But he has kindly brown eyes.

"It must be boring, all those little pieces," she says, wondering why she said this as soon as she hears her own words. He's very sure of himself and that makes her nervous.

"No," he says. "I like it."

He draws on his cigarette and smiles, and she feels his smoke and his smile all around her like a big friendly cloud.

∞

Late that afternoon Gina watches Giovanni kneeling above a mosaic as he examines the small stone pieces, says they are *tesserae*. She sits on the stone steps rubbing her foot and wishing she'd worn different shoes, and marveling that she is here at all, on this little island with him, looking at ancient mosaics. She likes to say his name: Giovanni. But he doesn't call her anything. Hasn't she told him her name? He looks up.

"Gina, come on. Let's get some water and clean a section. We can do the face." Apparently she had told him her name, of course, unless he saw it on the collage. They walk to the shore where the sea comes in over the rocks and fill old tin containers, dipping into the deep section between the rocks. The water is cool. On the way back Giovanni tells her about his studio near the museum, and how he first discovered the mosaics. He seems so at home on this island.

He uses a sponge on the face of a figure in the center of the circular mosaic. Above the beard he wipes off mud, exposing lustrous pink and coral *tesserae*. Grass is growing around the edges of the old mosaic floor, and Gina wonders why it was placed as a floor. After he explains that it was once indoors and this is all that remains of the structure, she still thinks it shouldn't be stepped on because it's too beautiful and she tells him so. He's quiet and accepts her comment and asks if she wants to help. He hands her a sponge. The mosaic is eleventh century, but in the Byzantine style of the sixth century, he explains. She works on the eyes. They're burnt sienna with one tile of deep blue in the center of each eye, which Giovanni says is Persian lapis lazuli.

Looking over at Giovanni she wonders if love is something instant, like instant pudding, that you just need the right ingredients and you don't need years and it doesn't have anything to do with time. Kneeling here above this mosaic, she too feels at home, and puzzles over what it is about him. He's like the man in the mosaic, peaceful like that, only alive.

Her eye catches a small group of tourists off the ferry watching them down on their hands and knees scrubbing away. Giovanni grins over at her and stops working. He stands up and beckons her away so he can take a few photos of the newly cleaned mosaic. He takes a candid one of Gina beside the old crumbling stairs before she notices what he's doing. A tourist snaps a photo of the two of them and offers to take one with their camera. Giovanni hands over his cell phone for their portrait. The man rushes to catch up with his group, which has already started to board the ferry. Their photographer waves from the boat as it takes off.

Sitting on the stairs, Giovanni unpacks cheese and bread from his backpack. "And last but not least, a bottle of wine," he says, pulling it out, magician style. Gina starts slicing the cheese and tells him it seems they've known each other before.

"I was thinking that too," he says, breaking off a piece of bread.

"Delicious," she says. "I forget to eat sometimes."

Giovanni proposes a toast.

"To his silent words," he says, looking down at the freshly cleaned face. He hands Gina the bottle and being thirsty, she drinks the wine like water, even though it's warm. Handing the bottle back to Giovanni she recites for him, making up words as she speaks.

I have always been both old and young,

this island of forever, is where I'm from.

He smiles, surprised at her poetic words.

"Oh, I'm not much of a poet, but I can rhyme," she says. She tells him about the greeting card company back in Colorado where she sells little sayings and rhymes. A small blue butterfly flits by, briefly lingering above their feet.

"A spirit," Giovanni comments.

"I love butterflies. Most bugs. Did you know that in Panama there are some very beautiful iridescent beetles, and women put little harnesses on them and wear them like jewelry? I saw it in a fashion magazine. They shouldn't do that," she shakes her head.

Giovanni leans back against the hard steps. He asks her to tell him a story, the story of her life. Says he's a good listener.

Well, she grew up in Colorado, an only child, she begins. She hiked in the mountains and was always afraid of rattlesnakes, though she never saw one. Her mom was a school counselor and her dad was a high school principal. She was a poor student. She only liked drawing and dancing. She's not quite ready to tell him about what a problem child she was. The sun has begun to set and she finds herself staring at Giovanni as his hair blows in the afternoon breeze.

Giovanni snaps his fingers in front of her face.

"Gina, are you there?"

"Oh, it must be the wine. Probably it's the wine." Her life story? Well, should she go on, actually tell him the truth? How many times in a person's life does someone ask you to tell the story of your life? Giovanni is leaning forward resting his arms on his knees.

Yes, she was a difficult child. Couldn't concentrate in school. One of those fidgety types who can't sit still and likes to stare out the window. In sixth grade she got into drugs. She starts to laugh.

"I'm just making this up," she tells him.

"Okay," Giovanni says, his eyes sort of sly and sincere at the same time. "Well, we need to leave." He says the boat doesn't run much longer, and not at all after dark. The last tour group has left so they'll have the Basilica to themselves, and Marcello, whom he knows, won't be closing the doors for another twenty minutes. "There's something I want you to see."

They pick up their picnic fare and walk toward the Basilica. Inside, they stand below a great ceiling of gold. Floating in its center is the Madonna in blue holding the blessed child, the most perfect depiction in all of Italy, Giovanni believes. It's all those thousands of gold *tesserae,* he explains, that emptiness of space all in gold that surrounds the Madonna and sets it off. Other mosaics fill in the space with saints and angels, but here the mother and child are alone. They stand below the Virgin in the golden sea of light until Marcello tells them its time to close up, that the last boat is nearing the dock.

They leave in silence and hurry toward the dock, hearing the motor of the *vaporetto* nearing the island. It pulls in and they board, the only passengers to be picked up from Torcello. Settling down in the boat, she feels like she has been commuting from this island for years. They're quiet together until they near the mainland when Giovanni starts to talk about Venice, and as they start down the Grand Canal he points out the play of color on the bricks of the buildings now at twilight. He says each building is a mosaic work of art, and that one building against another grows into a large mosaic of red and orange and sienna. He says the whole world is one mosaic, the outer world reflecting the inner one of atoms and ideas. Someday we'll see the mosaics in Ravenna, he says.

As they near shore, he points out the dome of San Giorgio Maggiore and its rosy glow, "like Saturn," he says. They dock, and Giovanni buys them each a bag of fried fish from an outdoor vendor and they walk toward the studio eating the greasy fish.

As they stroll along the canal Giovanni talks about the city, its history, the early days when they made and sold salt, and about the canals and the bridges they pass by. He says there are nearly 400 bridges in Venice, and as he begins to name them, Gina finishes her last piece of fish and thinks of the greasy creatures returning to life inside her, transformed into their original shapes and swimming around in circles in her stomach like goldfish in a bowl of wine and she doesn't feel very good. She has to sit down and rest. Giovanni tells her they can go to his studio, they haven't much farther to go, but she sits down.

"No, too far. I'll just stay right here on the steps." She curls up on the bottom stair and grabs hold of the beak of a wrought-iron bird in the railing. Giovanni sits down across from her. Spotting a gargoyle on a building across the canal, half animal and half bird, with ugly laughing teeth and cold stone eyes, she thinks of Anita and moans softly as she holds her stomach, to keep the fish inside. Giovanni helps her up, tells her they're close, that she can make it.

"My legs, they're shaky," she says, and doesn't think they'll work. He tells her to lean against him and she does. "I think I'm seasick, Giovanni." She holds his arm and tries not to look at the canal.

4. Giovanni's Studio

When Gina awakes, she doesn't recall going up the steps or lying down. It's dark and she can hear guitar music. She definitely feels better. The studio is enormous and it's like she has been sleeping in the center of a large church. There is light coming from a round stained-glass window, but the other windows are dark. She sees floor-to-ceiling pictures on the walls, of people and flowers and animals. The moonlight is just bright enough for a soft visibility.

Giovanni has lit a candle on the table next to the bed and she watches him walk out of the shadows and into the candlelight. He sits down beside her and asks if she's feeling better and leans near. She says she has to call Charles, her husband, who is in Vienna. He raises his eyebrows and moves the phone to the bed for her. She gets the number from her purse, but doesn't have the country code. What if the operator asks her something in Italian? When Giovanni sees her hesitation, he offers to place the call for her.

"Okay. I don't have the country code," she says, handing him the phone and the slip of paper.

He makes a call and after a minute hands her the phone.

"Oh, Charles, it's you," Gina says when he answers.

"Well, who did you expect?" he answers, annoyed. "You called me, didn't you? Gina, this is an odd time to call. Are you all right? Do you know what time it is?"

"Oh I'm sorry, I just know it's night."

"Three a.m. It's three a.m."

"Well, I thought I should call. I'm in Venice."

"Fine. You're all settled in then. Any special reason why you're calling so late?"

"Oh, I just thought I'd call," she says. "Isn't it interesting that I'm in Venice and you're in Vienna?"

"It is, but I have to be up early." She hears his exasperation. He tells her it's been raining all day there. She asks if he remembers the time that bag of cement mix was left out on the lawn and she forgot to tell anyone it had been delivered and it rained. "Do you remember that?"

"Charles, are you still there?"

"Yes, yes I remember," he says. "I still love you, Gina. I did then too. Why don't you go back to bed and call me in the morning."

"Okay. Good night. Sorry about the time," she says and hangs up the phone.

"Charles. He's fine," she says to Giovanni. "I'm married."

"Yes, I saw your ring." Giovanni takes her hand and she is aware that this is an unusual moment, highlighted by candlelight. They are in the center of an Italian painting, and she is both in her body and observing the two of them from afar. Giovanni touches her face and she closes her eyes. When he turns to blow out the candle, something grabs her, gripping her shoulder. Sudden pain. What is it? She pulls back and the lumpy weight of something stays on her back and the pain sharpens.

Giovanni yells, "Pascal, down!" He leaps up and grabs the thing at her back. She screams and moans and leaps out of bed and runs. Looking over her shoulder she sees the dark shape of a monkey with long arms and fangs jumping up and down, shrieking, just like her. She shudders and rushes away and finds the bathroom, locking the door behind her.

Breathless, she stands in front of the full-length mirror until her breathing slows. She uses a hand mirror and sees long red claw or fang marks on her shoulder, dripping, just like in a drive-in horror movie. She sinks to the furry white bathmat, sobbing and laughing, and curls up into a ball.

"Gina, come out. I'm really sorry. Now open the door. Let me put some disinfectant on you. Just unlock the door. Then I'll make us some hot chocolate. Come on now. Gina."

She curls up on the bathmat and picks at pieces of lint and recalls when Mario told her about his name—Mario Lanza O'Reilly—

named because his mother loved Mario Lanza, the opera singer. She used to play his records while she did the ironing. His mother liked Irish music too, especially the tenors. He told her that story of his name on the day they had yogurt sundaes to celebrate her final departure from therapy.

Giovanni has put on a CD of opera music and she tries to place the opera. Maybe it's not a CD. He would be one to have a turn table. She gets up, thinking about rabies, and where can she get a shot. Her head hurts and the morning church bells begin to ring.

"Giovanni, are you there?" she calls out.

"Well, you're sounding alive. Pascal's on a leash, asleep in his loft."

She unlocks the door and opens it a crack, sees Giovanni's one eye. "Okay, I'm coming out," she says and opens the door wide enough to slip out. He puts his arms around her and she can tell he feels really bad about the attack. The monkey is curled up on a platform above a ladder.

"Coffee?" he offers.

"Yes, sounds delicious."

"Okay," he says steering her back into the bathroom. "First we'll have a look at this." Giovanni gets out the antiseptic and bandages and she opens just enough buttons of her dress so she can pull the sleeve down over her shoulder. It stings but she doesn't cry out. She looks at his loafers while he bandages.

Patched up, she stands in the middle of the studio. It's so beautiful in the morning light that she almost forgets her shoulder. She must have fallen asleep on the bathroom floor. Now she can see the details of the large mosaics and frescoes on the walls. There are tapestries as well. She likes the tapestry of a monk standing in a garden of fanciful plants and flowers. There are animals in a row, and birds. Over her shoulder, she keeps an eye on Giovanni's monkey curled up as if asleep, though with his head turned away she can't see if his eyes are open or closed.

Settling back in a wicker chair near the balcony which overlooks the canal, Gina waits for the coffee and decides to ignore the monkey. Ah, the coffee. The aroma is divine and she stretches her arms. Giovanni joins her at the table, as casual as if they had been together for breakfast every morning for years. He tells her about the mosaic of vines and birds on the wall as they sip coffee. Several kinds of stone were used for the different sections, coming from various parts of Italy and beyond. The yellow stone is Sicilian jasper, and the greens Bohemian jasper. The pinks and grays are local stones, as is the white marble; the red-browns are from Siena. She recognizes the blue of lapis lazuli in the birds, and Giovanni says it is not Persian, but European, even though it was done later than the mosaic they saw on the island yesterday.

Giovanni talks about himself and his early days in California, after which he taught art in London and now gives lecture tours twice a week at the museum. He restores mosaics and frescoes, and travels around Italy buying marble. Giovanni speaks impersonally about himself, as though he's speaking of a casual acquaintance, or some historic figure. He tells her about a friend of his, a priest, who wants him to work on the mosaics of the Baptistery of S. Giovanni in Florence, a project which has become increasingly intriguing to him. This friend also has a small garden fresco in need of restoring, so those are his upcoming projects.

Gina remembers the wonderful doors of the Baptistery in Florence, and is quite sure that is where she saw the dazzling golden dome with many angels, and felt somehow golden herself for half the day after leaving the cathedral.

Giovanni retrieves oranges and biscotti from the corner kitchen. She leans back in the sun, keeping an eye on Pascal. The scent of orange and coffee fills the air.

"Why didn't you warn me you had a monkey? Such a bad monkey," she scowls, starting to peel a second orange.

"You're the first person he's attacked since Carol, and that was six years ago. She's my ex-wife," he says, wistfully stirring his coffee.

"Oh," Gina says, wondering if this is a compliment, being in the same category as his ex-wife. "I bet Pascal ended your marriage," she says quietly.

"Maybe. I don't know. She never did like Pascal."

"Do you like gargoyles?" she asks, and Giovanni laughs at her change of subject. Gina relaxes, trusting a person's laugh more than anything.

"Pascal is a little gargoyle, of sorts. They're all over Italy and I do enjoy them," he answers. "We have both angels and gargoyles in Venice. Probably more angels." He's looking at her like she was looking at him yesterday on the island, with a sort of hopeful and curious expression.

"Why don't we have a tour of Venice, see some sculpture?" he suggests.

"Sure, I'd like to," she answers. "You mean today?"

"Why not? I have time if you do."

"But I should talk to that guy at the gallery about my collage first," she says. He tells her there's a buyer for the collage already— one of the senior trustees of the museum who stopped by the gallery with him yesterday morning. All she has to do is decide on the price.

She is genuinely surprised and wonders why he didn't tell her yesterday.

"It is a nice piece, isn't it," she comments. They talk about what a fair price would be. What Giovanni considers fair seems high to Gina, but she relies on his expertise.

He makes a call. Gina expects that he will set up a meeting and she's grateful for his help. While he's rattling away in Italian she is anxious and fidgety, and starts shredding the ball of lint in her pocket. Giovanni's fluent Italian makes her determined to get back to her language lessons. She gets up and paces about the studio, having forgotten the monkey entirely.

"Okay, it's all set. It's sold," Giovanni says with finality. "Now we'll get you to the doctor. Then the gargoyles and angels."

She thanks Giovanni, quite astonished at how fast her life is falling into the unknown. She follows him to the balcony window where he points out the gallery down the way and says she needs to stop in and sign some papers, that Giulia at the reception desk speaks English and will help her. He'll meet her there after he takes care of Pascal. "Then we'll have a doctor take a look at you. Does it hurt?"

"No, not really," Gina lies.

"I'll meet you at the gallery then. Half an hour."

"Okay. See you soon," Gina says, starting down the staircase that she can't recall coming up the night before. Halfway down she stops and turns to ask how much she's getting for the collage. Through the half-opened door Giovanni throws one hand in the air in a snazzy Italian gesture and says 1,500 euros. As he gazes down at her she sees him framed in the doorway, smiling below his wild heavy curls. She feels his dark blondness following her as she walks down the rest of the stairs, ignoring the feeling of vertigo as best she can.

CR

Giovanni speaks quietly to Pascal while he packs his miniature travel case, just a few toys, the medicine and vitamins, and Pascal's ratty faded red security blanket. Pascal knows he's going to visit his "Uncle Luigi" as soon as he sees the travel case, and claps his long furry hands, keeping his feet firmly on the floor while bouncing up and down. He does his smile and flashing eyes routine for Giovanni, who's relieved to see him happy. Usually he likes to go to Luigi's, but sometimes he doesn't want to go and climbs the drapes and sits on the sill above the window. He'll only come down for canned peaches, a real problem when there are none.

Before they leave, Giovanni calls Dr. Fragalli to make an appointment for Gina. Though he's not a vet he gives advice on Pascal too, since he and Giovanni are friends. He thinks Pascal should see a vet for a complete checkup, that the unprovoked attack may be a sign of some new physical problem, perhaps some deterioration in his brain. "You'd better start thinking seriously about his future," Dr. Fragalli says to him, in a tone Giovanni finds chilling. The last time Pascal saw the vet the doctor said he was getting on in years, already into old age for his species, and that he would need more rest from now on. And he has been sleeping a lot the last few months. As they go down the stairs he notices the care

Pascal takes. He holds on tightly to Giovanni's hand even though he can still climb the drapes. He used to scamper down the stairs or slide down the railing.

Giovanni considers how comfortable he is with Gina and thinks they should skip the gargoyles and take a nice drive in the country. They can talk or just be quiet together. He likes how she's comfortable without a constant stream of chatter. It would do them both good to get away from the city. Certainly it would do him good. "Gina," he says to himself. He walks along the canal toward Luigi's and checks the water level as he does every day. Climate change is a big deal in Venice, yet he always thinks of Venice as a city that has risen up out of the sea. He's irritated with himself for constantly checking the water line on the canal walls.

Last week he dreamt of a flood, and as the water receded, it exposed an undersurface of rotted moldings and creatures that tried to hide from the light; white watery things that writhed and squirmed, half bone, half slime, mingled with bits of gold and sparkling jewels. The dream was part music, low twisted music of crumbling sounds and moans, yet beautiful too. At the end, termites came crawling up in a swarm, like the earth come alive, rattling and laughing in one big collective crackle of decay. He shudders, remembering, and how after he awoke he had taken a long shower to wash the memory from his skin.

He climbs the stairs to Luigi's and hands over Pascal. They exchange a few words, and Giovanni sets the travel case and monkey chow on the table. He waves good-bye, and Pascal waves back while eyeing the banana that Luigi always has for him, kind old Luigi. Giovanni leaves, and takes the steps down two at a time. On the street he takes long strides toward the gallery and lights a cigarette, anxious for the green rolling hills of the countryside.

5. The Fortune Teller

"Slow down, I can't hear you in this wind," Gina shouts, adjusting her scarf. He slows the Fiat and drives on as he tells her about the termite dream, not especially surprised that he feels comfortable telling her this dream. She's a good listener. He talks more about growing up in southern California and how he feels more at home here in Italy.

"Do you go back sometimes?"

 But he doesn't. Calls or email, that's about it. His father is a CPA and his mom directs a church choir in one of the largest churches in the area.

Gina has never been to California. She's been afraid, ever since her seventh-grade social studies teacher told their class that the state would one day crack off into the Pacific Ocean, right along the San Andreas Fault. But now they measure those things, have warning systems, better buildings.

Giovanni asks her to slide in a CD that he wants her to hear. "It's in the 9th pocket of that black folder. They're numbered," he says.

"Ouch!" Gina bumps her shoulder, already sore from both the monkey bite and the recent shot. She slides in the disc.

"Gregorian chant," he announces. "Early minimalist." A choir begins with low male voices singing in Latin, the words flowing in a mesmerizing repetition. She settles back to listen to the sounds, to the purity of the voices and Giovanni drives on in a reverie. Gina looks out the window and Giovanni stares at the road, and the music rides with them through the countryside. With the ending track, she looks at Giovanni in the rear-view mirror. The music has changed him. He pulls the car over and stops.

"Let's get out and stretch," he says.

"Wide open space, no fences," he says, stepping out and stretching his arms.

They lean against the car, taking in the distant hills, pale green and rocky, dotted with dark cypress trees. The field beside them is of golden wheat and the sky above a cerulean blue. The summer silence looms large, and very aware of one another's presence, Gina takes off to the edge of the field where she breaks off stalks of wheat. She hands a few to Giovanni and says she's going to do a large yellow painting, using wheat for a paint brush, in the manner of Cy Twombly. A noisy vehicle breaks the silence, as it rattles up the hill. It's a tractor pulling an old wooden wagon. They watch it poke its way toward them.

While they wait for the tractor to pass by Giovanni asks how long she'll be in Italy.

"September. We go back in September."

"And back to writing for the card company?"

"Maybe." She tells him about a computer program for writing verse. You choose the subject, whether it's for a birthday, funeral, or whatever, and then how many lines, number of syllables, whether you want it to rhyme or have a particular style. The computer comes up with several possibilities; some pretty funny or just plain bad, and others are really good. She says she is nearly as fast as the computer, at least with rhyming poems.

"So make something up. Something about us," he suggests.

As she's thinking, the slow-poke tractor chugs past. The farmer waves and they wave back.

"Okay. Here goes."

> Giovanni and Gina
> went for a drive.
> They stopped for a while
> in the countryside.
> A cow came along singing arias
> and asked for a coffee with cream.
> They gave her some coffee
> in a rose-colored cup
> and the cow provided the cream.

"Not bad," he says, laughing.

"Mostly I paint though," she says, running her fingers along the hood of the car, just short of reaching his hand. His fingers are long, and she likes his ring, a beautiful moonstone, with pale blue highlights. She looks across the field toward the horizon.

"What do you see?" Giovanni asks.

"Oh, just the beauty of the landscape. It's so vast. It seems like my future is no longer on the other side of the hills. Maybe I need a fortune teller."

Giovanni takes her hand and she feels the warmth of his fingers as she slides her hand away and the tractor noise fades to silence. They hear nothing but the sound of the breeze blowing over the field and their own breath.

"Funny you should mention fortune tellers. I actually know one," he says. "Well, I know of one. I haven't met her, but I know where she lives. In fact it's not far from here, maybe forty miles. You don't believe that fortune stuff, do you?"

"I don't know. I'm curious. Do we have time?"

"Sure, why not?"

She tells him about the Roma her grandmother used to talk about, back in old-time Sweden. They would come around and knock on the door and her grandmother and the other neighbors would give them their copper kettles to repair and clean. A few days later they were returned sparkling clean, though sometimes they just disappeared instead. She wonders if Giovanni's Roma will do this for her, shine her up, mend her wounds, and stabilize her.

"Okay. On to the future," Giovanni quips, considering how they'll be in the hills at nightfall, under a full moon, with no monkeys, no tractors, and he has a premonition the car may break down. He looks at her with just enough friendly lust that she needs to turn away. They climb into the Fiat, and after a half mile, Giovanni turns north and reaches into the console, pulls out a CD and slides it in.

"*Carmen*, the aria Don Jose sings to Carmen when he gets out of prison," he says, and is soon singing along.

"Giovanni!" she says, delighted and surprised at his beautiful voice.

He sings along with the aria, and she looks out the window as they ride, happy to be here listening to his voice. They continue on the country road for quite some time, along with the opera. Giovanni drives fast, like most Italians, and he drives easily, with two fingers resting casually on the steering wheel, as if steering the car is only an afterthought. He has an interesting technique Gina has not seen before: driving in a straight line even though the road curves, so that he is often on the wrong side of the road to achieve this as-the-crow-flies effect. He speeds up, and takes a firmer grip on the wheel, and she watches the speedometer rise to 140 kilometers. She's unsure what she thinks of this new sensation, traveling at this speed, but she doesn't want to tell him to slow down. He has stopped singing and she watches the tight concentration on his face, and knows it is echoed within her.

He accelerates as they climb a hill, and Gina braces herself. Even with a scarf, her hair is blowing like fury in the wind as the speedometer nears 160 and as they crest the hill the front of the car lifts off the road. Gina freezes and closes her eyes. Everything feels sucked out of her and condensed into the back of her head. They sail down the other side and she comes back to herself in a sudden panic.

"Stop! Stop the car!" she shouts.

Giovanni slows down and pulls over to the side of the road and eases to a smooth stop.

"Ah Gina," he says.

She blinks away unwanted tears.

"It's okay. We were flying, that's all," he says. "Let yourself go. We were safe, really. My reflexes are quick." He grabs her wrist and slides his fingers under her watch band, then leans back against the headrest 'It's good, speeding, if you'll let it be. Ride with it, over the curves and hills. Better than a roller coaster. We're just a little more in touch with life. You look like you think the grim reaper is in the back seat."

Gina takes off her scarf. "I was afraid, but I think I liked it until I got scared. Don't you get scared, Giovanni?"

"No. No, I don't." He hopes that's true; knows it usually is. He's in a sweet peace from the race, his personal race against anything: floods, dreams, death. It's better with her. She's the only one who loves it too; he saw that in the mirror, even though it didn't last. Gina, with her giant collage and wind-blown hair. Just drive on and on, like a river to the sea, to the ocean. Let the waves wash over us, slow us down, way down.

Gina reaches out to him, touches his shoulder, her arm near his chest feels the beat of his heart as he opens his eyes. "Let me drive for a while," she says. "You rest."

They trade places and he tells her to drive straight ahead ten more kilometers. She starts with a jerk. "Whoa, this is sensitive. What kind of Fiat is this?" He leans back and smiles, resting his hands behind his head and tells her he's worked on it, smoothed it out a bit. She moves forward and he watches as she adjusts the seat, puzzled at his own confidence in her. He's never let anyone drive his cars before.

"How did you end up in Italy," she asks.

Giovanni considers his beginnings here, five years ago, recalling the days that have become vague, blurred, like an old half-forgotten movie. There are gaps in his memory, and lapses of time. But it began after he and Carol parted in London, and she went home to Los Angeles and died of a ruptured appendix on a camping trip. He didn't go back for the funeral. He just walked around London in the rain, thoroughly soaked, recalling the squish of water in his shoes that day. Back at the flat, after a hot shower, he tried to read but he couldn't concentrate. Later on in bed, the day ended with great sobs as he listened to the rain on the roof.

"I don't know," he tells Gina. "My ex-wife died, and then I came here to restore a fresco and ended up staying. It just happened. A matter of chance."

"I suppose. You just never know what's ahead. You know, I wasn't even going to come to Italy. In fact I definitely had planned not to go, but then something happened and I decided to go." She remembers the night Mario told her he was moving to San Diego. He told her on the phone the night before he left. He said he couldn't pass up the great opportunity that had come up. She looks at Giovanni and taps out an inconsistent little rhythm on the leather of the steering wheel. Ahead is a small town.

"Is this it?" she asks.

Yes. "Take a right up here, the gravel road. Okay, about two miles."

She loves these green rolling hills and how the car handles around curves, and starts to tell him about Charles, how organized he is, how nothing happens to him by chance. Every step of his life has been planned. "Except me probably," she says. "He knows where he's been and where he's going, there's just never any doubt. He has teeth like a tiger, not quite fangs, but good and strong white teeth. And, no cavities." Well, he's a dentist, and he cleans her teeth once a month, on the first of every month. Rubbing her sore arm, she asks about his monkey, Pascal, but he says later. He'll tell her later.

"Here, pull in here, on the left, we can eat here. This is a good restaurant."

Gina parks under a shade tree by a gas tank and realizes she's famished.

CR

Stabbing curly pasta, she considers calling Charles and then decides to wait. "Nice wine," she says, and Giovanni tells her it's a local wine, the same as they had on the island yesterday. She decides to sip slowly.

Giovanni tells her about the B&B up the road where they can stay, since it's already late in the day. "One room or two?" he asks.

"Two. Yes, and I'd like to rest and change before we see the fortune teller," she adds, thinking she'd better call Charles. The thought of racing back to Venice in the dark is not at all enticing.

And the possibility of sharing a room with Giovanni at the Inn she chooses not to think about.

"You know, on second thought, I think I'm ready for the future now," she says, suddenly angry at Charles for being so far away, although she knows that's perfectly unreasonable. She needs to be angry at someone.

After their meal and refueling, Giovanni drives toward the abode of Livia, notorious enough that even the restaurant owner knows of her. Apparently, this particular Romany group in the hills are unusual, being an actual settlement, even though various members come and go, there is always someone available to tell fortunes. Livia is greatly respected and very wise, but somewhat suspect, even among her own people, as she ignores some of their traditions and has her own way of doing things. Giovanni has heard all of this second-hand through a Russian friend who has regular consultations, including advice on the financial market. Livia is in her 70s and no longer travels, or rarely so. He thinks arranging a reading should be no problem today, especially so late in the day. "Are you afraid?" he asks Gina.

"No. Well maybe. Yes, just a little," she answers, wondering what Livia looks like. She pictures a beautiful older woman with dark piercing eyes, wearing golden bangles and brilliant silk scarves. Giovanni turns onto the gravel road past a small wooden sign reading *Indovina*. "She speaks Italian, I assume," Gina says.

"I'm sure, and Romany, probably. That's their heritage, Romany. I'll translate the Italian," he says, and aware of Gina's powers of intuition, knows she'll pick up a lot through body language. He's surprised to find himself somewhat uneasy as they near the house.

As they near the end of the lane they spot her in the front yard. Livia is not the colorful figure either expected, but rather a small woman entirely in black.

Gina is scared. "You don't have to do this," he says. "We can turn around."

The dark figure watches their car move slowly in her direction. With a crooked finger she beckons, then turns abruptly and continues on toward her house, assured they will follow, just as day follows night.

They park where the road turns to a bramble of berries. Gina steps out of the car without hesitation, and although she's nervous, she's drawn to the old woman. Giovanni is curious. The path appears to be an old dirt road with grass growing in its center, and each step they take seems to bring them nearer to an older time. Instinctively Gina grabs Giovanni's hand.

By the time they arrive at the slate steps of the house, Livia is holding the door open for them. Her face is inscrutable, except for a playful gleam in her deep-set eyes. Livia waits for one of them to speak. Giovanni tells her in Italian what they have come for and she listens so attentively that her concentration is unsettling. *Prima i soldi*—first the money, she requests. He counts it out and she tucks it into her apron pocket, and escorts them into the parlor.

There is a pleasant, yet unfamiliar aroma in the room. They sit in easy chairs of purple flowered cloth. Gina sinks into a chair, clutching a silky dark pillow to her lap. Livia and Giovanni talk, and she follows their hand movements, their eyes and voice inflections, catching a word now and then.

The tiny room has an excessive number of windows, all on one wall and framed with dark red drapes. Bright paper flowers are tacked at random on the wall-papered walls, amid black velvet landscape paintings and mountain scenes. There are autographed glossy photographs on a shelf of spiritual figurines, including a brass many-armed Shiva, Indian god of the cosmic dance. A three foot blue-robed plastic Virgin Mary is lit from behind and stares serenely into space from a corner plant stand, her neck circled with a ring of dried purple flowers. Behind the Virgin and tacked to the wall, is an orange and green silk flag, while an assortment of twigs and roots dangle from a large basket. Other greenery is spread to dry on an ornate oak sideboard. From her chair, Gina can see into the kitchen where a profusion of variously sized copper utensils, mostly pans, but also small items such as ladles, bowls, and copper spheres, hang along the wall reflecting the late afternoon sun. Above the sink is a neon Blue Moon beer sign, rimmed in ivy.

"Gina, she wants you to tell her in your own words why you're here. She needs to watch you tell her. She wants to hear your voice."

"Is that Woody Allen in that photo with her?" Gina asks, pointing to a framed photo on the wall behind Giovanni, but Livia shakes her head adamantly, saying "No, no." Giovanni and Gina exchange a look.

"I'll talk some and then wait for your translation, and so on, okay?" He nods yes, and she composes herself, turning toward Livia, who sits now with her hands folded in her lap, content and motionless in her stark black dress.

She begins by telling Livia how her house reminds Gina of her grandmother's house, as she too had many things, knickknacks and pictures and postcards, shelves with books and walls covered with paintings, curly-legged furniture, and flags, and it felt like an antique shop, or a museum. It makes her feel at home, she tells Livia. Giovanni translates.

"Giovanni, is this working?" she asks.

"Yes, go on," Giovanni says, duplicating Livia's quick hand movements with his own. He looks eager. Gina clears her throat.

She continues: "Back in the beginning, before I started school, I was fine. But I had trouble in school, right from the start. I would get up and walk out of class. I'd walk home, which was close. Even in first grade I did that. Except for when we had art and used crayons. My parents tried different schools, but I couldn't adjust. I liked art and a dance class I took on Saturdays, but I just couldn't listen. I loved reading, though, but only at home and not in school.

"My dad is a high school principal and my mom is a psychologist. I was supposed to be the perfect child, but I wasn't. I just wasn't. I was totally unlike either of my parents. I liked to experiment. I liked to pick up trash and connect the pieces with glue. I did better at a new school, an experimental one, and I liked some of the older kids there. One boy, who wore a lemon-yellow hat, I especially liked. He was two grades ahead of me and I used to follow him after school. He noticed that I did that, and one day he asked me to steal a candy bar for him. He wanted a Heath bar. I said I'd just buy him one, but he said no, I had to steal it.

"I was small and innocent looking and quick, so I could get away with a lot and no one suspected that I was stealing stuff, and then by sixth grade I was selling drugs after school. Nothing like heroin or anything, just pills mostly. Benny with the lemon-yellow hat and I had a business and I got a cut of the money, but Benny got most of it. I hoarded and hid my money and planned to run away to Italy to live in a big cathedral. I had a picture of the cathedral that I cut out of a library book. I read spy novels for grownups, and I read my mom's books about crazy people. My favorite was a book of case studies that I kept in the back of my closet. I would mix and match from the case studies, or I would pick out a characteristic that appealed to me and try it out. It was interesting to experiment like that.

"Anyway, so it went on like that. I started drinking with my drug friends and they liked me. I could be a smart aleck with them and get away with anything. So, by eighth grade I was a tough kid and a mess, really. I spent most of that year in an institution. Which wasn't bad. I got to do a lot of art. That year definitely got me back to normal. I stopped acting out. Almost.

"Then I was good for about a year, before I went wild. Boys. I liked boys. I was pregnant at sixteen with my oldest boy, Danny. I wouldn't stay at home for anything. I was stubborn. I ended up staying with a friend of my father's, Charles, who was my dad's dentist, and whom I'm married to now. Charles adopted Danny and we had Chris when I was nineteen. Back then Charles had a big house and his sister, Cesca, who now lives in Vienna, was staying with him. She stayed there until I turned eighteen, and that's when Charles and I got married. Charles is good. I didn't really love him at first, but I did like him. He's a good man, but we're really different. He's twenty years older than me.

"Something I'd like to understand is about my therapist. He's been my psychiatrist since I was a child. He wanted me to call him Mario, but I always called him Dr. O'Reilly. Until I got better actually, then I called him Mario. Well, that took a lot of years. It was then that it started to change, when we started going to movies together. Charles doesn't like movies, so he didn't seem to mind. Mario was like part of the family by then. But he started to get to me, on my mind too much. I was attracted to him. Now I want to forget him. I need some magic potion.

"The other thing I want to know about is will I be a good artist? Will I still be painting and making art when I'm very old? I think I will. I guess I don't really need an answer to that."

Gina hesitates. She wants to talk about Giovanni, and how everything feels right when she's with him. Like she's finally where she belongs. She keeps it to herself.

Livia looks sympathetic and curious. Giovanni begins to translate her story objectively, as far as she can tell. She is aware of his surprise at some of the things she has said. As he tells Livia her story, she listens to the beautiful flow of the Italian language, and it seems amazing that her feelings, her story, can sound like that, and she watches Livia listening carefully. Occasionally Livia stops Giovanni, apparently to ask a question or clarify some point.

Finally he finishes and Livia sits in her chair absorbed, as if she were alone, her gaze internalized. Then she nods, tucks a stray hair into her black-fringed bandanna and indicates she is ready and she tells Giovanni to translate for Gina as they go along. She looks at Gina as she speaks.

"Too many men; not enough art," Livia says emphatically, slapping her hand on the table. "My creative friend, I will help you see without shadows or delusions. You will learn quickly and soon you will not be afraid of the brilliance of the sun, or the cooling rain, or the power of love, for you will become all these things. I need to see what you face more clearly. I will consult the crystal ball. Come. Come with me."

Livia slides a small table in front of them and removes a black cloth from the crystal, which she moves from the center to within a few inches from her edge of the table. She holds her hands above the crystal and her eyelids flutter. She stares into the crystal ball as if in a trance. Gina feels her skin burn feverishly from some invisible fire circling them both. Livia speaks slowly, and Giovanni, like a masculine echo, translates her words.

"First, your aura, as I suspected, is fire. Fire as wild as the aurora borealis. Now, the person you want to forget, he is good to look at—I see him juggling pinecones in a forest. There are red clouds above him. They bring rain and I cannot see through rain. The crystal fades."

They sit in silence. "Now another scene forms, Gina, and I see him again, and this time he is rowing a large rowboat with great vigor, but he is rowing in circles. The boat is filled with many people in old-fashioned party clothing, women with parasols and young men in black tie are drinking champagne. A clown serves hors d'oeuvres on a golden tray, but the rower looks straight ahead and continues to row in circles, with great determination. Giovanni is swimming in the water. He is swimming the backstroke. And you, Gina, you are on the shore digging in the sand. Now the pictures begin to fade. This is all that is revealed."

Livia covers the crystal with the black cloth and looks directly at Gina, before walking slowly to the plastic Virgin Mary where she takes one of the dried flower leis and places it around Gina's neck, chanting a rhyming verse all the while. She goes to Giovanni to give him instructions for her.

He translates again, sentence by sentence: Gina is to fast for four days, although she can have juice and tea, and she must spend four hours outside each day in the fresh air. She is to sleep no more than six hours each of these nights and is to write down her dreams immediately upon waking. Livia gives Giovanna paper and pen and insists that he write down the instructions. She makes him read them back to her to insure he has recorded it all correctly.

She then adds that at the end of the four days and before the last night, she is to go to a deserted place and make a fire and sit before the flames and think of her dreams and her life. When the fire dies down she is to take an ash from the fire and make a mark on her forehead and then she is to sleep outside under the stars. When she wakes, Livia says she will see a ravishing sunrise and will feel herself to be part of the sunrise, and just as this is so, she will become part of everything. Livia looks at Gina with kindness and a gentle smile. Her last words are of a lilting rhyme, which Giovanni doesn't understand and says it must be Romany.

CR

Next Giovanni and Gina switch places. It's his turn. Gina settles into the flowery chair and he moves to a hard-backed chair at the table. She stares out the window at a flowering shrub, its leaves and white flowers fluttering in the breeze as she listens to Livia tell Giovanni what she sees for him in the crystal ball. She understands nothing of the Italian. Livia goes on and on, and Gina tires.

The sun is setting. In her restlessness she walks quietly to the bookshelf. Most of the titles are in Italian, but she recognizes a few names: Svevo, Dante, and there are several German books, including the writings of Freud, and Jung's dream symbolism. She reaches for a volume by Otto Rank, but jumps back, as Livia snaps out at her.

"You can't touch her books," Giovanni tells her. "They're sensitized with her personal vibrations and she wants you to go back and sit down and wait."

Gina sits down again and pouts, getting increasingly sleepy listening to the droning sound of Livia's voice. She certainly has a lot to tell Giovanni. But finally she finishes and hands him something small which he slips into his pocket.

At the door as they say their good-byes, they all seem to be bowing to one another in a quasi-religious ceremony and Giovanni and Gina end up bowing to each other in confusion as they make their way to the outside of the house. As they start down the road the late sun is blinding after the dark house, and the air seems fresher. Gina turns back and sees Livia's small dark figure through the window, staring out at them with her inscrutable stone face.

6. At the Inn

A t the Inn, Giovanni lies in bed looking at the shadows on the white plaster walls below the wood beams of the ceiling. A pale spider stirs in its moonlit nest in the corner above the bed. Gina is asleep next to him and her hair is pale as cobwebs in the bright moonlight. He shoves his too large pillow off the bed and tries to settle into a corner of the puffy quilt. Turning, he sees the moon out the window, neatly framed by Spanish lace curtains. The crystal ball and the fortune teller's eyes hover in his mind, dangling like parts of a mobile.

He gets up as quietly as he can and pours a glass of brandy. Settling into the chair by the fireplace he prods the dying embers with a poker. Gina fell asleep while he went to buy brandy and he had decided not to wake her upon his return. After her night on the floor of his bathroom in the studio she was exhausted, and now he can't possibly sleep beside her. He wants her too much.

He's slumped over like a broken old man, remembering Livia's prophesy. The first image she had seen in the crystal was of a monkey with wings. Pascal, she explained, was being weakened by a force or spirit returned from the dead; one who was not buried deeply enough. The spirit returned from the dead would be Carol, he thinks, if there's anything to this. No, he mutters to himself. But again, Livia said the spirit was filled with jealousy of the living; it needed to be confused or consoled into returning to the dead. To do this, Giovanni must leave Venice as soon as possible, only to return after the death of Pascal, who was dying of old age and brain fever. Giovanni finishes his brandy and gets up. "The hell with it," he says to the night.

Lighting a cigarette, he sits at the edge of the bed. The angles of Gina's face are like his own, and he sees the skull beneath her pale skin, his sister twin, as she breathes in and out. Looking at his own hand, he remembers iridescent red bones, a flashlight held beneath a hand at night once, long ago in a tent.

Gina moans quietly in her sleep. She sits up and rests her head on her knees, holding her head, and rocking back and forth. "A dream. A long dream," she says, and jumps out of bed, looking for her purse. "The pen, I have to write it down, before I forget". Giovanni finds the Inn's stationery and signature pen and directs her to the chair by the fire. He puts another log on and pours two brandies. She writes frantically. He hands her the brandy and lights two cigarettes. She takes hers without hesitation, having forgotten that she quit. She inhales as if drawing in something vital.

"Can I see?" he asks.

She reads the scrawls across the paper:

The moon-eyed Gypsy
counts the banshees one by one,
as spades upon the cards are charted,
ancient rhymes begun;
one-eyed jack turns up,
she gently touches this,
with gaudy rings, and finger circles,
says, beware the bliss.

The smoke of her cigarette is drawn into the fire. "Look," Giovanni says, "smoke rings." Three perfect rings float up in the air between them.

"I'm not stable," Gina says to the fire. "But I feel stable." She slips on her borrowed robe and grabs the bed quilt and heads outside. "Come. There's a moon," she says. They follow the foot path toward the hill behind the Inn. Climbing under the moon light, without shoes, the ground is soft with leaves and grass, the scent of night, of earth, and a faint herbal scent from flowering bushes of rosemary and sage scent the air. Near the top of the hill is a clearing with a smooth expanse of grass. She gathers wood and he starts a fire with a cigarette. As he fans the fire, the flames leap up, and their arms glow orange in the firelight. Soon the fire is warm and intimate, and the old magic of red flames rise, forming smoke dancers, soft vaporous creations in the night. The fire crackles and Giovanni blows smoke down Gina's neck, into her ear and his voice is a low secret whisper. He licks at her ear and slips off her robe. The pale curls of his hair glow from the fire and Giovanni and Gina make love like ghosts on the pale quilt beneath the moon. Afterwards, disoriented and dizzy, they are silent, and rest against one another in the cocoon of the blanket. The air is filled with the scent of pine and the black sky is filled with stars.

They listen to the night, a bit stunned at their union, and brush leaves and bits of moss from one another. Gina curls up beside the fire and Giovanni leaves for supplies, returning with another blanket, a pillow under each arm, and the bottle of brandy in one hand.

"It's nice. No bugs," he says. "Here," and he tosses her a pillow, sits down and takes a drink. He hands her the bottle. "Couldn't manage glasses."

"I'm decadent," she says, taking a sip before lying down. She wiggles into a comfortable spot, pulls the silky edge of the blanket over her nose in the Indian veil position, sighs, and falls asleep.

Giovanni adds wood to the fire. He scans the horizon and listens to the crickets. They are on one of the higher hills in this rolling countryside and he follows the silhouette of the dark hills, recalling similar hills in Africa, and a jeep trip at night with his father-in-law on a night like this once, some years ago. The only light visible is the one from the Inn, though there must be a million stars, and he lies on his back looking up into the dome of the sky.

Carol used to say the stars were diamonds. Her father told her each star was a diamond when she was a girl in Johannesburg, and she couldn't quite stop believing that. He remembers the time she wanted him to help make a jeweled mosaic icon in their London bathroom. They used mirrors for the eyes, and she wanted a circle of diamonds around each eye. She thought of them as toys. He had a cigar box full of fake jewels someone had given him as a silly present, which they used to finish the mosaic. She couldn't tell a real ruby from a fake. It didn't matter. After Carol died, he sold the London place to an old pal, and wonders if the jeweled icon is still in that bathroom. He couldn't convince her to have it on the bedroom wall, where it wouldn't be damaged by steam.

"Giovanni," Gina says in a sleepy voice.

"I thought you were asleep."

"I was, but I rolled onto something hard and hurt my shoulder." She reaches back with her hand and twists her neck awkwardly, trying to see. He leans in to look.

"It's where Pascal bit you. It's bleeding a little where the scab came off. Lie down on your stomach and I'll fix it." He lies next to her and licks the wound. Gina starts to laugh, says she's ticklish, and he runs his fingers lightly over her back and she is still laughing and then can't stop laughing.

"Stop it," she says, through a laugh. "No, Giovanni, stop it," and he does.

"Too much of anything hurts," he says. "I love it here, on these hills under the stars. With you."

"Yes, falling asleep looking at stars," she answers, and it is fine outside, except for the bumpy ground. They watch the last of the embers of the fire die out and feel the chill of the night come on.

"Let's pack up. I'll take you home."

"You mean the Inn?" she says, yawning.

"No, your beach house on the coast. When does Charles get back?"

"Oh, down there," she says, puzzled. "Well, I don't know exactly. Not for a while yet. It's pretty far. I don't know just how many miles, or kilometers. Why do you want to leave? It's so nice here. I feel at home here with you."

He takes her hand. "The moon will follow us. Wherever you are, when you look at the moon, you'll have this night."

Gina toys with his ring, turning it in circles, absorbed. Giovanni lights two cigarettes and hands her one. He tells her he might leave Venice; thinks he needs a change. For now he just wants to follow her, and he has a marble quarry down near where she's staying. He'll check out the marble. He blows smoke through her open fingers. "I'll tell you about the quarries on our way. And the diamond mines," he laughs.

"Okay," she says, yawning again, and asks what Livia gave him, what he put in his pocket.

"I'll show you, but not now." They wrap blankets over their shoulders and start down the hill, each holding a pillow.

"We're two fat religious pilgrims," she says.

"We're in an everlasting life, the two of us, but we can only see a little bit of it, that's what I think," he says.

They traipse down the hill slowly in the dark. At the bottom of the hill Giovanni bursts into song, a rousing version of the afternoon's opera aria.

"Shh, shh. You'll wake everybody up," Gina whispers.

But he takes her arm and spins her around in a midnight dance as their pillows drop aside, their blanket capes flair out under the moonlight. And arm in arm and half holding each other up, the revelers of the night make their way back to the Inn.

In the room Giovanni tumbles onto the bed and mumbles that they'll go in the morning. His last few words are smothered into the pillow, and mid-sentence, he falls asleep.

Gina climbs into bed, tired and happy. She closes her eyes and falls asleep.

7. Giovanni the Baptist

In the morning Gina waits for Giovanni to get out of the shower. She is glad they are going for a long drive, and looks forward to the ride, to just being quiet with him. From the beginning they have had a friendly and comfortable ease with one another. Lying back on the bed she can hear him singing in the shower and allows herself to daydream. She pictures them in Africa, like Tarzan and Jane, bathing under a waterfall surrounded by a lush tropical jungle filled with beautiful singing birds. Pascal could be there too, if he behaves.

Giovanni comes out of the shower rubbing his hair with a towel.

"You need to learn Italian, Gina."

"*Buon Giorno*, Giovanni."

"Not bad. More pizzazz. And use your hands."

"*Buon Giorno*," she says, then flings her arms in the air. Giovanni laughs and tells her to do it all together. There's a certain rhythm to it, the words and the motion.

Another try and he tells her she's got it, soon she'll be almost a native.

"My barber says this is a natural cut. All I have to do is shake my head and let it dry by itself," he says, shaking his head like a dog just coming out of the water.

Lighting a cigarette, she sits on the edge of the bed and watches him. Giovanni appears to have stepped out of a Botticelli painting, with skin so fair in the morning light. What a miracle we are. She pictures his insides, all the red parts, the heart and liver, all the long and winding veins like roads, and muscles, the tenderloins Charles would broil on the grill. She shudders.

As he smiles before her she looks through his chest, which last night seemed so mighty and sleek. She pictures lungs, delicate air, like fanciful white balloons. He lights a cigarette and walks toward her, beautiful and amazing. How can we walk at all, with all these weird things inside of us? She starts to cry.

"Oh come now," he says. "I'm going to give you a bath and baptize you into someone new." The water is so hot she can hardly stand it at first. He says he's Giovanni the Baptist and there's soap and steam and his hands move over her like velvet; his voice, his calming voice, then as her tears stop, and she starts returning, the white porcelain is nice and warm. Something he says seems funny, and being bathed, the father and mother caress becomes the sensuous touch of Giovanni, who carries her to bed and she doesn't know who she is, what she is, she's the sunrise and a part of everything, just like Livia told her, though she hasn't even fasted.

Then it's quiet. They rest. A knock on the door breaks the silence. The innkeeper. Gina pulls the covers over her head and lets Giovanni answer. There are still leaves all over the floor and their bathrobes are stained with ash. But apparently there's no problem; it'll all come out in the wash. Gina hears the door close, and Giovanni lifts the pillow off her head.

∞

Driving toward Venice, her hair dries quickly in the breeze. The country air is clear and fresh; a perfectly beautiful day of blue sky and hills as green as spinach salad. Gina laughs out loud.

"Ready for breakfast?" Giovanni asks.

"Yes, aren't you?" she asks, but he's not and says it's because he smokes. She remembers how she used to have a cigarette instead of breakfast. They're going to the *pasticceria* Rinaldo told her about.

"I'm going to quit," Giovanni says, looking confident on this bright morning.

"Oh," she sighs. "But it's so hard. Why?

"I'm tired of it. It's stupid, of course," he says.

She recalls what happened when she quit. It was awful. One day without nicotine and it seemed life wasn't worth living. She had it planned out, ready to sleep and exercise a lot, and keep to herself, away from any one she knew who smoked. When she walked into a room she would tell herself not to say anything, but she couldn't keep quiet and ended up saying something mean to someone, to Charles. Even to the boys. It got so they would just leave the room when she came in. She would walk in, and they would walk out. That first week, anyway. The second week was pretty bad too. What she ended up doing was to withdraw from herself. She became an observer of her own suffering, a technique she learned from Mario. "It's just really hard, Giovanni. It's like being temporarily insane. But I'll try to help you, being a former addict and all, if you're serious."

"I am," he says, lighting a cigarette before reaching into his pocket. He hands her the charm Livia gave him. She opens the small cloth bag that's tied with a black string. "It's an amulet of magic herbs," he says, "and a petrified shark's tooth. There's a hole in the tooth and it's on a string." She touches the dark glossy tooth and sniffs at the herbs. "Scary," she says, half smiling. It brings to mind cellars filled with old potatoes and onions and asks if he ever had a cellar.

"No. No cellar." But he recalls a vague memory from when he was a kid. The cellar was at someone's house, maybe a neighbor's. He had to go down the stairs with an old woman to get something, a jar of fruit from a dark room.

He grabs the amulet from Gina and flings it out the window into a field. She still has the shark tooth in her hand. She watches him in the mirror, glaring at the road, and braces herself, excited. The red dial of the speedometer moves slowly to the right.

"Last night on the hill," he says. "So good. Something to think about when I'm old. The two of us, the fire, and all those stars. Though I'll probably die young."

Gina's hair is flying wild in the wind again. She drops the shark's tooth into her purse and rummages in the accumulation at the bottom. There is a tiny dog-eared book by Gertrude Stein, old envelopes, her passport, a good-sized piece of driftwood and a cork. And what she was looking for, an Italian phrase book. She can choose a few things to learn each day. She leafs through to the section called 'Restaurants: Ordering a Meal.'

By the time they near the outskirts of Venice, she is ready to order *cinghiale* –wild boar, convinced she could pass for a native, as long as she doesn't have to say anything else. She asks Giovanni how to say "well done."

"*Ben cotta*," he tells her, and she writes it in the back of her book.

CR

They drop off the car in the usual lot and board the train for the short ride into Venice. He plans to stop at his studio, and the museum. She needs to get to her hotel, call Charles, pack, and check out.

On the train they discuss art, and both agree that they like paintings in private homes better than in museums; that the setting is more natural, but of course more people can see art in museums, and Italy has some of the best. Still he likes talking about paintings and sculpture. He is interested in artists and their lives, and he enjoys some of the questions he gets from people on the tours. Why do artists paint? Why did Picasso keep changing from one style to another? How did they grind their paints?

"So what do you say?"

He explains how he talks about how the artist has something to say that can't be said any other way, the usual. And that if a painter could say in words what he said in the painting, he would have written a poem or a story, but he could only make this particular statement in paint. But he doesn't really know. "Why do you think artists create, Gina?"

"You gave me a good bath this morning, Giovanni, but you forgot to dry me off. You just carried me dripping wet to the bed."

"Now why do you do that, change the subject like that? Am I talking to the windshield? Here, smoke with me." He hands her a cigarette. The train pulls in and they leave the depot to wait by the water's edge for the next *vaporetto*. The soft waves against the dock welcome them to Venice as a boat pulls up.

8. Marble Dust

Their stop is closest to Gina's hotel, so after walking her to the door, Giovanni walks past the museum and his studio and continues on down the block. He opens the heavy door of the palazzo and takes the steps up two and three at a time and calls out "Natasha!"

After a moment, a woman's husky voice replies "Da, Giovanni," and the door opens.

Natasha gives Giovanni a friendly hug and her hands, coated with marble dust, leave white marks like flour on his dark green shirt. Behind her, in the center of the studio, a white marble sculpture glistens in the morning sun, and on the podium near the window, Jesse, the handsome welder, her current model, nods in greeting to Giovanni. The sculpture looks finished, he tells her. She's working on the hair and ears, the last refinements, she says, but yes, it's nearly done.

He asks her to take a break, that they need to talk, and he takes out a handkerchief and wipes a streak of marble dust off her rosy cheek, wondering if her high color is from vodka or from physical exertion, or both. It's hard to tell anymore since she's taken to chewing strong-flavored bubble gum.

They speak quietly to each other in English and he asks Natasha if she would like to do the lectures at the museum, as he's leaving Venice for a while. After a considerable pause, she agrees, at least for a while, she says, asking when he's leaving and is surprised to hear him say today. He had considered asking if she would move into his studio while he was gone, knowing she's fond of it, but considering the weight of her work, her equipment, he realizes the move wouldn't make sense, especially since she's returning to Russia so soon. But he does ask if she'll stay there occasionally, to keep an eye on the place.

She looks at him with a glimmer in her eyes, a rare secret possibly available, and heads to the heavy wooden worktable by the window and picks up a letter. Even from a distance he recognizes the look of the Russian language in print. She waves the letter in the air saying the university has approved her grant for the new project. Another marble statue for a building in St. Petersburg, and she has permission to do the work in Venice. She puts her hands on her hips and laughs.

"No Russian winter for Natasha this year. Crazy Russia. But I love winter, oh how I miss snow, beautiful snow! Crazy me. But yes, I'll watch your studio. I love your studio. Best light. I'll keep my large work here and do my clay at your studio. Yes, should be good."

She's quiet for a moment, chewing gum, and slowly, expertly, blows a large pink bubble. It pops with a crack, and she thanks Jesse and dismisses him for the day. One more morning, just the ears, she says. He steps down from the podium where he's been eavesdropping and smoking. Still stiff from sitting in the same position, Giovanni and Natasha listen in silence to the wooden clumping of his boots on the stairs, like the echo of an old forgotten war.

Giovanni has many times sat watching Natasha at work in her studio. She is like a beautiful demented orchestra conductor, always watching, measuring, circling, shouting instructions in Russian to models who speak only Italian. Head to the left, arm higher. She demonstrates positions, paces the floor, hands behind her back, and then the lonely sounds of the hammer and chisel tapping and pounding, tapping and pounding.

Natasha is an odd, cold, beautiful woman—a straightforward person. Sometimes Giovanni thinks she's like frozen vodka, a woman of ice. And definitely an enchantress, probably most at home under her own cold Russian sun. He shudders at the chill of her love. Gina tells him he's pale. But Natasha doesn't go out in the sun; Natasha is like white marble, snow, a winter butterfly.

The heavy door at the bottom of the stairs closes in a polite slam by the departing model as Natasha pulls the scarf off her long thick red hair. She puts the samovar on the stove to heat and comes over and puts her arms around Giovanni. He smells the piney scent of vodka through the bubble gum, and with a sad guiltiness, tells her he's had a long night, he's tired, and has a lot to take care of yet today.

"All right," she says matter-of-factly. "We'll sit down and have tea." They sit on a bench, using raw marble blocks for their tea tables, as always, dusty with fine marble dust. Natasha pours them each a cup and they discuss the details of Giovanni's studio. He glances at the marble figures, so enormous and heroic above them, staring out into some vast Siberian landscape.

They discuss the museum schedule. She knows the artwork as well as he does, or nearly so, and is just as opinionated as he. Many times they've gone through the museum together, arguing with animated enthusiasm over one painting or another. She loves Kokoschka, and Chagall. Michelangelo. To put her in a good mood, he tells her the tea goes well with the color of her hair, something he has told her in the past, but now he wonders who will drink from his teacup in the future. She always gives him the one with the red peacock, with a chip near the handle. She doesn't ask him where he's going or why he's going. He knew she wouldn't; she's like that. She was the one who said from the beginning that she couldn't have a relationship with anyone who wished to pry into her life, and she wouldn't ask for details of his life. We will just accept each other just as we are and for now, she had said.

But she does ask about Pascal. Giovanni is going to give him to Luigi, which surprises her and she says she'll miss him. Pascal, or Giovanni, he wonders. Natasha gets up and slowly circles the statue, quietly staring downward following her shoes. All right, yes, yes, she mutters.

"Come here, I'll get you something." From a drawer she pulls out a photograph of herself and hands it to Giovanni. In the lower corner of the photograph, written in ink, are the words *Moscow, early winter*. In the photo, Natasha is wearing a black coat and high black boots, standing in front of an enormous snowbank under a white sky. Her thick red hair stands out like a burning bush, even though the photo is in black and white. He thanks her and she asks that he leave her a memento in his studio. "Just in case," she says.

Of course, he tells her. "And I'll leave the key at the museum." After a polite kiss of ending, he leaves quickly and heads down the stairs, the photo in his hand, a piece of his history becoming small, months of his life turned into a thin paper photograph as he walks out onto the street, thinking dust to dust, snow to snow, ice to ice, God, where's the sun?

Giovanni walks down the street breathing in the Venetian humidity, conscious of the city's saltiness, a taste of sea and crumbling brick. Down the street he spots Luigi walking along at his usual snail's pace. Luigi is holding Pascal's hand, and in the other is a grocery basket overflowing with vegetables. Giovanni crosses the canal and Pascal leaps up into his arms, screeching and smiling, and he pats Giovanni on the back with a long hairy arm.

He smiles at Pascal, in spite of the rock he feels in his chest for a heart, thinking you're better than people, Pascal, and he tells him he's as ugly as ever and tickles his chin. Up in the apartment Pascal has a banana while Giovanni and Luigi talk. Luigi is delighted at the prospect of having Pascal for his own, though he makes a pretense at the difficulties involved, the expense for a retired man of maintaining an exotic animal like Pascal, and all the extra trips to the store and the vet. Luigi shakes his head slowly, old-time checker player that he is. He scratches his chin and frowns, holding his jaw tight. He avoids looking at Giovanni. Giovanni had expected this and offers him a monthly sum for his expenses, and tells Luigi he's going to give him the Fiat to use for as long he likes, for his drives in the country.

Giovanni has heard him telling his cronies how he drives the car for him often and is almost Giovanni's chauffeur. He recalls the one time Luigi drove, out in the country when he was driving Luigi to his sister's place. Luigi could drive well enough, though he is a very slow driver. Still, his reflexes are okay, and Giovanni is not worried. The car seals the deal.

He reminds Luigi that Pascal needs a check-up. He gives Luigi some money for the first month, and as they walk to the door, he tells Luigi he'll be calling in a few days, and he should make an appointment at the vet this week. He gives Luigi the extra Fiat key and tells him he can pick it up in a day or two; he needs to get his Ferrari out of Orazio's barn first. He pats Pascal on the head, and feeling like a deserter, he smiles on his way out the door, feeling both sad and relieved.

Giovanni heads to the museum. Inside, he doesn't waste time but goes straight to Samuel and explains the situation. Sam barely disguises his delight. Natasha has filled in before, and Giovanni chooses not to think too much about this, but feels certain he's turned his peacock teacup over to Samuel. He pictures Sam's immaculate dark suit with handprints of marble dust, what Natasha leaves, as other women leave lipstick on collars. Samuel is formal, efficient, always meticulously groomed, down to a neatly placed gold tie clip. He is distant, though polite, with Giovanni. They've gotten along okay, nothing more, and it's Samuel who keeps the distance. The top of his bald head shines under the museum track lights, and pale salmon tufts bush out above each ear. Natasha will like the sculptural qualities of that fine head. Why doesn't he shave those off? Those clumps above the ears give him a comic, almost clownish appearance, yet without them he might appear too grave and forbidding, the scraggly little brooms his humanizing factor. Giovanni asks for an envelope and paper, says he has to write a note to Natasha, would he be so kind as to give it to her, taking up this wordy politeness that comes over him whenever he speaks with Samuel. He hates himself for it, but it always happens. He sits down and writes:

Dear Natasha,
 Here's the key, and a photo. Take care of
yourself.
Love,
Giovanni.

He folds the note and puts it in a museum envelope along with the studio key, then looks through his wallet, pulls out an old British driver's license with his picture and adds it to the envelope and seals it up. After writing Natasha on the front, he brings it to Samuel, requesting that he give it to her today; that she'll be stopping by later. They shake hands, and that's that.

As he leaves the museum he senses the eyes of the first floor Picasso portrait following him out the door, and his head throbs. Damn, not the rain, he says to himself as he walks out onto the sidewalk. Despite the rain he decides he needs a gondola ride. As he gets in it starts to pour. They move a block down the canal before the gondolier pulls over. They sit out the downpour under an old stripped canvas awning, and water leaks down through its cracks. Giovanni leans against the dry side of the boat, holding Natasha's picture on his lap; it's been splashed. He folds it in half, opens it and starts tearing off pieces and dropping them into the canal. He watches a torn piece with Natasha's leg bob in the water, before it drifts away.

He listens to the rain on the old awning and on the water of the canal and lets his mind drift with the rain, rain and more rain. Waves of rain gush down, splashing onto the cobblestones next to the canal. He closes his eyes and leans back. Faces float past: faces from the museum, portraits with eyes, swimming off like schools of fish in tangles of seaweed. Hair, women's hair, falling like rain. Then Carol, sitting on the side of the bed drying her dripping hair, always asking something with that dryer noise, he couldn't hear, but then the voice is Natasha. No it's Gina. The gondola jerks from a wave and startles Giovanni out of his reverie.

His head throbs. Opening his eyes he feels good. The rain bounces in the water and he starts humming and begins to sing *Singing in the Rain,* softly at first, until his singing wakes the gondolier from his rain trance and he joins in on the chorus, singing to the rain, in the rain, with a sudden joy from nowhere, and renewed and refreshed, Giovanni and the gondolier sing while the rain pours down all around them on the grey canal.

9. Orazio's Mural

By the time the rain lets up, Giovanni and his new friend have gone through several versions of *Singing in the Rain*, and are well pleased with their harmonizing. Antonio moves them out with a graceful shove, expertly moving along the canal. He must take Gina for a gondola ride, but now he is impatient and absently watches the canal walls. Since Carol, his involvements have been with temporaries; women in Italy for short periods of time: tourists, teachers, anyone who catches his eye and interest who is in Venice on a short-term basis, but beyond that, he turns away. But now Gina is another matter. He's puzzled at the way he is drawn to her, almost as if he has no choice. She's like a magnet for him.

Rain drips off the rooftops and balconies and the sun comes out, brilliant and shining over the city. A crazy cheeriness within him makes him anxious and the slow movement of the gondola becomes excruciating by the time he nears his stop. Getting out, he walks quickly from the canal to her hotel and through the revolving front door. He asks the desk clerk for her room number and is told 307. The clerk smiles apologetically and shrugs his shoulders. "Lost a tassel," he explains, rubbing an epaulet-less shoulder of a very faded purple uniform. Giovanni tells him it'll probably turn up, then takes the jerky elevator to the third floor and walks down the gloomy hallway to room 307.

She answers in a silky white robe, and he steps inside and pulls her to him.

"Giovanni, get me out of here," she says, half laughing, then pointing to the bare light bulb dangling from a black cord like a lonely suicide creature growing out of the ceiling. The bulb sways slightly above them on its skeletal cord.

"Why ever did you pick this hotel, Gina?" He grabs her leather suitcase from the floor and flings it onto the bed. She explains how she found it on the map and it was pretty close to the museum so she thought it would be convenient. Gina slips into a blue cotton dress, steps into open-toed sandals and folds her robe neatly into the suitcase. Giovanni picks up a pair of shoes. "Don't forget these. They look new."

"They are, but they give me blisters. I bought the wrong size." She points her right foot out so he can see the bandage, from that day on the island. Before he arrived, she had been standing at the window watching the rain and thought Giovanni might have been a ghost, it was that kind of weather for those kinds of thoughts, but when she felt the blister she knew he was real. Anyway, one blister is enough. Someone will use them if she leaves them behind.

Giovanni sets the shoes on a chair, sure they cost someone a gold crown. They take the steel cage elevator to the lobby, getting out as it clanks shut behind them. Gina has already paid so they wave to the clerk and Giovanni calls out that he hopes he finds the braid.

"*Arrivederci. Ciao,*" the clerk calls out, confused, trying to wave and touch his shoulder and salute all at the same time, coming across as the good-natured young guy he is. He gives up further communication attempts and puts his hands on the desk counter and watches them leave through the revolving door, wondering who they are, maybe movie stars from Hollywood, with all that shining hair, staying here incognito.

Outside in the sun, Gina and Giovanni take a motorboat to the train station, and after a quick train ride, arrive at the car lot, where they find the Fiat clean from the recent rain. She wants to know if he took care of whatever it was he needed to do and he assures her that yes, all is in order, more or less, and he's as ready as he'll ever be, though for what, he isn't quite sure. "On to the future," he says, half to himself, and laughing, slams the car door.

"Luigi has Pascal for good now."

He tells how he had to bribe Luigi with the Fiat, which means they have to see Orazio, a guy he knows. A poker player. Giovanni has a car in his barn, so that's where they're headed. That's the last stop before the beach house, he assures her, and asks if she has ever worked on scaffolding.

"What?" she asks, somewhat perplexed.

"There's a mural on the side of a barn," he tells her, a hand combing through his hair. He promised Orazio, he would restore it, but he's put it off for two years. "Wait until we get to the hill by his place and you'll see it as soon as we start down the other side. Joseph and Mary are riding a motorcycle and Jesus is on Mary's back like a papoose with a golden halo. The background is mountains, with lakes and animals, even Orazio's dog, Michelangelo. There's a rainbow and a lot more," he says. "I swerved off the road when I first saw it. And that's how I met Orazio."

"So my car is in his barn. We were playing poker and I got drunk and lost a lot of money, made a deal with Orazio to keep the car until I repainted the mural on the barn. I was a fool," he says, incredulous, even today. "The sweetest car," he continues. "Do you want to paint? You could touch up Mary and Joseph, brighten the haloes. Or you can work on the motorcycle."

"I'll do the faces," she says, already thinking of technique. For the hair and the beard, she'll use an almost dry brush, without much thinner or water.

"What color is the car?" she asks.

"Red. Sort of old, but classic." He's more peaceful now, and his hands on the steering wheel are eager for the Ferrari.

She thinks Giovanni is crazy just like she is, but she's already game for painting a mural on the side of a barn and asks where this friend lives.

"Pretty close now," he says, glancing at her, his eyes blazing like a tiger fresh out of the zoo. He speeds up, and the road surface shines from the recent rain. He makes a sudden swerve and parks beside the *pasticceria* with an 'open' sign.

They're both famished. Inside the *pasticceria* everything looks and smells wonderful. There are fresh breads with shiny brown crusts, crisp *cornetti* sprinkled with sugar, golden flaky treats filled with fruits and almond paste, and enticing little white powdery balls made of ground nuts. They decide to have a picnic on the hill above the barn's mural, so they can look it over while they eat. The plump and efficient baker fills Giovanni's basket with bread and pastries, plus cheese he just happened to have available, and asks if they need wine, but Giovanni has a couple of bottles in the trunk. He adds a bottle of orange juice to their purchases.

Gina wants to know what's in the oven that smells so good. A conversation between the two men proceeds with much animation. The baker starts through a swinging door to the back of the bakery, glancing over his shoulder at them before letting the door swing back, winking one dark eye at Gina.

"A specialty he bakes on Tuesdays," Giovanni says. "He uses grated orange peel and some herb he grows in his yard, and star anise. Said he doesn't let just anyone buy them; they're usually reserved for him and his daughter, Gina. I told him your name, so that's why we're getting two, hot from the oven. Good thing you asked."

The baker returns with two warm braided rolls on a wooden board, each as large as a small loaf, and he tucks them into their basket. They thank him effusively, and as they leave Gina sighs, having thought her face would crack from smiling so much, her compensation for her silence, the lack of Italian made up for in smiles.

Giovanni slides the basket into the trunk and joins Gina in the car and starts off. She fiddles with the radio looking for a popular station, then settles back, pleased with what she has found. Giovanni hums a vague little phrase, harmonizing with the radio's song, and they are on their way.

After the rain, the countryside smells clean and inviting. They drive past fields of wheat, and hills with picturesque rows of olive trees. They see green fields with grazing horses, and trees scattered near streams and along the edges of fields, like quiet guardians. Gina notes a hawk sitting on a fence post, and later, a white cat stalking along a ditch, a fleeting glance indeed, at the speed Giovanni drives. He sings snatches of songs along with the radio, and they drive for a long time, neither wanting the hills and fields to end, nor the drive. A gnawing hunger for lunch has a pleasant edge. As they drive further away from Venice, and are not yet somewhere else, they are carefree and relaxed, happy as kids on the way to a fair.

"We're almost there," he says. "Just over one of these hills."

Gina expects to see Mary and Joseph and the babe on a big motorcycle just over each hill and looks expectantly at the top of each hill they crest, until finally, after the fifth hill, there it is.

"Wow!" She wasn't expecting it to be this huge. It seems like there should be some words, like for Harley-Davidson, or the Pope, or something. She understands how he could nearly go off the road the first time he saw it and they agree it's both comical and beautiful, and totally awesome.

He takes the ascent slowly so they can get a good look before pulling into the gravel road to Orazio's place. A small black dog runs toward them from the porch, barking ferociously. Giovanni gets out and pets the dog, which becomes friendly, or remembers Giovanni. He asks Gina to wait so he can see if Orazio is home as there is no car in the drive.

She watches him walk to the house, the little dog leaping around in the air after Giovanni, its tail wagging erratically and enthusiastically, but somewhat crookedly, like a broken toy that still works, but is not quite right. That must be Michelangelo, his dog. She watches as Giovanni calls out for Orazio and knocks on the door. Finally, after no response, he returns to the car.

"No one home. We'll just go eat."

They arrange the basket with the braided bread and cheese and the bottle of orange juice. Giovanni grabs a blanket, and they start toward the hill. Michelangelo joins them, running and prancing ahead, then circling back.

"A whirling dervish," she comments. "Michelangelo, big name for a small dog. He's cute though. There's something wrong with his tail. It wags crooked."

They pause before a small stream at the base of the hill and the dog takes a drink before bounding off along the creek bed. "Probably after rabbits," Giovanni says as he leaps over the brook and sets down the basket and blanket. Gina stands on a half-submerged rock and leaps across.

They continue on up the hill, choosing a picnic spot midway from the top. Giovanni spreads the blanket, a shade of green nearly the color of grass. They have a perfect view of the mural and settle down.

"I feel like we're the first ones here for some event," she says. "The Fourth of July, or Shakespeare in the Park, something like that. Well, I rather like it." She is sure she can do a good job of touching up the faces, and the flowers. And the mountains. They definitely need work.

Giovanni will take care of the bodies and the motorcycle, and he'll redo the sky, which will be much easier for him to reach. And that dove near the top with a poker chip in its mouth which has almost faded out. Giovanni bought the paint two years ago and expects it'll still be in the shed behind the barn, along with the brushes. They can start today. He saw the scaffolding leaning against the far side of the barn when they drove in. He's sure they can finish the whole thing in a day and a half if they start today, if Orazio gets back. "Maybe sooner," he says, taking a chunk of the special bread. "Great bread, isn't it? Nice and crusty, and tasty," he says without waiting for an answer. He wants to do a mural of Adam and Eve someday, or a mosaic, in the garden, he tells her. The Garden of Eden was before they had children. He asks about her children. "Two sons, didn't you say? Here, have some juice."

Gina is proud of her sons, Danny and Chris. She thinks a woman's version of the Garden would have included children. They are the miracle. Giovanni wishes he had children. They sit quietly and he reaches out to hold her hand and asks if she's going to let him fit in somewhere. "I could be an uncle," he suggests.

"Well, I don't know." She takes a bite of the bread, and says that Charles is really good, but they're not alike, not at all. But he's so reliable. In a way he's like one of those old mythical Greek gods, she tells him.

Giovanni laughs, and says somewhat bitterly that god could be a dentist, but that Charles is just not a god's name. He takes a drink and fumbles for his cigarettes. He doesn't offer her one.

"That's the first cigarette you've had since Venice, isn't it?" she asks.

He stares at the mural without answering, communing with his cigarette. He fiddles with the grass and picks a blade, and holding it between his thumbs, blows through the grass reed, making a high flute-like whistle. "Here try it," he says, handing her a thick blade of grass. She blows, and Giovanni starts to tell her about his parents, and how he woke up alone in the house when he was, maybe six years old and saw a fire down at the beach and went down there in his pajamas. They were sitting by the fire, one parent on either side of the fire, and his sister, his senior by fifteen years, sitting nearer to the water. He sat next to his mother and they all sat there with only the sound of the crackling of the fire and the breaking of ocean waves, until he fell asleep. What he remembers is that they were a family, but they were each separate, and he felt lonely, even though he was snuggled up against his mother. He woke up in the morning in his bed with a strange feeling, like he had grown up somehow. Giovanni lies down on the blanket and looks up at the sky. "I feel so empty," he says.

Gina hands him a piece of her bread. It's satisfying, just sweet enough.

"So you lived with Charles for two years before you married him? You were underage. That's illegal."

She leans on an arm and tries to explain. How his sister, Francesca, lived with them. Cesca, they called her. She was getting over a divorce and taught voice lessons. Charles was from a big family, with many brothers, and Cesca. One of the brothers was in jail and they never saw the others, who lived in New Jersey. "Someone just drove in," she notes, sitting up.

"Orazio," Giovanni says. They fold the blanket and start down the hill with their belongings and jump the creek. Michelangelo comes running at top speed, flying across the brook, and water splashes like glitter in the midday sun. He runs ahead to greet his master in the driveway, well ahead of Gina and Giovanni.

When they get to the driveway, Giovanni greets Orazio with a hardy slap on the back, with something that seems to Gina to be a friendly vengeance. He makes the introductions in Italian and Orazio shakes Gina's hand and doesn't let go, as he eyes her appreciatively. Giovanni has to take Gina's wrist to disengage

Orazio's prolonged handshake. After stowing their picnic things in the car, he grabs Gina's suitcase, and puts his arm around her as they walk to the house, subtly moving her away from Orazio.

"I'll get my bag later," he says.

They have been invited to spend the night, and Gina wants to rest before starting the mural. She's tired from the lack of an ordinary night's sleep, and yawns at the very thought of a nap. Giovanni is tired too, but anxious about his car, and after showing Gina to their room, he and Orazio start down the stairs. She hears the door slam and then reopen, and footsteps bounding up the stairs. Giovanni opens the door and says "Lock your door. I'll be back soon and have a good rest." He smiles and is off.

Gina locks the door and runs water in the adjoining bath, which has an old-fashioned tub on elegant claws. The house, what she's seen of it so far, is a mixture of cozy farmhouse and elegant Baroque. There are marble lions next to potted geraniums, rosy cherubs painted on pine panels. The paintings on the walls astonish her. A portrait in the bedroom could actually be a Titian, though the signature is vague. She is sure she will fall asleep quickly in this room after a bath. It has heavy oak paneling polished to a warm amber, below wallpaper of roses and butterflies, which remind her of her childhood room where she would nap in the soft afternoon light of lowered shades.

Out the window she watches Orazio and Giovanni open the barn door. Behind the barn, part of a racetrack is visible. For jogging? Orazio hasn't the shape for it with that stomach. Horses maybe. She turns off the water in the tub, undresses, and pauses before an ornately framed mirror on the bathroom wall and sees the Titian portrait reflected in the mirror, watching her from the partially open door. The house is full of surprises. Maybe there are hidden panels that open into dark hallways and hidden rooms. She closes the door on the possible Titian and steps into the water, which is just the right temperature and luxuriously filled to the limit. Eyeing a gold unicorn faucet, she sinks under the water up to her ears. Here there is no gypsy to hear her thoughts, and she becomes something warm from the sea that floats, a young woman with a pink covering of skin.

Her hair floats like seaweed as she slithers back to the surface and wiggles her toes, splashing quietly like an otter swimming through water at night. Sitting up, she gets down to business, and washes with a new bar of reddish soap which smells pleasantly spicy. She dries off on a plush mauve towel, taking care near the unicorn towel rack. She looks around for other possible dangers but sees only a plump pigeon on the window's outer ledge, fluffing its slate feathers as she nears the window.

"Too much pasta," she tells the pigeon. In the bedroom she climbs onto the canopied bed and gets under a fluffy white feather bed. "Mmm, down pillows. Clouds," she murmurs, and falls asleep the instant her head touches the pillow.

A loud knock at the door wakens Gina. She sits up in bed, disoriented, and rubs her eyes, surprised to see that it's already dark outside. "Who is it?" she calls out sleepily.

"Come and find out, if you dare," answers Giovanni.

She turns on the lamp nearest the bed, slips on her white robe, and opens the door. "Good grief!" she says, seeing his face streaked with splotches of red and blue, and his clothes all splattered with paint, like a Jackson Pollack battle victim. He holds his hands in the air, and tells her not to worry, he won't touch her. "Just fill the bath."

She doesn't comment; he looks exhausted. She runs the water and he comes in while she's looking over the contents of the medicine cabinet for something to put in the bath. He tosses his clothes in the waste basket as he takes them off.

"I finished the mural," he tells her, stepping into the tub. Gina pours bubble bath as the tub fills, and Giovanni settles back with a sigh. She hands him a towel for a headrest, and refills the tub with hot water, the bubbles climbing near the top while she admires his sun-burned face and muscular arms.

"My arms are ready to drop off," he says with a drowsy smile, a desire to be taken care of quite evident. Gina takes a washcloth and moves near to wash an arm, says she's Florence Nightingale, and starts to rub the paint off his skin. She hadn't noticed how muscular he was before, only how trim and lean. The water-based red paint washes off easily, but the blue is not coming off. "Turpentine. The only blue was oil. There's a bottle in the back pocket of my jeans."

She finds it and uses his discarded shirt for a rag and works on the blue. She finishes his arm with the washcloth, and he takes the shirt and rips off a section and does his other arm and his hands. She holds a mirror while he cleans his face, and he makes a beard out of bubbles when he's finished. Gina checks in the cabinet and finds an aloe lotion that smells like grass, and sets it out for him.

When she turns, Giovanni has slid under water, but comes up laughing. "I love singing underwater, he says. And making love too. Come on in," he invites her. She finds him very charming in his bubble bath, but says "No, but kiss me," and leans near. Giovanni slips off her robe and before she knows it, she's in the tub.

Meanwhile, downstairs, Orazio has come in with Michelangelo. He's been out on the hill looking at the mural under the floodlights. Clicking off the outdoor light, he sees water dripping down from the ceiling onto the center of the dining room table where it splashes off the head of a favorite horse statue. He takes one look and dashes up the stairs like a charging bull. The door to their bedroom is ajar, and the bathroom door is wide open. He sees them in the tub resting against each other in the bubbles. They see him and he says "Artists!" with exaggerated disgust; he can't take his eyes off Gina, and he tells them the water is dripping onto the table downstairs. He turns to leave, his mind a blank, trying to think of an excuse to linger.

He's never done anything like that. His wife lives down the road with her sister now. He never saw her naked. Not once. It was always dark, and she would never turn on a light. As he backs out the door of the bedroom he yells back: "Better mop that floor," and he slams the door. He's aware of a slight trembling of his hands as he goes down the stairs, and the beautiful richness of the deep red oriental carpet on the stairs begins to look wobbly by the time he gets to the dining room.

Michelangelo stands in the doorway of their room wagging his tail as Giovanni and Gina soak up the water on the floor with towels. She tosses a soggy towel in the tub and starts laughing. She tells Giovanni that they're getting to be like a Laurel and Hardy team, remembering the night before and the blankets covered with pine needles.

"Maybe," he says, yawning.

Gina lets Michelangelo out the door, then climbs in bed and watches Giovanni at the window. She tells him that in his velour robe he looks like a prince.

"I thought I was Oliver Hardy," he says, climbing into bed with its nest of fluffy pillows.

"I feel good," he says, though his arms, his whole body aches. "And ready to drop dead," he adds, as he stretches out, and his stretch is so expansive and soulful that Gina is touched by the gesture. It's like a prayer, or the stretch of a satisfied cat, though it's simply the stretch of a tired and happy man.

He looks sleepily at Gina. Would she go to Africa with him? Carol would never go. They could wear hard hats with lights and go down the mine shaft with a bucket and pick diamonds like blueberries. They could sit on the hill and wait for nightfall and watch the orange African sunset when the trees turn black and then the sky turns black. When all of the stars are out they could throw diamonds by handfuls up like fireworks into the sky. "Stars," he says drowsily, closing his eyes, but Gina can barely hear.

"Cars?" she asks, not expecting an answer. He falls asleep. Gina gets up and locks the door, wide awake after her long nap. She goes to the window and looks out at the night. There is the barn, and the brook beyond, sparkling as it bubbles over the rocks in the moonlight. Settling onto the high, deep-set window ledge, she sits with her legs hanging loose, dangling above the floor. As she watches Giovanni sleep, she twists her wedding ring back and forth like a knob, then wiggles it off and puts it on her little toe. She runs her fingers along the window casing. In the corner of the window ledge is a funnel-shaped spider web. The spider isn't visible. She slips the ring off her toe and drops it into the center of the web. Nothing stirs in the web and the moonlight shines on the gold of the ring. She waits for something to happen—for a spider to peer out at her with tiny iridescent ruby red eyes, but the web remains quiet with the ring in its gauzy center.

Her hand looks wrong. Lacking. Mario once told her in a therapy session that she was lacking. She lacks a capacity for guilt, which means she has no conscience. She has an incorrect balance of chemicals in her brain. Tonight, she knows he was wrong because she is blushing red with guilt here in the night with no one to see.

She eases herself down from the window ledge and looks around the room for paper. In the bureau drawer she finds a few sheets inscribed *The Grand Hotel* in English, with a palm tree growing out of the final *"L"* of Hotel. Giovanni's matches are on the bedside table. She turns out the night light and lights the candles in the brass sconces on either side of the window. He doesn't so much as stir. Now to find a cigarette. In the bathroom she finds one in the pocket of what's left of his torn shirt, and lights it ceremoniously on the way to the bed.

As she settles down on the end of the bed, she begins to draw Livia's face using a book for a table. The cigarette tastes stale. She leaves it to burn down in the crystal ashtray by her feet and works on the drawing until she is pleased with the result. Holding the drawing of Livia by a corner, she lights the paper with her cigarette, but it doesn't catch fire. Then she uses a match and lets it burn to round the edges, and then just below to give the paper a yellowed smoky look. Giovanni turns over but doesn't wake. Last, she burns holes with the dying cigarette in the Roma's eyes and peers through the eye holes as through a mask, looking at Giovanni, like a character in the middle of a burning book.

With a second piece of paper from the bureau she climbs quietly across the bed and begins to draw Giovanni asleep: the delicate lines of his face, the sculptured mouth and brow, the zygomatic arch she loves, the mass of curls on the pillow, a loose arm with a perfect hand, the hand with the moonstone ring. She draws his lashes, their shadow on his face from the candlelight. She looks at him for a long time, then gets up to blow out the candles, and looks out the window, one last look for a sign, a signal, but even the crickets are silent. Softly, unconsciously, she says "Charles," to herself and goes back to bed, settling under the covers with her vague, fleeting guilt mingling with the shapes and shadows on the wall.

In the morning, Giovanni comes downstairs to find Gina and Orazio having *cornetti* and coffee and big bowls of raspberries with cream. They're eating standing up at the island. Orazio is telling Gina the origin of the tiles on the wall above the sink. They are from Siena. He has an art history book open between the two of them. Gina waves good morning to Giovanni with her spoon. She pours Giovanni a cup of coffee, and gestures to the berries and *cornetti*. He kisses her on the cheek and sits down.

Gina and Orazio seem to be getting along all right despite her fifteen words of Italian, though he is standing a little too close. Her Italian phrase book lies unused on the counter, and there's an excitement in their attempts at communication, with much pointing and gesturing.

Giovanni sips the strong coffee and watches as Gina pages through the art book, looking refreshed, glowing and animated in the morning light. Orazio looks his usual self, though his hair seems to be slicked down in some new manner. Maybe it's just still wet from a shower. Giovanni eats with gusto, devouring the fresh raspberries in cream. He walks around with a mouth full of berries and steps between Giovanni and Orazio, giving him a friendly slap on the back, feeling generous and wonderful this morning.

"Did you fill it up?" he asks Orazio.

Orazio tells him he has a full tank and it's ready to roll. Says he's even washed off the barn dust. Giovanni takes a last swig of coffee and heads out toward the barn. Orazio and Gina follow, and Michelangelo comes out of nowhere, barking and dashing underfoot, his tail wagging its off-centered jazzy rhythm.

Orazio unlatches the door to the barn and they each pull open a side of the heavy door, which creaks dramatically. The red Ferrari is awesome. It looks out of place in the huge quiet barn, which smells of old hay and gasoline. Inside dust floats above the empty horse stalls in the morning light. Leather saddles, bridles and various horse trappings hang from the beams, and cracks in the wall let in streaks of sun. The light from the door floods onto the red car, making it shine like a dazzling jewel.

Giovanni blows a piece of straw off the hood and runs a finger along the window. He gets in the car, honks the horn and a few pigeons flutter up in the rafters. He backs out of the barn and stops just outside the door.

"Well, we'll be off, Orazio. Gina, come on, you can drive to the house and I'll run up for our luggage. Come on, go ahead. I'll walk over with Orazio."

She asks how to open it, seeing there is no door handle. He shows her the handle camouflaged in chrome at the door's upper edge. She gets in, Giovanni has left it running, and she drives the half block over to the house with white knuckles. It's silent, like gliding through calm water. She is careful to come to a smooth stop; they're both watching. Giovanni loads the bags, and Gina says she's forgotten something upstairs. She hurries to their room, and cautiously, with a pencil, retrieves her ring from the spider's web and slips it back onto her finger, and turning, is startled to see Giovanni standing behind her waiting. Did he see? She can't tell. He just says *Pronta*?

Pronta, she replies, and they leave.

Giovanni gives Orazio directions for dropping off the Fiat for Luigi, at a lot outside Venice that Luigi will be familiar with.

"You did a nice job on the mural, Giovanni," Orazio tells him, and hands him a carton of raspberries for their trip. After a quick dash to the Fiat to retrieve his CDs, they are ready. They shake hands and Orazio gives Gina a kiss on each cheek. Michelangelo comes running as they both pet him good-bye, then climb into the Ferrari.

Giovanni pulls out like a bolt of lightning and Gina barely has a chance to look at the mural as they speed by, but it seems Joseph and Mary and Jesus look happier now, and Mary has a pair of sunglasses resting stylishly on her head.

As they fly over the hill and speed down the roadway Giovanni starts to sing. To Gina, the Italian song sounds like '*ta romeo row, ta romeo row*,' and it's catchy. She hums along each time he comes to the chorus. The speeding car transports them along the road, filling them both with the exuberant joy of a roller coaster ride, and Giovanni drives them on into the timeless summer morning.

Riding like this, Gina wants to go around the world, see what there is to see, find out what would happen, what's around the corners, and she settles back at the pleasant thought of the day's drive. She takes a scarf from her purse and ties it around her head, feeling ready for anything.

"Gina, the Gypsy," Giovanni says. "You need a golden earring. I'll buy you some earrings. Some bangles, some bling. We'll stop in one of the towns down the way," and he reaches over and tousles her hair, and asks her when she's going to fast, and follow Livia's orders.

"I think I'll just be my own gypsy," she says. She tried fasting once but couldn't do it. She got too hungry by lunchtime. Giovanni laughs and speeds up, telling Gina he's going to take it to the limit, that there's a straight stretch ahead past the next vineyard so she'd better hold on. They come around a sharp curve and the road straightens out, straight as far as the eye can see, and he accelerates, making a move like a racer out to win on the home stretch. The speed is intense, and Gina concentrates on the horizon, aware of vibrations like a train whizzing by, only it's the car and she's inside it. She is disoriented and a pressure pushes her back against the seat. Her heart leaps.

Finally, Giovanni slows down and pulls over by the side of the road. He's breathing in that ecstatic way she's seen before, with pure joy. Not knowing what to say, but in a confused rapture, she starts laughing. Tears stream down her face; she closes her eyes.

"Slow down," he says, stroking her hair. "You have to slow yourself down; save something," and he calms her. They sit quietly, until Giovanni gets out of the car and climbs over a fence. He returns with a cluster of grapes. "Try these."

She tells how her boys like to peel grapes and make eyeballs. He asks if she ever did anything like that, as a kid. Yes, on vacation when she was seven, she and a friend made a stew. They made a fire on the beach and cooked a bunch of empty clam shells and a dead fish from the beach that didn't look too old. They used driftwood and she had matches. Neither wanted to chicken out and not eat the stinky stew, but then they were saved by her mother calling her for supper. They both agreed to leave the mess for the seagulls.

"I wasn't really afraid when you were racing, Giovanni."

"I could tell. God I love this car," he says, and reaches for his cigarettes, then remembers he quit last night, there aren't any, and he honks the horn at nothing instead.

Giovanni drives at a normal speed to the next town. They stroll the streets, stopping at outdoor markets selling cookware, tablecloths and flowers, and head up a narrow street past a black cat. He wants to buy something for Gina, some remembrance. "I don't want you to forget me," he says. "I don't know what's ahead for us."

∞

IN THE BOUTIQUE—Gina comes out of the dressing room wearing a dark green sundress. Giovanni greets her with a wave of a big straw hat which he plunks on her head and tips to a jaunty angle, but the clerk shakes her head in disapproval, one hand fluttering no way, it won't do. Nevertheless, Gina likes the hat. The clerk leaves to fetch a pair of sunglasses for her to try.

Giovanni ponders the jewelry counter and points out an oval piece of amber on a gold chain. "Just right for you," he tells her, assured of his own good taste, but he's glad she likes it too. "I like these too," she says, pointing to a pair of gold-looped earrings on an earring rack.

The clerk comes up beside them and hands Gina a pair of black wrap-around sunglasses and Giovanni tells her what he wants to buy. Ignoring him, she removes a long dangly necklace with a cloisonné parrot from the locked jewelry counter and puts it around Gina's neck and winks knowingly at her, saying something that, though in Italian, Gina knows is, *It's you, darling.* Gina shakes her head, and removes the necklace, setting it on the counter. She doesn't know why the clerk is being so rude to Giovanni, standing with her back to him. Maybe she's having a bad day, or she doesn't like men.

The clerk boxes and wraps the amber necklace and earrings, pushing the items toward Gina while Giovanni pays. Amber is made to last. Gina imagines the amber necklace around her neck when she's a skeleton, decorating her bones like a piece of petrified sun. Still, she's extra happy. Sun streams through Giovanni's hair from the window and shines down through the glass countertop.

Now what can she buy for him? Something Italian, something really nice. She can use some of the money from the sale of the collage. Looking at his profile as he counts out euros, he looks like someone from an old American cigarette ad, a slightly more delicate version of the handsome rogue who lights up, though she hopes he can quit. She doesn't like the smell, and his beautiful fingers are yellowed. With his sunburn, his poetic edge has hardened. Maybe a pipe, a fine sculptural shape he might like. No, that's still tobacco. She'll think of something. Maybe a book, an art book. As they're about to leave the shop, Giovanni returns to the counter, takes the parrot necklace and puts it around the clerk's neck and says something to her in Italian.

Back in the car Gina puts on the amber necklace. "I love it Giovanni," she says, fondling the light warm amber. "What did you say to her?"

"You don't want to know," he replies without a smile, and drives off. Must be the lack of nicotine already unnerving him. She decides to be quiet and curls up into a comfortable position. She's also thinking about smoking, so will try to sleep.

Later, Gina wakes up. Giovanni is looking at a crumpled map spread over the steering wheel.

"Where are we?"

So deep in thought over the map, he's startled by her voice; she's been asleep for over an hour. He tells her no one has ever slept while he was driving before, and that they're getting close. She has a red line like a scar across her face from leaning against something while she slept, probably a seam on the leather seat, and a round mark, from a button, on her flushed cheek. She pushes hair out of her eyes.

"You're always here when I wake up," she says, stretching and yawning. She tells him about her dream. He had given her a handful of tiny candy hearts with words on them, but instead of saying *Wow*, or *Cool*, these were all in Italian. A waiter came and offered to pour pasta sauce over the hearts, but she had wanted them plain. There were a lot of people at a long table and it was quite confusing. Giovanni had come over and put his arm around her shoulder and told everybody, very knowingly, that she was new at hearts. Giovanni was wearing a tuxedo, just the top and boxer shorts and she had wondered if everyone else at the table was also half dressed.

"What an odd dream," he says, realizing he hasn't celebrated Valentine's Day for many years.

"Giovanni, let's get all dressed up and go to the opera. Charles hates opera, so I rarely go."

They decide, yes, they'll put it on their list of things to do. La Fenice, the temple of opera, in Venice, for sure. Opera is one of his great loves, and he admires the Italian passion for the art. He tells her about an intermission at a Puccini opera when two guys were arguing over who was singing better, the tenor or the soprano, and Giovanni was almost caught up in the middle of a fist fight. He had been standing nearby smoking a cigarette, taking it all in until they were about to start a brawl. Fortunately, the bell for the next act rang. He slides in another opera CD and sings along.

Giovanni makes a sudden stop. "The bridge is out. If we'd been driving at night we'd be in the river," he says. Someone must have stolen the sign. Some prank. They will have to detour but decide to stop for a rest in the meantime.

They walk along the riverbank, stopping at a pool to watch two large fish swim in circles. The shallow water is clear enough to see sand at the bottom with water plants waving around in the commotion of the playful fish. When the fish swim upstream, Giovanni puts his arm around Gina's shoulder, and they watch the water gurgling along the stream.

Soon they're focused on the stones of the creek bed, and Gina finds a few perfectly shaped small black stones she thinks are perfect eyes. That sets them off and they begin gathering stones. With a stick, Giovanni draws the outline of a face in the dense sand.

He organizes stones by shades of black and white, reddish colors and in-betweens, and starts filling in the face, instructing Gina in the ways of mosaic as they work together on the outline and the eyes. Outlines come first. They stand to get a bird's eye view before proceeding, both lost in time under the warm Italian sun, finding just the right stones for each part of the face, continuing until they have a remarkably ancient appearing mosaic visage looking up at the world from beside the river, complete with white halo.

"You're a good teacher, Giovanni."

He tells her she's the perfect student, and he is definitely going to teach in the spring. He's going to accept a position in Florence to teach art history, plus a workshop on fresco painting in the spring and then a mosaic class in the summer. Still, he'll keep his studio in Venice. Giovanni uses his cell phone to take a photo of their masterpiece.

"It's not long for this world," he says. "A few rains will wash it away."

They drive the last stretch to the beach house listening to the music of Spanish steel string guitars. Gina thinks it is the same music that was playing when she awoke that first night in the studio after Pascal's attack. How odd that life is like that; such horror in the middle of the sweetest songs. She wants to know where Pascal came from and settles back to hear the story.

Pascal was a wedding present from Carol's Uncle Pete. Pete the Pirate, Carol used to say. He got him in Africa, and Carol was furious at the dumb present. She never liked that uncle, and thought it was supposed to be a joke. She expected all the proper things like crystal, silver. No monkeys on her list. "I can still see Pascal looking scared to death sitting in the corner of a huge black leather chair looking up at us with those big eyes and hanging onto a little red hat for dear life," he says.

Carol's family lived in California but had ties to Africa because this Uncle Pete lived in the Congo where his dad led safaris back in the old days and knew a lot of politicians. Both Carol's dad and his brother Pete were in real estate. He was shrewd and reckless too. Thet both were. Together they bought property in Africa that was said to be studded with undeveloped diamond mines. Well, it turned out to be true. The mines were priceless and Pete, and Carol's dad, who went in on it, became wealthy men. It was an old story by the time Giovanni met Carol.

Giovanni said he was pretty indifferent towards wealth back then, and now finds their dealings in the mines an ugly business. Anyway, in addition to Pascal, they each received a diamond mine for a wedding present, and then another one for a birthday. "I still own them," he says. "One is the *Bright Diamond* and the other *The Southern Cross*." Even though he hates owning them he hasn't been able to make himself get rid of them, but now he's ready, thanks to Livia.

He looks to Gina for her reaction. She's playing with her new amber necklace, but she's obviously been listening. She's hard to read sometimes but he suspects she's like him, with an inability to appreciate the almighty dollar. Fate of the artist.

"Old Pete," he goes on. "You couldn't help liking the guy. He had charm; I'll give him that. Very physical—a back slapper, or an arm always draped over someone's shoulder, and good looking. Distinguished and elegant, too. Everybody wanted to know Pete—thought some of his charm might rub off, even though you would know the whole time he'd stab anyone in the back in the blink of an eye if they got in his way." He pauses, remembering, and slows the car.

"Carol was a little like him. Maybe that's why she always hated him," he says, more to himself than to Gina.

"I'm glad she's dead," Gina says, surprised for having said so. Giovanni's expression doesn't change, remaining thoughtful, serious, showing no shock. "Well," she goes on. "It's easier. I mean that's one reason I like opera. It's so clear cut; death, with all that murder and suicide. If there's a problem, you just kill them off. Have them drink poison or find a snake. Or a duel at dawn like in the old Russian novels. Dramatic. No malingering. But still I'm sorry what I said about Carol," she says, realizing she doesn't really know anything about actual death, only what happens in plays and in books.

Giovanni laughs, a sudden laugh of alarm, and looks directly at Gina and asks if she wants him to kill for her, and in his eyes, intense and glassy, she senses the possibility of anything, and a hypnotic power holds her, and she likes it. Yet he probably wouldn't even think that way if he was still smoking, she's sure of that. Some immense energy was harnessed by the smoke, and now that expression of the wild, a madness looking out from the forest edge has emerged.

"If my life were an opera or a play, I'd say yes," Gina tells him, and feels some life force flow between them, a manic connection taking place as they drive along the road, speeding with the wind. Soon Gina is giving directions, as she recognizes the road and the local vineyard of her neighborhood. They pass the turnoff to Rosa's, the steep winding road past the cove with its sharp curves, never traveled before at this speed. Then down the hill past Rinaldo's and on to the driveway of the beach house where they pull in beside the garage.

"Looks like Charles is back," Giovanni says, noticing the car in the garage. He shuts his own car door carefully; he used to slam the Fiat door, Gina recalls. But she assures him it's not Charles's car; she doesn't know whose it is. Then, looking closely through the glass windows of the garage at a blue car with a bicycle on the back, she feels a jolt as if she had been hit by an electrical charge, and knows the car, of course, belongs to Mario.

A sense of falling and rising at the same time comes over her and she stiffens. A forewarning, such as this, has come to her before, of something irrefutable, unchangeable. She's always persevered when it's come before, and now with her backbone a tense rod, she feels a steady flow of adrenaline. Her blood is throbbing with an invisible fiery excitement both inexplicable and wonderful. Here we go, the angel-demon of amusement park tracks, the old irrevocable ride, the speed and the tracks, the demon laugh and scream, the demented thrill. The last time she felt like this was the weekend before she was committed. But she's standing still in her driveway, staring through the window pane of the garage. At the blue car. The beautiful blue car that she's never seen before in her life.

"What, are you having a nicotine fit?" Giovanni asks, taking her trembling hand. An uncanny steadiness has come over him. As soon as he touches her she knows they could walk through flames together; something has been conjured, and she pulls her hand away. He wanted a star-light blue car once, but this is darker. She touches her lips, like rose petals, too soft, in her mind they are black leeches, at night when she can't see. Giovanni grabs her upper arm. "Gina, pull yourself together," he says.

"I'm all right," she tells him. He's hurting her arm, or is it the hardness in his eyes that hurts. What am I doing, bringing you here? Retrieving her keys from the mess at the bottom of her purse, she picks up the shark's tooth, and it seems funny. She pictures a shark smiling, and her own teeth pointed, a glossy charcoal gray, what would Charles think? She turns the key in the lock. It opens easily; it must not have been locked. Where is he?

"Whose car is it?" Giovanni asks, demands, as the sound of saxophones drifts out as soon as the door is opened, a breezy jazz from the speakers.

"Mario's," she says.

"The Roma's Mario, of course. I should have known. Christ, Gina, did you know he'd be here?"

Gina stands there, half puzzled, half stunned. She doesn't know what to say or do. Her hand seems glued to the doorknob, she can't unclench her hand. Then with concentration she pulls, and her hand comes loose, and she's thrust back, regains her balance and a semblance of composure. He's looking at her hard. She tells him Mario was never her lover; that they were just friends. He was just her therapist. Suddenly she feels calm, even with Giovanni's current rage.

"Well, let's go in. You can meet each other, and I'll start dinner," she says, as though life is going to be normal.

The phone rings. It's Rosa, checking to see if she had gotten back. Rosa chatters on, and Gina listens as well as she can, watching the scene taking place before her. Giovanni enters the living room as Mario opens the sliding glass door from the patio. He's smoking his pipe. She understands the smoke signals, their hazy winding shapes in the late afternoon sun: war clouds.

Mario, as cool as ever, walks into the room with his masterful pipe, Chief Mario. Scenes of cowboys and Indians, Saturday afternoon matinees of childhood flicker before her, arrows flying, whooping sounds, guns, smoke, oh the smoke, the tobacco makes her dizzy, the aroma. We're all adults here, she hears herself telling Rosa. Rosa is speaking in Italian, and Gina holds the phone away from her—she knows she doesn't understand Italian, what is it, Cherokee, Apache? She starts tapping on the table like a drum.

10. Mario's Pipe

L ate in the evening while removing the mostly melted icepack from Mario's pillow, Gina notices a black notebook in the half-opened drawer of the bed stand and knows it must be his journal. Quietly she slips it from the drawer without so much as a guilty swallow, keeping one eye on Mario, who appears to be sleeping soundly. She moves stealthily to the door and turns out the light. Taking her prize to the patio, she sits down at the wrought iron table, using her last match to light the candle of the antique Chianti bottle.

She leans forward and stares at the notebook, its black cover, as though trying to absorb its contents by the sheer act of concentration until the black cover takes on a life of its own, the slick cardboard becoming a skin, like the dark red apple of a psychical eggplant. She runs her fingers across the surface of the smooth black cover, slowly, as one might move across a Ouija board. Then with a sigh, she gets up and returns to the bedroom with the unopened journal, thinking, not today, there has been enough, not wanting to admit she's simply afraid.

Inside the bedroom door, she stands waiting for her eyes to adjust to the dark, and watches the sleeping form on the bed come into view, much as an old-time Polaroid photo would develop: gauzy white bandages are wound around his head as he sleeps on the apple blossom pillow case. She slips off her shoes and walks over to the drawer to return the journal, touches the fold of the blanket over his shoulder, and leaves the room.

Feeling wounded and tired, she wanders to the kitchen, turns a burner on high, gets down a bottle of wine and opens it with the angel de-corker and pours half a glass of orange juice, adds red wine to the top, then rummages behind the cans in the cupboard for a bendable straw. Leaving the kitchen light off, she sits down on a bar stool in front of the stove so she can watch the spiral of the red-hot burner in the dark while she sips her sangria concoction. Time passes. She continues to watch the burner, waiting for the red burning circle to spin. It doesn't, but she feels a sensation of something—a friendliness in the heat, a reassuring piece of a star, near her on the stove, that fell out of somewhere and fits into place, as Africa fits into South America. She relaxes into a cozy oblivion in the darkness of the kitchen with the memory of a huge pit in the west somewhere a comet had fallen, connected, and the memory mixes with the moment and the parts of the day, slowly, as thick soup stirred with a wooden spoon.

Finally, with the last slurp of her drink, she turns off the burner. She wanders around the house, pacing back and forth carrying the wine bottle and chewing on the straw. In the den she picks up an old issue of the local newspaper, and one of Charles's blank notebooks—he doesn't use that kind anymore, the one with a full set of teeth at the top of each page, each tooth numbered with the rest of the page lined for writing. Gina uses them for sketch books now that computers have taken over.

Back in the bedroom Giovanni has fallen asleep stretched out on a lower bunk. In the moonlight he looks more wounded than Mario, perhaps because he doesn't have a beard like Mario, so he's more vulnerable, and one's eye is drawn to Giovanni's bandaged head. She goes closer. The line of his jaw seems so intimate and the angle at once determined and mortal. Why do I always see the skeleton within, she wonders, and wants to touch his face. A thief in his room too, she checks his pants pockets for matches, and leaves with a box of them.

Back outside, she heads down the hill, taking the path past the cypress trees and on down to the beach where the moonlight brightens the shore. She gathers driftwood, dry to the touch and crumples newspaper and starts a fire, which is soon blazing. One of her most rewarding gifts, she's sure, is her ability to start fires.

Sitting on the side opposite of the smoke, she starts to write: "Dear Diary."

She crosses out the words and starts again, writing the date, August 25, between the lower and upper teeth at the top of the stationery.

"Arrived at the beach house with Giovanni today. Mario was at the house when we arrived and there was a fight. I think it was because Giovanni hadn't had a cigarette all day, and then Mario's pipe was certainly an aggravation, on top of his just being there when we arrived. When they were fighting, I could only catch a word here and there, although they were yelling at each other the whole time. Giovanni was yelling in Italian and Mario was quieter but spoke more steadily, just under his breath. I was horrified, but it was also wonderful, just the same.

I had never seen an actual fight. It was nothing like the karate movies the boys watch, the actual sounds are much dimmer, not much like whips snapping or bones cracking, but a duller sound.

It was Mario who started it, in a sense, the way he swaggered up to me like he did, always just a little too cocky. He shouldn't have asked me like that: *Who's your friend, Goldilocks?* So Giovanni with his nicotine left back in Venice just socked Mario in the jaw before he could even get the pipe out of his mouth. It went sailing across the room and hit the wall. It all happened so fast.

I don't know what would have happened if I hadn't finally picked up that brass duck from the table. I didn't know whose side I was on—both I suppose, but I knew I had to do something, and I struck, and it was two with one blow. I got them both with the mallard and they crashed to the carpet, the good Persian one. The silence in the room is what scared me then, even more than the blood. I got down on my knees. I thought they were dead, and I was just kneeling there like that with the mallard in my hand when Rosa came in the door.

She got the doctor finally. I don't know how long that took. I just kept moaning and rocking back and forth on the floor, waiting.

The doctor said concussions weren't so unusual and they would recover but would need absolute rest and quiet. Rosa took the duck away from me before the doctor arrived. She said the doctor told her all the blood was from the nosebleeds and the blow from the brass duck was softened by the felt on the bottom of the brass duck. It could have been worse, and wasn't, thank heavens.

Gina tears the pages out of the notebook, crumples them up and tosses them into the fire, then lies down on the sand to listen to the crackling of the fire and the waves against the shore, the rhythm bringing her to the edge of sleep. The fire shadows bring half dreams. She falls in and out of sleep—the fight, the blood, strained faces, sweaty arms, the awful cries and groans, until they merge, like sand, into one—Mariovanni, until she pries them apart, each into his self again. Their dream images walk down the beach in opposite directions and vanish into the air. Gina sits up, and although she is next to the fire, she is shaking with cold.

Taking off her shoes, she sets them beside the fire and starts to walk toward the cove, walking on the cool sand, along the edge of the sea where the sand is wet. The waves wash over her feet, washing away her footprints, one by one as she moves toward the darkness of the cove and away from the fire, past the driftwood log, and on to where the cliff forms a point and the waves slap harder over her feet, splashing against her ankles. She continues around the corner to the beginning of the cove's dark shadows. Something splashes and swims into the smooth dark water and she stops. Here she is the only living human being.

She sits down on a rock and rests her head in her hands. Her head feels like granite. Closing her eyes, she wiggles her toes in the sand and listens to the sea. She drifts off and wakes when her head slips off her arm. A fish jumps, and it's bright enough to see the water rings circling out, wider and wider until the surface is smooth, and she feels the need to go back to the house, in case they wake.

Moving along quickly, she doesn't notice that her footprints have all been washed away. As she passes the cliff she can see the light of the fire and follows it along the beach. Her shoes sit waiting for her, warmed by the fire. She sits on the log and brushes the sand from her feet and slips on her shoes and puts out the fire from the water pail, covering the embers with sand before hurrying up the hill. Under her breath she whispers, no one is going to die.

Back in the house, she looks in on Mario. Next to the bed she stands very still and holds her breath until she can hear, as she did when the boys were babies, listening to the sweet reassuring sound of breathing in the night.

Next she goes to Giovanni's room and listens. His breathing is heavy and rasping, and he's thrown his blankets onto the floor. She doesn't know where to sleep. She would wake Giovanni if she used an upper bunk, and the second lower bunk is covered with books and puzzles. The couches are made of separate pieces that come apart so they can be rearranged—she tried napping on them once and they slid apart. Mario is in the big bed. It's too soon for Charles to return with the boys, she's pretty sure. Yawning and painfully tired, she takes a couch pillow and the old quilt from the foot of the bed and curls up on the floor and falls asleep.

CR

Early the next morning Mario wakes, and is surprised to see Gina asleep on the floor in her clothes. He steps around her carefully to get to the bathroom. He feels pretty good until he looks in the mirror and sees his black eye and swollen lip, and an ugly slash high on his cheek and a cap of white gauze bandages wound round his head. Mainly his jaw aches, but he laughs, thinking of the wedding next week, and the photographer Anita is having flown in. She's so excited. "Anita," he says to himself; he loves to say her name.

Mario kneels down next to Gina and gently wakes her, a hand on her shoulder and says, "Good morning," when she opens her eyes.

"Morning Mario," she says drowsily, and her face starts to burn with shame at the sight of him, his swollen mouth, the black and blue eye, remembering how heavily she brought the mallard down on their heads. Was it harder than necessary? She recalls the girl she read about in the newspaper who stabbed her boyfriend 52 times, though the first would have been the fatal one. "I didn't mean to hurt you," she says and smiles. There is something irresistibly joyous in the morning, and in his eyes.

She's so stiff, and reaches to her back. "Hardwood floors," she grimaces, and asks Mario how long he's been staying here.

He's been here since Tuesday, thought she wouldn't mind, and the door was unlocked. "Did you know that?"

"Oh. I left in kind of a hurry."

"So, I just made myself at home. Nice beach—I've been swimming every day. Good record collection too. I've been playing a lot of Mozart, and Jarbarek. He was playing when you came yesterday, with what's his name?"

"Giovanni."

"How is he? Is he here?"

"Sure. He looks worse than you. Why did you call him that yesterday?" she says accusingly.

"Hey, I'm hardly awake. Don't you feel sorry for me?" he asks.

"No. You're too radiant, too happy. I can feel it right through all that black and blue."

Mario smiles, says he's been using the deck hot tub, hopes she doesn't mind. She and Charles hadn't used it because they didn't want the boys to, but now she's glad it's filled. She sits up and thinks about breakfast. No one ate last night. They can eat outside. Maybe smoked salmon and fruit. She looks toward the ceiling dreaming up the menu. Some eggs too, and orange muffins. Coffee.

"You need to apologize to Giovanni," she says.

"Look, Gina," he takes her arm. "He came at me like a maniac. You think I should apologize?"

She shrugs a shoulder and he loosens his hold. She touches the cuff of his black velour robe and leaves the room, wondering why they have the same robes—black, such an unlikely color.

◌ঽ

Mario sinks deep into the spa up to his neck, thinking of Anita as he soaks his aching self. Feeling a pain in his side, he hoists himself up to examine his hip, surprised to see a fist-sized black and blue mark. He slides back in, choosing to ignore the injury. He closes his eyes. He must have been four, maybe younger, when he hit his finger with a hammer, missing his target, and the blood blister seemed to scream out of him, but he didn't make a sound, didn't tell anyone. He blinked away his tears.

Gina wrote a poem for him once, about sawdust and wood shavings, the late afternoon sun and shadows of a carpentry shop. He never told her how moved he was by that poem. He could never tell her much, though he would want to. It was always easier to listen, to just be the therapist. It's easier with Anita. No complications. It's never confusing, thinking of Anita. He's in a circle with her where it's peaceful—the right place. He has to finish writing his vows, after breakfast, can't seem to get anywhere. Damn, his head hurts. He's got to call his office. He needs another week. Get someone to cover for him. "Giovanni." He says the name to himself. Funny, he doesn't look like a Giovanni. So blond.

Mario closes his eyes and lets his legs float out, concocting a vow. No, a statement. Something about the circle and the ring, journeys, discoveries. Gina could do it. No, I haven't even told her. Maybe two bikers riding in unison, a unicycle. No. Shit.

"Hi."

Mario looks up. It's Giovanni standing in the doorway with his bandaged head. Both of his eyes are black and blue. After staring at each other they both start talking at once. Mario starts laughing, and says, "You look like Hell," and motions for him to join him. Giovanni stands with his hands on his hips looking at Mario, like one animal measuring another's intentions, and decides it's safe. He lowers himself into the hot tub.

"Gina's taking a shower," Mario says, glancing at the bathroom door.

"Where did she sleep?" Giovanni asks.

"On the floor. Honestly. That's where I found her this morning."

They're both silent, neither knowing what more to say or where to look, like strangers on an elevator, they take turns clearing their throats. The silence becomes uncomfortable, so they make small talk, which they both abhor. The temperature of the water keeps them going for a while. Finally, Giovanni asks Mario if he has an extra pipe. "Always carry a few," he says, and climbs out to retrieve the smoking paraphernalia, wondering if his good one broke last night in the fight.

"Which one?" he asks, returning with the pipes in hand. "Corncob, or this one?"

"I'll try the cob," Giovanni says, never having tried one. Mario fills the pipes and lights both. Soon they are soaking and puffing away on their pipes, the morning is good again and smoke clouds float up with the steam above their bandaged heads.

Gina strolls in wearing her gold oriental robe. She stops short and freezes—hadn't heard them with the shower running. She stands there feeling like the horse of a different color in the Wizard of Oz turning from blue to green to rose. Yet she's transfixed at their strange beauty—these handsome young men home from battle, both smiling and happy, talking to her; saying the water's fine.

"Good morning," she says. The fight apparently forgotten, replaced by all that smoke. She leaves for the dressing room where she rummages in a drawer for clothes, finds only scarves, just mixed up scarves. Where did she get all these scarves? The wrong drawer; they're not even hers. From the next drawer she retrieves her favorite tennis outfit, the green and blue batik, always comfortable and cool even on the court. Now, a scarf, and she's ready. Funny, she has not looked for a tennis court the whole time they've been in Italy and their rackets sit unused beside the umbrella stand. Being the good tennis player that she is, she feels more in control and clenches her hand around an invisible racket and heads back to the men in the smoking spa.

"Good morning again," she says, interrupting their conversation. She heard snatches of their talk while she dressed, about a Gaudí building in Barcelona, and about curved staircases, and how they both like a certain mausoleum in Ravenna.

"I'm so glad you're both alive," she says very seriously. They laugh.

"Come on in Gina," Mario says.

"No, I don't think so," she says half to herself, and tells them breakfast will be on the terrace in half an hour. She's both terrified and fascinated by the sight of the two of them in the spa, and part of her wants to sit right down and sketch them, but she leaves for the kitchen.

On her way she stops in front of the stereo. What to play? A requiem? Certainly no jazz. The South American flute suite will do. The music follows her into the kitchen as part of the summer morning. Mixing up muffin batter, she grates in fresh orange zest, waiting for the joyous savage cries she knows come early in the CD, the calls of birds, monkeys, and creatures of some great unseen rain forest. There it is, and for a moment she holds her breath, until the flute drifts on and the muffins go into the oven.

The melons are still good. She mounds the orange and pink melon balls and licks the sweet juice from her fingers. She arranges the smoked salmon on a glass plate and picks young dill sprigs from the window ledge plant from Rosa. Chewing a fresh dill seed, she heats a pan and starts the eggs. Coffee should be ready by the time she gets everything out to the patio.

"I didn't know you were there," she says, startled at seeing Giovanni in the doorway. "How are you?" she asks.

"Not bad, except my back hurts and my head hurts and I think I have a loose tooth."

She wipes her hands. He leans over for a kiss, pauses, and says Mario's an okay guy. But he wishes he weren't here and offers to carry something to the table. He's starving. She hands him a tray. On the way to the terrace he tells her he and Mario are going to the marble quarry after breakfast.

"You never told me he knew so much about architecture," he says.

"No, I guess I didn't. Tell him we can eat now, if you would."

Gina returns for the coffee and butter, puzzling over their quick recovery, and their friendliness. They're at the table by the time she gets to the deck.

"One more thing," she says and returns for vitamins. Back at the table she pours coffee and passes the vitamin bottle around. Looking at their bandages, she pulls the scarf off her head, and points out a white boat down on the sea, a big yacht. Those big ones rarely come this far north. "I wonder where they come from, who they are," she ponders.

"The idle rich," Giovanni says.

A melon ball in her mouth, she keeps chewing.

"Are we the idle rich?" she asks.

They laugh, and Mario says, no, he just owns a bike. But he's not so sure about Giovanni, having noticed the Ferrari in the driveway earlier. No way, Giovanni says, his hands out defensively. Mario looks at Giovanni, puzzled, thinks he's more like Gina, and senses an understanding between the two of them, an ease he's never really had with her.

Well, Giovanni says, waiting for Gina to say something. She says she's not the idle rich, and that she's going to paint this morning, and anyway, it's not that big of a yacht. Refilling coffee cups all around, they listen to Mario tell about his biking trip. The men clear the table while Gina has an extra cup of coffee. On his way to the kitchen Mario leans over and tells her he has to talk to her alone.

Sipping coffee, which tastes extra good this morning, she watches the yacht turn south and sail away. Like her boys, they'll get bigger and bigger and then they'll sail away. Off to their own lives. She wonders what Mario and Giovanni were like as boys. The sea is the blue of a Madonna's robe this morning. Almost a French ultramarine. She'll have to point that out to Giovanni.

Sudden hands on her shoulders.

"Gina," Mario says, pulling up a chair.

"Giovanni's loading the dishwasher. You couldn't find an Italian to do that for you. At your house I always used to end up cooking for everyone. Remember?"

"You're a good cook," she tells him. He's looking down at his hands. She's only seen him like this once before—that night after *Hannah and Her Sisters* when they took a short cut to the car and walked down an alley past the lilacs. You could smell the heavy scent of lilacs all along the alley that night, in that old part of town. He talked so distractedly that she wanted to do something, help out. It was always hard for him to talk to her and she knew he left things unsaid. He was used to being the listener. They would talk for hours about all sorts of things, always being so considerate of each other, but mostly she did the talking. He's as fragile as he is tough, she knows, and wonders if anyone else knows that. She used to think of him as a wild stallion that would come to visit her and if she wasn't extremely cautious, he would run off into the mountain valleys and meadows.

"What is it?" she asks.

He coughs and clears his throat, clasps his hands, pauses, and sets his hands firmly on the table. "Anita and I are getting married. Next week. I needed to tell you. I thought you might come to the wedding. You and Charles. The boys are welcome too. The wedding is in San Moritz." He looks at her, his eyes asking for approval.

She rests an elbow on the table, the fingers playing with the muffin crumbs. She scoops them up and takes them to the bird feeder, letting them fall like snow. She leans on the railing and stares out at the melted sea. Mario comes over and stands beside her, confused, like he's given her news of someone's death and he feels close to her. He puts his arms around her and holds her like a true friend. She kisses his beard, laughs a little laugh and wipes her eyes with the back of her hand, surprised that she's partially relieved at his news.

They watch the sea, and Gina tells him about the time her brother's fiancée came home for the weekend, shortly before their wedding. Gina had liked her very much but cried all that first night because she knew she was losing her brother.

"You didn't really lose him though, did you? Isn't he always your brother?"

"Well, yes and no. They moved far away, but still he's always with me. You know, always part of me. But mostly I lost him." She gives him a hug and tells him she wishes him well, both he and Anita, and is surprised to realize she really means it.

He doesn't let her go. Giovanni puts on a record, and they move to the music, a waltz that seems appropriate for the bitter-sweet moment.

"I missed you when you got well. I missed hearing your dreams, your stories," he says. He can't explain to her why he left, how Charles knew they were getting too close. Charles could be rough, almost threatening him. He doesn't want to tell her about that side of Charles. He sighs, his fingers stroking her hair. "What's this?" he asks, fondling her amber necklace. "The color of honey."

"Amber. A present from Giovanni. The Vikings used to trade it for gold."

"He's good for you, isn't he?" Mario says.

"Yes," she nods her head.

"Well," he pauses. "Ready?"

"Yes, let's go in."

Giovanni is out in the driveway, and his feet are sticking out of the car, apparently looking for something when they come out. He gets out and asks Mario if he's ready, but he avoids looking at Gina. Mario's appropriately enthralled over the Ferrari. Giovanni gets in, says "Come on, Mario," and says *"Ciao"* to Gina without looking at her. She watches them drive off in the gaudy red car, the backs of their heads visible. With their bandaged heads they look like mummies in a scene from a really bad movie. She watches until the dust settles on the road and there's nothing more to watch.

Inside she tapes a large sheet of gessoed paper to the wall and gets out her brushes and paints. She chooses the darkest colors, black, raw umber, sienna, Prussian blue, and then the bright colors, the reds, and an odd purple she rarely uses. She squeezes a blob of white onto the center of the glass palette, which is an old windowpane from the garage, then begins to pace, glancing at the white paper. She paces and waits, waiting for the animal with teeth that paints, that frees her to paint. She pours a glass of wine, continues the restless walking, and her emerald eyes glisten as she starts in, scooping up white with a palette knife, she begins spreading, smearing. The images form—faces, skulls, and the black. She's taken over. She sips, paces, looks, talks to herself—here the delicate line of a shoulder, teeth, and hollow eyes. Movement, red, intense, something moves in with hands, hands like candles, selfless, her hands work, the painting becomes alive, completing itself, a creature fully formed that she allows, guides, into being. She stands back. It's finished. She accepts the painting; knows that it is good.

Cleaning the knives and brushes meticulously, mechanically she puts everything away. Though it's still morning, she's exhausted, ready to nap. The smell of rubbing alcohol and tobacco whiffs up from the pillow where Giovanni slept. She falls into a deep sleep.

Gina is wakened from sleep by a bell. She doesn't know if it's a telephone or a doorbell. In the living room she realizes it's both the phone and the doorbell. She gets the door first. It's Rosa, and she welcomes her in, points to the phone and goes to pick up, rubbing her head, waking up. It's Charles.

"Charles. It seems like you've been gone so long. How are you?" she asks, quickly alert.

"We're all fine. How about you? I haven't talked to you since that night you called me at a rather ungodly hour. Are you sure you're okay?"

"Not quite. I mean I'm just sleepy, I was napping. I'm fine. Didn't you get all the emails I sent?"

"Yes, but they were odd. Really odd, Gina."

"Rosa just stopped by. I just let her in."

"That's good to hear. She's a reliable neighbor. Anyway, I just need to know if you can pick us up at the depot," he says. "We get in tomorrow night."

"Oh, I left the van at the train station," she says. "I took the train, like you suggested. I didn't fly. Do you have the extra keys?"

"Sure, sure. I suppose Rosa picked you up. Just as well, no waiting that way. So the boys want a party when we get back, and we'll probably be late tomorrow night. I'll tell them we'll have the party the following night. For some reason they have a Hawaiian luau in mind. Something to do with a movie they saw. I think I'll order a boar and roast it on the beach. Talk to Rosa about it," Charles says. An operator comes on the line.

"Okay. See you tomorrow night," Gina says.

"One more thing. See about pineapples and coconuts. See what you can get. And flower leis, like in Hawaii." The operator breaks in again, and they end the call.

Gina hangs up and with her hand still on the receiver she tells Rosa that it was Charles and that the boys want to have a luau, a Hawaiian cookout with a roasted pig and tropical fruit and lots of flowers.

Rosa loves the party idea but asks about the patients, surprised they aren't resting but have gone off to a marble quarry together.

"And I forgot to warn Mario about Giovanni's driving. He drives too fast."

"Gina. First of all, I don't approve." She looks at Gina through lowered eyes that more than affirm her statement, yet she says she is her friend and will stand by her. They are very handsome men, both of them, although she only saw them when they were unconscious. So she can see what Gina sees in them; she's not that old. "But Gina, if you can keep one man happy you can be proud of that. You don't need so many. All you will do is stir up the devils."

Gina wishes she didn't sound so much like the fortune teller, yet, looking at Rosa, she wishes she could be more like her. Rosa seems so satisfied, and sensible, like Charles says.

Rosa brought a big covered cooking pot of her special sauce, good for a number of meals, she says, so Gina need only cook the pasta. She lifts the lid off the still warm sauce, the kind Gina knows simmers for hours and is cooked with anchovies and sun-dried tomatoes.

"Yum, it smells so good," Gina says as they walk to the kitchen with the pot between them.

"Thanks, Rosa. And you take some of these cooked tomatoes," she says, setting two of the containers from the freezer that didn't explode, down on the table, explaining they're from Rinaldo's garden. She's happy to have something to give in return.

Gina heats coffee in the microwave and they sit at the kitchen island. Rosa looks out of place at the modern barstool counter. She likes Rosa's old-fashioned kitchen better, while Rosa secretly admires the modern look and roominess of Gina's kitchen.

"I like the blond one better," Rosa says. "He looks kinder. The dark one, I bet he started the fight."

Gina sighs. Rosa only saw them when they were unconscious. But Mario does affect people like that. He has a kind of dark mysterious look. She was on an elevator with him once and a little boy looked up at him and then stepped back behind his father. The child was afraid.

Giovanni, the blond one, actually hit Mario first, she tells Rosa, who listens attentively without commenting. They both sip their coffee. Rosa has become accustomed to Gina's weak American coffee that you can drink so much of.

"What are you looking for at the bottom of that cup, Gina? You're looking so hard; the cup is going to start leaking. Just drink the coffee. So, what's on your mind?"

Gina takes a sip. She was thinking about the angel God kicked out of Heaven because he was jealous. The angel knew too much and He wouldn't allow that. They're both like that, Mario and Giovanni, beautiful fallen angels. Or is she the fallen one?

"It's hard to understand Mario and Giovanni," Gina says.

"Yes, men are like spaghetti sauce," Rosa says simply, as though she were stating an obvious fact.

Gina laughs. "That's good Rosa," she says, and hears a screech in the distance, and knows they're back.

Soon Giovanni is honking the horn, playfully, rhythmically, in the drive.

"What are they honking the horn for?" Rosa asks. "Maybe there's something wrong," she adds.

"No, they're just feeling good. Showing off."

Soon the men come into the kitchen, and Gina introduces everyone. Giovanni is smoking a cigarette. They must have stopped in town. Both show the effects of a day in the sun and their wounds are vivid and raw looking. Rosa is polite, smiling with her mouth, while expressing horror with her eyes, taking in the black eyes and bandages, the various wounds and abrasions.

"Gina, I have to be off now. I'm going into town," she says. "You two better go straight to bed," she tells Giovanni and Mario, and departs with her frozen tomatoes. Gina walks her to the car.

Back in the kitchen, Giovanni tosses Gina a pack of French cigarettes, the kind she thinks taste like stale Camels. She catches them in one hand and thanks him.

"She's nice," he says. "But it's just as well she had to go, because we have to talk to you alone."

"Two people can't talk to me alone," she says, feeling a bit panicky. They sit waiting with their beautiful eyes.

Mario starts in: "We sat up at the edge of the quarry today talking."

She breaks in "No, don't. Don't talk to me."

"Just calm down," Giovanni says.

Feeling trapped, she picks up the coffee pot and pours coffee for the three of them, standing behind the counter like a waitress in a hospital coffee shop serving her battered customers. The doctor is pressing charges, they'll say, for her mallard act; she'll end up behind bars. They'll put her into a medieval dungeon, force her to wear rags, put her picture on the cover of the National Inquirer: WOMAN SLAYS LOVERS WITH DUCK. She'll spend the rest of her life in jail.

"We've been talking," Giovanni says again.

"Okay, go ahead," Gina says, waiting.

Mario takes a sip of coffee, and says "What was it Giovanni? I forgot."

"Well," Giovanni says seriously, as he adds cream to his coffee. "I can't remember either." They both laugh.

Gina cocks her head, starts stirring the sugar in the sugar bowl, lifts up a spoonful, lets it fall back in the bowl. Mario walks up to Gina, brushing against her shoulder. Too close. And she can smell marijuana. So that's what they've been up to at the quarry. She shakes her head in disbelief. She walks back and forth behind the counter. They've been drinking too, of course. She can smell it as she walks past Giovanni. It's the pot talking. They sit there waiting for her to do something, say something.

"Okay, follow me," she says, looking from one to the other, then walks off toward the studio and they follow along. In the studio Giovanni lights two cigarettes and hands one to Gina. Her hands are shaking and she notices that his are too. They all stand looking at the large new painting.

After a silence, Mario says "I think it's the Holocaust."

Gina says the painting is her personal holocaust. Giovanni comes near, draws deeply on his cigarette, stands close to Gina and tells her he thinks that the blue is the sea and the sky, and the black is a scramble of hidden things, like hieroglyphics, all mixed together.

A silence hangs on until Gina says she wants to take their picture in front of the painting. "I want you to see yourselves," she says, looking from one to the other. She borrows Mario's cellphone, and both stand in front of the painting. "Smile." They smile unnatural smiles and she takes the picture, knowing she'll remember the actual image more clearly than the one just taken by the camera. They all look in the viewer and laugh. It's the comic relief they needed.

"I don't feel so good now," Mario says. "Slight headache. Too much sun."

"Me too," Giovanni says. "Do I really look that bad?" he leans in and clicks on the photo again, the black eyes, the bandages.

She says they really should lie down for a while, like Rosa said. She'll bring some aspirin and ice water.

"Just some Excedrin or something; whatever you have," Giovanni says.

"I have some codeine pills and something else—very strong. I'll get those too. Charles always has those." Giovanni and Mario leave to lie down. She finds them both half-awake in her oversized bed.

"Those bunk beds—that mattress I slept on last night. Really bad. Springs poking every which way. God this bed is big, extra big king size. Must be czar size," Giovanni says, having changed his mood with the room.

Gina says it is bigger than king, at least the king sheets don't fit. She has to keep washing and using these same sheets, thinks the bed is custom made. They take their pills with water and settle back on the abundance of pillows. She's given them the strongest pills.

I used to want to be a nurse, she tells them.

"Do you have any beer?" Mario asks.

Okay, she'll be the bartender nurse, and leaves to look in the kitchen. Giovanni calls out that he wants one too. Returning with the beer, like it's a normal thing to do, she purposely goes to Mario's side of the bed first, though she wants to go to Giovanni. She gives Mario a bottle of Swedish beer and tells him to have a good rest. With a hand on her shoulder he thanks her, but quietly asks her why she didn't warn him about Giovanni's driving. It wouldn't have helped, she says. They both look at Giovanni, who heard the comment about his driving, and laughs. They are able to joke a little and talk fondly, a delicate camaraderie developing among the three of them.

"Not bad," Mario says of the beer. She passes a bottle over to Giovanni, thinks he looks extra pathetic with two black eyes, and tells him so. He bursts into song, a *canzone* he makes up which sounds vaguely familiar. It's Italian but she recognizes her own name and that of Mario and Giovanni in the lyrics. He laughs one of those outrageous operatic tragic-comic laughs, says he might write an opera. "About the three of us. But Gina, you have to stay with us for inspiration."

She looks at Giovanni, at his irresistible resilience. Mario looks on with concern.

Impulsively, Mario asks Giovanni if he'll sing at his wedding.

"Sure, what should I sing?"

Mario says "How about *I've Got to be Me.*"

Giovanni slumps down on his pillow, laughing hysterically.

"Mario, no, no, no."

Mario is momentarily indignant, takes a long draught of his beer and tells him to pick something. He's feeling too close to both Giovanni and Gina not to go along with whatever Giovanni might choose and he really wants him to sing; he is as captivated as Gina by Giovanni's voice.

"I propose a toast," Gina says. "To Mario's wedding!" She raises her bottle, and they all clink their bottles together, and Mario's eyes tear up.

"Don't be so maudlin," Giovanni says, regretting his words as soon as they're spoken. "So am I," he says in apology. "I always cry at weddings," he lies. "Schumann," he says, mostly to himself.

They're all drinking the beer a little too quickly, the afternoon is hot, but mainly they need the excuse of beer for the tension among them, and the exuberance waiting to break out. Gina goes for a second round and turns on the radio on the way back. She passes out the bottles and sits on the edge of the bed by Mario, comfortably tucking her legs and half curling up.

Suddenly, the room feels much too warm to her, and dangerous. She feels as though she's been picked up and swept into something—a painting, a fresco. She is in the midst of angels, fallen angels, and the bed is a cloud of down. The room is almost spinning. Giovanni's blond curls, the gauzy bandages, Mario's beard, the murmur of their voices, their breathing, and it is too warm. She slips through fingertips, and quickly gets out of bed, leaving them to their rest, aware that she has made a narrow escape. And she doesn't even like beer. At the door, she turns to tell them that Charles and the boys will be back tomorrow night.

In the kitchen, she lights a cigarette and calls Rosa. Thank heavens Rosa answers. "You're back from town," Gina says. "Can you come and rescue me? Can I stay in your guest room tonight?"

"I'll be right over. Pack your toothbrush." Rosa isn't surprised. Those two men. She doesn't know that Gina needs rescuing from herself.

Gina picks up the mallard in the living room and examines it for blood. It's clean. She packs a small bag, writes a note and leaves it on the kitchen counter, then exits through the side door. She wants to be ready to leave with Rosa as quietly as possible.

CR

Later: Mario finishes writing an entry in his journal and puts the book aside. He takes up his pipe and rearranges the pillows before lighting up. On the wall is a print of a horse race. He had wanted to take Gina to a race once but she wouldn't go, saying it was unnatural. She preferred to watch horses run in the fields and there weren't enough fields anymore. She got upset about it, the races and the fields. He sees Giovanni sitting up in the living room where he has arranged the furniture into a long bed. Mario brings him a pipe.

They sit and smoke together in silence. Finally Giovanni asks where he and Anita are going to live.

"San Diego. His business is good there, and that's where Anita has her practice. She's a pediatrician."

"Suppose you'll start a family then?"

"No," Mario says. "Anita doesn't believe in it. She wants to keep the population down. There are too many people, too much traffic, and robots are taking over the jobs." Mario confides that Anita has had an operation so it's out of the question anyway.

"Still, I like kids" Mario says. "Especially the little ones, the way they roll around in the grass and wrestle like puppies." He laughs, picturing some tots he saw in the park, giggling and picking dandelions they kept throwing at each other. "Oh well, you can't have everything." Anyway, kids seem to shy away from him, though he doesn't know why.

Giovanni has one sister, no brothers. He draws on his pipe, wondering what it would be like to be a father.

Mario pulls out his billfold and opens it to a picture of Anita, proudly handing it over to Giovanni.

Giovanni studies the photo of Anita, taking in the beautiful insincere smile, and the fabulous red hair. He decides not to mention Natasha.

"Brown eyes," Mario says. "Very unusual for a redhead," he adds.

"Yes, she's beautiful," Giovanni says, but has summed her up by her smile and feels sad for Mario, whom he really likes. Anita looks like she couldn't love anyone but herself; just like Carol.

Mario says he has to call Anita, and his office. He puts down his pipe and replaces the photo. The bandages on Mario's head are lopsided and he adjusts them. "I don't know what the hell good these are now."

"That old doc did it to scare us into taking it easy," Giovanni says.

"I believe it," Mario says, wondering if he'll stay long enough to see Charles and the boys.

"Charles treats me like a brother," Mario says. "Well, not quite. He has something like seven brothers back in New Jersey. One's in jail. The rest are questionable, to say the least." Mario sits on the edge of his chair, his hands together, thinking of how hard it's going to be for Giovanni when he sees Gina with her boys.

They hear cars outside. Mario steps outside and sees his blue car go over the hill, and Rosa driving away in her old clunker. He must have left the keys in the car. He's sure Giovanni wouldn't leave keys in the Ferrari. He circles the beautiful Ferrari, then steps into the garage from the side door. At least Gina left him his bike. He's not worried about the car; Gina knows it's a rental. Still, it's a bit puzzling.

Back inside, Mario calls Anita's relatives in St. Moritz. The cousin who speaks English answers. Anita is out shopping. He says he'll be there soon and he's found someone to sing for the wedding and Anita should get at least three hotel rooms for guests he's bringing. Yes, yes, yes, her cousin Berle keeps repeating. Yes, yes, she's writing it all down, and she has to go for a fitting soon. What kind of flowers does he like? All kinds, wild looking ones, he tells her before they end the call.

After the call, he remembers what he likes. Iris. Purple iris. Oh well, it doesn't matter, it's probably not the right time of year for iris. Next he calls his office to see if there have been any emergencies, and arranges for someone to cover until he gets back, since he'll be away another week with the wedding. That taken care of he's feeling in charge, somewhat. This finalizing is tensing him. He sighs, picturing Anita, and how beautiful she'll look at the wedding. She's always so agreeable, especially when she gets her way, which is nearly always. He doesn't mind. And she's practical, unlike Gina.

He hears Giovanni in the kitchen and joins him. He's going through the refrigerator, says Gina left a note saying she's at Rosa's.

"Oh. Anything good in there?"

"Smoked fish, cheese, tomatoes, more cheese—let's see," he says, hauling it all out. Mario gets out glasses and plates, feeling in charge. He's been here a few days and knows where things are. He gets the bread, mustard and olives. They settle down at the table and start making sandwiches.

"I don't know why they leave the head and tail on smoked fish, all crinkled up like some dried-up dead fish from the beach," Giovanni says, cutting into one, and offering the plate to Mario.

Mario thinks it's too early in the day for fish and settles for cheese. "Gina loves smoked fish," he says. "Don't take her out for sushi though—she thinks it's full of worms."

After cleaning up the kitchen, Mario comes up beside Giovanni in the den. Giovanni is reading a print-out of an email from Danny to Gina.

"She sends the boys a joint email every day," Mario says.

"See here, about a book Chris wants. She printed it out to remember. Even when they're all at home she does that. Little jokes, funny words, something somebody said or saw that day. Could be about a ladybug or firefly, or mashed potatoes. Anything. Danny answers and Chris has just started to. It's how they learned to read young. Danny is already writing little stories, all on his own."

Giovanni shakes his head, genuinely surprised, though he occasionally found her sending messages. He had assumed they were mostly to Charles.

11. Friends and Enemies

"Gina, hey, come swimming with us," Giovanni says, looking down at her. She's sitting on the carpet with a bucket of water and a scrub brush. No, she has to get the blood out of the rug. He offers to help with it later, but she tells him to go on, and insists she wants to do this herself. "I can't seem to get a good night's sleep," she says, yawning. "Really, I want to do this myself." And she wants to clean the freezer when no one is around. Doesn't want anyone to see the tomato explosion in there. "You go on ahead," she waves him on with her brush.

You sure?"

"Yes, yes. I'll see you later." She can't stop yawning now that she's started. The bed in Rosa's guest bedroom must be a hundred years old. Back to scrubbing the rug, she recalls cleaning the mosaic on the island with Giovanni. He was so quiet that first day.

Mario is already at the beach when Giovanni arrives. He's found Gina's sand monkey she must have made the night before. He's standing in the water looking at it. The tide has already started its erosion. They walk into the water where it's shallow for several yards, before it slopes off and drops deep. Mario takes the lead— he knows the water and currents, checks the strength of Giovanni's strokes, and they swim south. Mario gradually increases his speed, and a rivalry takes place for a good quarter of a mile. They're both surprised at each other's strength. Giovanni stops to tread water and laughs. They rest, and swim on.

Mario turns at the rocky point and they start back, moving through the water now in unison, Giovanni's greater height compensated by Mario's greater strength and experience, and their earlier rivalry has vanished. They swim as one against the reality of the sea, and they are quickly back near shore.

Walking out of the sea and breathing heavily, they're renewed, their bandages lost to the sea. As they walk along the sand, Giovanni slaps Mario on the back with his towel, says he thought he was going to die out there at first, keeping up with him. They take the long path up to the house, Giovanni talking about growing up near San Francisco and a childhood spent on the beach. He loved to swim and did it a lot until he moved to London.

"I never liked pools," Giovanni says, as he slides open the patio door. Too predictable. Swimming back and forth is monotonous. He likes the sea.

Mario likes pools. He's practical and likes to know what's in the water, what the temperature is going to be. Still, it was great swimming today, and he still feels the exhilaration. Lately he's been falling out of sync with his usual ways, even becoming a stranger to himself. That old staid, practical Mario is slowly being taken over by some hidden self, doing things he's not used to doing, things he doesn't expect of himself. He laughs aloud, says he just feels good.

They dry off and dress in the main bedroom where Gina is sleeping soundly.

"Look at these," Mario says in a whisper, picking up one of the Hawaiian shirts at the end of the bed. "This one's yours," handing it to Giovanni. Gina has written their names on pieces of paper taped to the shirts. Mario's is blue and Giovanni's green, both bright with tropical birds and flowers.

They both agree the shirts are good, of a comfortable material; neither likes scratchy clothes. She must have bought them in town. Strange though, a small Italian village selling Hawaiian shirts. Mario plans to read down at the beach and tells Giovanni about the folding chairs in the shed down there, if he wants one. "And bring a cup if you want coffee. I'm bringing a thermos down."

Giovanni notes how at home Mario is here, and much more relaxed than he should be. He may go back to the beach after he calls Luigi. He answers on the second ring, sounding happy, surprised, and more animated than usual. Yes, Pascal is fine, he's been to the doctor and had his prescription refilled and he has some orange pills too now, just before bed he takes those, for his blood. Luigi is thinking of moving to the country, in with his sister. He thinks Pascal would like a yard with trees and now with the car he can get around, and yes, Orazio brought it in.

Giovanni gives Luigi Gina's phone number and tells him to call him here if he needs him or leave a message with Natasha at his studio. He hangs up.

Unable to ignore his uneasiness, though assured of Pascal's health, he had thought that news would calm him. He runs his fingers through his wet hair and pours himself a drink. He wanders out to the deck, where he saw Mario and Gina having a dramatic discussion when he was fiddling with the CD player. A small boat is passing by. Watching it move away into the sunset, he leans on the railing. Mario is in a beach chair below, an unopened book on his lap. He's watching the boat too.

What was he trying to do, when they were swimming so hard? That glance, between strokes—Mario was measuring him, and his eyes were like a wolf's—a cold, icy blue. As his face went under the water he felt physically pierced, and could imagine those eyes watching him drown, just watching him with the steady arctic stare he had caught in a split second while they swam.

That's when he had stopped to rest and laughed from the tension. After that, Mario relaxed, as though he had been conceded to, had won. The ice hurts his loose tooth, and he flicks his tongue along its edge. Drinking straight Scotch on ice, he lets it burn his throat as he watches the sunset. Gripping the emptied glass, he's ready to smash it, like Natasha when she's drunk, but doesn't, thinking of bare feet running down to the beach, Gina's boys. He pictures them, both blond, little Vikings—people would think they were his if they were together.

ଔ

Back in the bedroom he searches for his shoes. Gina is asleep. He stands looking at her with his socks in hand. In the living room, he slips on his socks and steps into his shoes. He takes the side door to the garage, gets in his car and drives off in the silent Ferrari.

Meanwhile, Mario has picked up his book and started reading where he left off earlier, the chapter on architecture today: *Relatives of the Renaissance.*

"...the moats and crocodiles of yesterday have been replaced by security guards and electronic detection devices...."

He skips the print and looks at the pictures, turning pages absently, stopping to look at a small stone house. The caption reads simply: *Small stone house, 1600, built into a hill, Italian, local stone mason.* He leafs through the glossy pages of cathedrals, skyscrapers, fast-food restaurants, a fish house in the shape of a whale, which you enter through the mouth; and then some predictable government buildings. Turning back to the stone house, he checks the note for a more specific location, finds nothing. He closes the book and shuts his eyes.

The vows, Mario tries to think, but the more he concentrates the emptier he feels, and nothing comes. There's still time. His mother will be there. He should call her. His dead father comes to mind, and the old woman who sang with the organ at the funeral. It was like a dream that you walked through playing your part, with all the people from the old neighborhood so glad to see him and talking and smiling as if they were at a party. Mario had been horrified when old Martha Hartwood came up behind him to talk, just at the moment he saw his father in the casket. If he could have been alone with him; he should have come the night before. So many old people chattering, patting him on the back, perfumed old women with powder in the cracks of their soft faces, so tender towards him. Too many people and names he couldn't remember.

Afterwards at the house, people kept bringing casseroles and cakes, and Mario's mother sorted through cards, counting money with a pained expression, making lists, trying to keep track of who brought what. He saw faces that had haunted his dreams that day: Prim Aunt Greta in a proper black suit, quiet and kindly condescending, and Aunt Janie, pink and puffed up, bustling about in a shiny black dress. Uncle Matthew sat in Dad's old easy chair and got slowly drunk, staring at the TV even though it was turned off. There was some sense to it all though. His mother was kept busy with the casseroles, making room for them in the refrigerator, heating them up, counting money—it helped her through the day.

He wonders if his wedding will be like that, just going through it, one step and then the next, never really knowing what the hell he's doing.

The first stars come out. He watches the scene in front of him, the sea and sky and the long smooth line of the beach as the waves wash against the shore. Gina's sand sculpture has been washed away. They'll live at Anita's house and sell his. They've been living in both and it's been good, but he liked being able to retreat to his own house in La Jolla at times. Yet it was he who insisted on the marriage and said they should make a commitment. Her independence—always talking about how she was a free spirit, in his heart he didn't believe it and so he challenged her with this marriage. She agreed a little too quickly and he regretted the confrontation. He had just wanted to know if she would agree; he didn't know if he really wanted it. Why didn't she turn him down? Now she gushes over those bride magazines. In St. Moritz she turned into a commando, planning the wedding like an upcoming battle. He wonders what part of her he's getting.

Gina. She told him once that someday they would have an affair when they're old and rheumatic and rickety, in a nursing home somewhere. What did she say? Rheumatic affair, instead of romantic affair. She came right out and said, *When Charles is gone.* Charles is older, certainly, but not that old. Mario was surprised at her talking like that. Still, it was just a joke to her. She has almost a child's view of age. Of course, she's barely twenty-five years old. Danny is nine and Chris is six, so she grew up pretty quickly.

Certainly, marriage is bound to change people. He's seen it in people who have lived together for years, with their little fetishes and dislikes. He's heard it in the background sometimes, when visiting friends, and their terse quiet words of anger to one another over some triviality—someone purposely trying to hide the salt, someone forgot to buy the right kind of mushrooms, again, or someone bought the wrong kind of olive oil, not cold pressed. Frantic kitchen scenes held in undertones—years of emotions, cultivated and compressed into tight little words, then they emerge, all smiles, coming to the table. Gina had laughed telling him what a wonderful dotty old man he would make. He would fall asleep at concerts and wake up when he dropped his program, pretending he'd never been asleep. He does that already. Now he knows enough to tuck in his program so it won't fall when he dozes off.

He's pretty sure Anita will get back to normal after the wedding. The bride magazines will go out with the garbage, along with that façade and it'll be like before, only better. His restlessness is only normal. He strokes his beard, staring out at the sea. It's quite calm tonight. He heads up the hill with his book and empty thermos, ignoring the unrest that makes him shudder, and he plods along up the path.

Back in the house it's quiet and Gina is still sleeping, curled up under the covers. He stands close looking at her, feeling protective, and sorry, as though she's slipping away, breath by breath into the night away from him.

Mario walks through the house looking for Giovanni, and not finding him, steps out onto the patio and looks down over the beach. He sees no one. He steps out to the garage. The Ferrari is gone. A guiltiness creeps over him and a hard sort of pleasure sets in. Back in the kitchen he sniffs at the glass on the counter—melted ice and Scotch. He takes an empty glass and pours himself a Scotch, pouring it slowly like a prize. He's always liked Charles's taste in Scotch. While Gina is sleeping, he'll just drink.

On the patio he sets the bottle on the table and walks to the railing. Giovanni's lighter is on the ledge. He flicks it over into the bushes with a finger, and although no one watches, he lets it fall as though by accident, unwitnessed even by him, then settles down in what he now considers his chair. Putting his feet up, office style, on the opposite chair, a sudden pain cuts into his hip. "Damn," he mutters in the dark. Have another drink. Who was it she told him about? Some fallen soul who had repented, given up his worldly life and got a job washing corpses and wanted to die and be buried outside a churchyard, some place where everyone would walk over his foul bones for all eternity. His foul and wretched bones, he laughs, says "wretched bones" aloud, already quite inebriated, enjoying the sound of his own voice. The time goes by as the level of Scotch goes down. He half dozes off, and only wakes when he leans too far off his chair. Half rising, he says he'll do his own singing. Doesn't need any Giovanni and laughs raucously to himself.

"Just a little too much. Scotch," he says out loud, feeling terribly clever. He gets up to look for the lighter and sees the gold shining on the ground and leans far down from the patio to pick it up.

"Mario, what are you doing there?"

Startled, he gets up with the lighter in hand. "Giovanni," he says, and ambles over and grabs Giovanni by the shoulder. "Your lighter," he says, laughing, delighted at everything. "Just look at these stars Giovanni," he says, wiping his hand across the sky, inviting him to enjoy the evening sky.

Mario stands looking at the sky, pointing to various constellations with a wavering hand. Giovanni sits down with the Scotch, taking a drink straight from the bottle, and listens to the mumbling professor of the night give an impassioned lecture. He watches Mario's flashing eyes, the rise and fall of his brows, his voice conveying the secrets of the night. Giovanni is fascinated and lets him go on. Finally, he gets up and goes over to him and says: "Mario, you and I are going to see Livia tonight."

"No, no," Mario says, moving his hands as though to shoo away invisible bats. "Enough women already," and he grabs the back of his chair. Mario holds his mouth tight in a grimace, shaking his head back and forth.

"No, you don't understand. Livia is a wise old woman," Giovanni says.

Mario looks over his shoulder at Giovanni, without humor, and drunk, Mario's face has an intimidating strength and the raw ugliness of a handsome man. Giovanni takes another drink, and tells Mario that Livia is a fortune teller.

"We're just going to take a ride to see a fortune teller," he says reassuringly.

"Oh, okay," Mario says, sitting down, staring at nothing.

"I'll be right back. Wait right here," Giovanni tells him. He leaves for the den and writes a note to Gina.

Gina,
 Mario and I went to see Livia. Back tomorrow
night.
Love,
Giovanni

He walks from room to room, picks up Mario's two pipes and
tobacco, throws what he needs in a bag and sets the bag by the
door. Mario has fallen asleep in the chair. He wakes him and Mario
follows docilely to the car. Giovanni sets back the passenger seat so
Mario can sleep, settles him into the car, and drives off to the north.

12. Lint

The following morning Gina puts Giovanni's note in her pocket. She'll clean the house. First, she gathers up all the sheets and laundry and starts a load in the funny washer, a combination washer and dryer built into a wall behind a folding door. She found it after nearly giving up. There's blood on the pillowcases from the fight. They'll need bleach. It's good she has a surge of energy this morning so she can clean everything, but first she puts on some lively music: Bizet's *Carmen*.

The bathrooms are first on the list and she wants to make them shine like in the ads, sparkling clean with pine fresh toilets, lemony fresh floors, and dazzling mirrors. She'll cut some flowers for vases and put out the new blue towels. She flies around the rooms, spraying and shining, picking up, putting away, making it look like no one lives in the house, all clean and sparkling as in a magazine.

She keeps coming across things of theirs—matches, pipe tobacco floating in the hot tub. She catches bits of tobacco like little water bugs, meticulously, one by one, but they keep oozing away when she's ready to pinch them between her fingers. Finally, she uses a sponge to pick them, up, determined to get every last piece of tobacco. She sits down and scrutinizes the surface of the water, waiting, in case she's missed a bit. Staring at the water, she has to laugh at her fanatical cleaning, and recalls the caretaker in the building where an old friend lived. She was waiting for the elevator and the janitor kept pacing back and forth with his hands behind his back, looking at the carpet, pursuing some lost item so intensely that she had offered to help look. He said he had a big ball of lint that he dropped, and he couldn't find it, didn't know what happened to it.

Later, she had always wanted to ask him if he had found it but couldn't bring herself to ask the question. Sir, did you find that big ball of lint? She can still she him pacing, a dignified old man on his lint-hunting safari in an apartment lobby.

Satisfied with the cleanliness of the hot tub, she heads to the bedroom to see if Mario's journal is still in the drawer. It is. She slides it under the mattress, above the springs. She finds a sock under the bed, throws it in the laundry basket for the next load of wash. Already five mismatched socks have surfaced from the last dryer load. Poor lonely things. She wonders which are Mario's, which are Giovanni's, or maybe Charles's. There is no way of telling them apart at all. Men's socks are totally boring.

Well, it looks pretty good to her as she walks around the house, then, recalling the cars, she has to decide what to do about Mario's blue car. Should she leave it? Move it? Drive it to Rosa's again? She liked driving it to town when she bought the colorful shirts and made photocopies from Rosa's scrapbook. There's no reason to move the car, but she may still have the keys in her purse. Yes, they're dangling from the pocket in her purse on his Gaudí souvenir key ring. She'll drive it over later. Everything is in order.

Now, for coffee and Mario's journal. And why shouldn't she read it, considering all he knows about her, all those years of therapy. If someone leaves something like that around, it's an invitation, isn't it?

CR

MARIO'S JOURNAL—New Year's Eve: Missed the party. Anita's on call night. Sat in the lobby drinking instant coffee. Saw one child brought in scalded. Pulled hot chili off a counter. Later, a kid who put a coffee bean in his nose. Dreamed about driving, having to get somewhere.

January 1: Golf 2:00 p.m.

January 2: Mrs. Green Bean again. Good session. She's making good progress. Shut the drapes and had calls held. Opened the drapes and looked out the window. Watched traffic and people below. Lunch with Ted. Heard all about his root canal. Had crab. Ted had soup.

January 4: Worked on my paper. Meeting in pm went well. Made grocery list. Watched TV. Started Crime and Punishment.

January 6: Stopped for drinks at new outdoor café. Warm for January. Felt timeless under umbrella in the sun, Anita across the table. This is right. Where I want to be, the right place, the right time, or lack of time. Feel no sense of yesterday. So good it scares me.

January 25: Saw faces in the clouds and long streaks like pipe smoke. Ready for a vacation, change of scene. Yogurt for lunch. Called travel agent. Called Gina. Don't know why, maybe to see if she was still there. It was snowing there. They are going to Italy this summer. Went biking with Anita after work. Talked about going on vacation somewhere, maybe take our bikes. Stayed at Anita's.

January 26: Talked to a man today who looked like Uncle Matthew. Eerie feeling. The whole day like that. Started when I remembered my dream—back home coming to the table at breakfast. One extra person and I knew it was someone in the family who was always in the family, had always been in the family. I didn't let on that I didn't know who it was. Felt like I was crazy. Going to the pool for a swim.

With restlessness, as if someone might come, interrupt, Gina skips to the last entry, rather lengthy, for this Friday. There's a black hair sticking out of the page. Just a stray? Or a subtle marker? He's a Hitchcock fan she knows, and carefully places the hair on the chair arm beside her.

August 23, 11:00 am: She always looks at him. All the time. She hardly ever looks at me, even now. She looks at my face avoiding me, my eyes. I'd like to know why. I feel like we're two blind people sometimes. Can't remember if she looked at me when I told her about Anita. I don't know what's happening to me here. I don't know why I can't leave.

Writing in bathroom: Blond hairs in hairbrush. Med. Prescription, empty, says 4 times daily, Charles del Tredicci. Quarry now. Giovanni is waiting.

Later: The fight. I like thinking about it when I'm talking to him. When he starts talking about something he gets that faraway look but he's trying to bring you there, really wants you to understand, be his friend. His openness is appealing. I think he's better than me.

Gina stops reading and closes the notebook, not knowing what she had expected to find. She replaces the hair in the book and lifts the mattress as high as she can to set the book carefully back where she found it. Then, smoothing the bedcover, leaves to wash her hair.

IN THE STUDIO—Gina spreads out the copies of newspaper articles and photos she photocopied in town from Rosa's scrapbook, arranging them in various positions, tearing the edges of some, and spattering paint on others. She paints over a large stiff paper with a shade of blue, pressing some of the papers straight onto the wet paint. The acrylic dries rapidly as she works with the glue and photos, alternating paint, glue, and her own drawings which she does quickly with a pen, then swishing over sections with clear pale blue, using her favorite wide Japanese brush.

Rosa's scrapbook started with family weddings, births, sporting events, and obituaries. The most recent clippings shocked Gina. The immigrants from North Africa in boats, in groups, close-ups of people wet and worn from the sea. The collage is scaring her as it comes to life. It's that sandal she found floating in the cove she set out to dry on a corner of the deck, part leather, part cardboard, and string and some type of twisted grass.

13. Livia

J ust off the dirt road near the bridge by Livia's house, Giovanni and Mario are lying down, waiting.

"She should be back by now," Mario says, sitting up, absently tossing a stone into the creek. Giovanni doesn't answer, though awake, he's drowsy from waiting, and from the same question.

"Why'd you come back for me?" Mario asks, watching the clear water, not looking at Giovanni, listening to the water.

"I don't know," he answers, nothing more, thinking maybe someone needs to take care of the psychiatrists.

It's quiet, just the fresh water moving along, leaping over the same boulder, rushing over its sides. Birds are singing in Italian in the trees.

"Tell me about your wedding," Mario says.

"Oh," Giovanni answers reluctantly, resting his jaw on his hand. "I was the little man on the cake. That was long ago." After some minutes pass he continues. "I don't even like white cake."

The conversation progresses with the slow motion of the lazy stream, or the forest behind them, as two trees holding a conversation. There's no rush, neither moves much; they're simply planted there with plenty of time.

"Chocolate. I like chocolate cake," Mario says.

Giovanni raises his eyebrows in agreement.

They sit at the riverbank, the sweet image of chocolate cake lingering, and it seems enough for the moment, as slow and pleasant as the river in front of them. A bird flies down and flutters its wings in a shallow pool near the shore, flicking off water and shaking its tiny head. Giovanni and Mario watch the bird until it flies off. Giovanni begins to draw in the sand with a stick.

"I don't know what I'd do. I mean if I didn't have to work like you," Mario says, tossing stones one by one into the water where the bird had been bathing. "I'd probably work though. Maybe I'd write," and he slings a rock hard into the trees across the creek, pondering what he would really do. He's always liked architecture. Maybe build something, a tower or a rock wall.

"I do have to work," Giovanni says. "I mean I like it. I like teaching. I like painting, working on frescoes. But mosaics, I could work on a mosaic forever." He takes a handful of smooth wet rocks from the stream and begins to arrange them where he's drawn the outline of a bird in the sand. Mario moves over to watch, thinking how Gina does that too, makes things out of nothing.

Giovanni finishes the stone mosaic, placing the stones easily, fitting them quickly into his puzzle with an uncanny perfection, with subtle color variations in the bird's wing, the darker background stones making the white pebbles of the bird stand out. He scrutinizes the stream and pulls out a smooth red stone for the bird's eye. Just right, he's pleased.

"A dove?" Mario asks.

"Yes, maybe. Or just a bird."

"Picasso liked doves," Mario says. He tells Giovanni about his book of photos of Picasso in his house in southern France where he would let the doves fly around inside his house, and he had a goat in the house too, at least in the pictures the goat is in the house. There's a series of pictures in the book showing Picasso forming a plate out of clay, where he takes the fish skeleton from his lunch and presses it into wet clay forming a fossil image. In the last picture he's looking at the clay plate when it's finished, and you can just see how much he's enjoyed making the thing, in those pictures. "Picasso was having fun. Just like you just now," Mario says, alluding to the bird mosaic in the sand.

"Sure. We're like kids sometimes. Artists, I mean. It's not always fun though," Giovanni says, thinking of the picture Gina took of he and Mario standing beside her holocaust painting.

Mario used to marvel at the drawings Gina did of dinners, especially the vegetables before they were cooked. It's a matter of looking at the ordinary, plus talent, and he's tried but he can't get past the ordinary. Still, psychiatrists are important too. How many people has he helped? He's pretty sure quite a few. Now here he is needing help himself. And his head aches. He hasn't been this drunk since he was a freshman in college.

As if reading his mind, Giovanni asks Mario if he can be his own therapist, "not that you need it," he adds, though he's sure he does need help. They both do. Maybe everyone does, at least this week.

Mario talks about one of his patients, a woman concerned about her son who was in a nursery school. The child was always alone when she came to observe the class, and she was concerned. But the teacher had said he was fine, that each child needed to do whatever they needed to do at the time, whether it was playing alone, or even climbing the walls. Every child didn't need to fit into a mold and be like everyone else.

Apparently, I need to climb the walls, or some equivalent, Mario muses. Giovanni keeps tossing stones in the water, deconstructing his mosaic bird, when they hear a car motor, and are brought back to the moment near the Gypsy's little stone house. Giovanni's Ferrari is parked in the center of the road just beyond the bridge. As they walk up the bank toward the car, Giovanni says "Mario, I'll play my guitar at your wedding when I sing."

Mario doesn't comment. Just too much talent in that guy. He feels at a loss.

Livia gets out of a black van on the other side of the bridge. The van is old but highly polished, with gold tassels visible in the windows. A pair of dice dangle from the inside mirror. A plump dark-skinned man gets out from the driver's side and goes around to the back and removes two large baskets of groceries. Mario and Giovanni cross the bridge to the van and stop. Livia hands them each a basket without comment, as if she had been expecting them. She exchanges a few words with her driver friend and then simply nods to him as he backs away down the narrow road, obviously quite accustomed to driving backwards out here.

As the three walk on together, Giovanni notes a peculiar expression he can't make out on Mario's face. Mario, not one to be intimidated, is having a time maintaining his composure. Giovanni remembers when Gina held his hand, like a child, when they walked down this road together.

This time, Mario is the listener, as Giovanni and Livia speak to one another in Italian, but Mario is able to follow the gist of their conversation, catching a word here and there—money, euros, tossed back and forth in clipped sentences. They're bargaining, and he's surprised at Giovanni's insistence, but Livia seems to be a stone wall, hard, yet still enjoying the banter. Mario's known the type, but it's bizarre, seeing it in this old woman with her fierce pointy jaw and keen round ageless eyes. A lull in the conversation ensues, and they keep walking.

Giovanni's laugh breaks the silence, and he pulls out some bills for Livia, who tucks them neatly into her pocket, a tight smug smile barely detectable on her face.

"She says we're high-priced clients, and we'll get our money's worth." Under his breath, Mario promises to pay his share later, blaming Giovanni's Ferrari for the high price.

At the house, Livia tells Giovanni to wait. She wants him to go up on the hill and wait, and points out a worn path leading to the hill. Go think, she tells him, and she'll call him when she's ready. Giovanni protests and they bicker in Italian, Giovanni insisting that Mario needs him there, almost forgetting his reasons, Mario's meager Italian, and he's incensed at missing part of what he came for. Finally, he sees that she's going to have her stubborn way.

"Oh terrific. I'm going to have my fortune told in Italian. Really get my money's worth," Mario says. "Go on then. Go sit on the hill." And to Livia, "After you," throwing his hand toward the door dramatically, for Giovanni's benefit. He'll try almost anything once, willing to go along with Giovanni's game, Livia's game. Walk straight into the dark, at least Giovanni won't hear it.

She closes the door gently, stands at the window watching Giovanni climb the hill. He stops to look back and sees her in the window before he continues up the hill and out of sight behind the pines.

Mario follows Livia like a lamb and helps her unpack the grocery baskets in the kitchen. She puts the groceries away, then sets out two small red crystal glasses and fills them with brandy.

"Sit down, Mario," she says kindly in English, and Mario shudders. "I'm glad you came," she continues in perfect English, her British accent has a romantic lilting edge. He sits down and takes the drink, looking at Livia, at her eyes which are now warm, like condensed brown oceans.

"We don't need a crystal, you and I," she says. She raises her glass, motions to his. "To your future." They drink and Mario leans back in his chair and Livia leans forward, her hands folded and relaxed in front of her on the table. She tells him that he is changing faster than he can understand, and that it happens like that sometimes. She laughs and says it's for the good. He has been temporarily ahead of himself and trying to pull his past up to where he now resides, but it's already jumped to a future point of his life and it will all come together in time, and as smooth and sweet as the brandy they're drinking. She tells him he is a shining light. She lifts a finger into the air, and with one eyebrow cocked, refills their glasses.

"You have been troubled lately. Tell me. Talk to me. It's part of your transition." Mario rubs the back of his head. "I've not been myself lately." He pauses to look at her. Says he understands what she means, but that he's not much of a talker, he's more of a listener. Still, he finds himself telling her about the mountain lion.

Two years ago there was a young mountain lion roaming Charles and Gina's neighborhood. It took a small dog a few houses away from their place, and their son Chris's best friend had seen the lion walk down their driveway one morning and couldn't stop talking about it. Gina's boys were both having nightmares. Apparently, the entire neighborhood was having nightmares, including her parents who lived half a mile away on the next street.

He seemed to be counseling the whole family, but particularly the boys, Danny and Chris. It was because of the lion that Gina's parents decided to leave Colorado and move back to Minneapolis, and after that, Gina came into her own, and no longer needed therapy, for mountain lions or anything else. That's when he and Gina started to get too close, going to movies together—Charles hated movies, he only went to documentaries. With Gina, it was nothing but trouble waiting to happen. More trouble than the mountain lion. So that was when he moved to California. He had to move. He cared too much about her, as well as Charles and the boys. Plus Charles had threatened him.

Charles called Mario in California asking for a referral for Gina; he thought she needed more therapy as she was staying up nights and acting peculiar. But he told Charles to let her be, that she was fine now and could handle anything on her own. He still believes that. And the authorities finally relocated the mountain lion, the boys were doing well, everything seemed fine, and that was that. He met Anita, and now he's not sure if he wants to get married.

"Funny how the truth sounds so odd to yourself when you actually hear it. Almost corny," Mario says.

Livia takes another drink, sits back with a sigh, considering. She taps on the table slowly, deep in thought. "You just needed someone to listen to you." Refilling their red crystal glasses yet again she tells him to look at her. He looks straight at her, feeling no need for defenses, explanations, or anything. What he needs seems to be there in her eyes as he receives and gives of himself, and in seconds, it's over. Just sitting there like that looking into one another's eyes, he feels something significant has happened. Another human being has understood. He finishes his third brandy in one gulp. Livia gets up and says "You can go and get Giovanni now. Stay up on the hill. Enjoy the forest." She walks him to the door and pauses before he leaves. "Mario," she says quietly, "Giovanni and Gina are twin spirits."

"I know," Mario says. "*Ciao*, Livia." He leaves and starts toward the hill. Walking up he feels light-headed, the taste of brandy still on his lips, and he walks into the forest, which smells heavily of pine. A chipmunk chatters on a mossy log, watching him pass by. At the top of the hill Giovanni is lying down in the grass, resting his head on his arm. He turns his head, hearing Mario.

"Your turn."

"That was quick," Giovanni says, sitting up. "Well?"

"It was okay. I don't want to talk though. She's waiting for you."

"Mario, are you okay?" He senses a remoteness in Mario, who turns his head away from Giovanni's questions and says, "Go see her."

Giovanni gets up, thinking he shouldn't have brought Mario here, but he has, and it's done and he feels uncomfortable, and doesn't know what he had wanted to happen, but now it all feels wrong, Mario sitting there lost in another world.

"I'm going down now," he says over his shoulder. "We can eat afterwards. I know a good place," and he goes off down the hill.

Mario lies down on the grass. It's cool and soothing. His headache is gone, even after the brandy. Maybe it wasn't even brandy. Feeling detached and alone, the people of his life seem abstractions, and he doesn't really mind. Floating off, he feels the earth next to his body, its contours against his thighs, his arms, his chest, as he breathes on the ground, and his hands clutch the grass like hair as he falls asleep.

14. The Luau

It looks like a grave. Three-feet-deep, by a good six feet in length. Gina stands resting with one foot on the shovel. Now the wood. She arranges the logs in the pit, climbing in and out, piling the wood at angles, an intuitive pit maker. She keeps in mind what Rosa read over the phone from the cooking encyclopedia, and the luau section from *The Joy of Cooking*: "Grape vine cuttings give a unique flavor to the meat." The pile of cuttings smell green and viney. Using half driftwood and half hard wood, she layers the grape cuttings using the lasagna technique; making a handsome weaving and setting aside the extra vines for later.

She pauses to admire her work before leaving for the house to get a drink. Her brow is dripping with sweat by the time she gets to the kitchen. Letting the water run in the kitchen sink, she cools her hands, then drinks a full glass of water before letting the water overflow the glass, the cold water running over her hands and wrists.

She watches the water run against her wrist and over the veins, the hidden blue river, so cold, when it dripped into her—plasma, all the plasma after Danny was born, how cold it felt—death into life, life prepackaged in plastic, wheeled in on a stainless steel rack. But Danny was perfect, beautiful. And there she was, a mother at sixteen years of age. Someday she'll tell Danny about his father, her high school art teacher. He took a job in New Zealand before she even knew she was pregnant. He doesn't know that Danny exists. She turns off the water and wipes her hands carefully with a towel.

"Giovanni," she says to herself, walking through the house, listlessly, mumbling his name, stepping out onto the patio. She leans against the railing. "Mario." Back then, the end of that lake where they walked past that old tree stump, and a willow, with its fallen curve against the beach. Those icy days with Mario and their walks after the movies. She remembers how stark and still she felt. She was vacant. They walked to a frozen lake where the ice was thin and had cracked up into large sheets in the bay. A gentle wind blew the broken panes of ice, ice against ice. The sound of chimes, winter chimes; melted summer waves frozen into ice.

Giovanni is summer. Mario is winter. Except for the movies. At the movies Mario laughs more than anyone. He loves movies, even the dumb ones. He could always find good things to say about what he admired, who had the best part, and he could talk on and on about a movie and then abruptly, would become his more reserved self. Maybe he's in the wrong field. Maybe he needs to make movies. Or be a movie critic.

Against the railing, she runs her fingers along the weathered wood, considering her life, and the sea beyond, standing like a carved piece of wood, precise, and pointing ahead like some ship's golden mermaid.

Voices. Car door slams. They're back. Danny and Chris. Charles. Another door slams, luggage plunked down. Kisses. They brought presents, everybody talking at once and the air is electric with the energy of the boys. They all want to show her at once: brochures, little snacks from the plane, presents to open, souvenirs, a new fire engine, everyone talking at once in German, Italian, showing off.

Danny collapses onto a chair, his head thrown back laughing, his long gangly arms and legs sprawled out. "I feel like I've been around the world three times, Mom." She leans over the back of Danny's chair, smiling down at the top of his head, brushing the hair out of his eyes.

"Me too," Chris says. "I think I'm Christopher Columbus del Tredicci. Look at this." He takes a large black plastic scorpion out of his pocket and dangles it on its string. "From Vienna," he says. "Made in China," he adds, coming up and leaning against Gina. Chris starts speaking gibberish – German, Italian and words he makes up, nonsense rolling off his tongue. "My poor brain," he says with a sigh.

Charles is resting in his easy chair, obviously exhausted. He watches Gina and the boys quietly in their reunion, and then tells them to put on their suits and go for a swim. They can stretch out after the long trip. Much scrambling around, everyone wants a drink first, before they run down the path toward the sea.

Gina sits in the chair opposite Charles.

"Well?" She says.

"I'm tired. Just tired. It went well though. And guess what?" he says, perking up, "I got a call from New York just before we left. We're getting the center, and in Denver—the Charles del Tredicci Dental Research Center," he says slowly, a weary, yet contented smile on his face.

Gina moves to sit on the arm of his chair. "Congratulations," she says, kissing his cheek. "You work so hard."

"I do, don't I," he says fondly.

Gina tells him to go soak in the tub for a while and she'll give him a backrub later. He gets up and she tells him she's dug a pit for the luau and has the wood and rocks almost ready, and a pile of grape cuttings.

He tells her she could have let the boys do that, but that the boar is on its way. He had some help from a German orthodontist who is having it shipped to the butcher in Cecci who'll drive it out. It has to be prepared, rubbed with salt, trimmed. You stuff it with red hot rocks, tie it up with rope, then lower it into the pit of hot rocks on a wire basket and cover it all with leaves and wet gunny sacks and then shovel dirt on top and let it steam.

"Complicated. And gruesome," Gina comments.

"Yes. But I want the boys to see it from beginning to end. They see too much of prepackaged meat. I want them to be aware of what we humans do."

Charles goes for his soak and Gina leaves to watch the boys swim. They're all superb swimmers. She went through baby swimming lessons with both. Now Danny has been watching a DVD about lifesaving, although he's too young to enroll in actual classes. The boys are good about staying on the shore side of the rope Charles set up, unless an adult is with them.

A horn honks in the driveway and Gina goes out to look. It's the meat market van. Way sooner than she expected. The butcher comes down the drive waving. He jumps out, rattling away in excited Italian. She catches the word *cinghiale* as he opens the back of the van.

"Where you want him?" he asks in English. She sees that he has a lot of ice in the van, and the poor furry thing, head and all, looks like it's asleep in a clear plastic bag, except she can see the slit of its empty stomach. It'll have to go in the bathtub she tells him, but he doesn't understand, so she gestures for him to take it along and follow her. He slings the boar over his shoulder, and Gina leads him into the house and down the hall to the bathroom. She knocks on the door.

"Charles, you have to get out. The boar is here. It needs to go in the tub." Charles comes out in his robe and they stand waiting for the water to drain down. Gina rinses the tub and the butcher lowers in the boar. Charles tells him to bring in all the ice he has and the butcher returns with two large plastic bags of ice which he pours in around the boar. The boys come in, still in their bathing suits, both fascinated and horrified at the creature in the tub. Charles walks the butcher to the door, then returns to the bathroom and says, "Okay boys, we'd better heat up those rocks." And to Gina, he says he didn't expect it until morning. Gina notes his new bathrobe—black. "You got a new robe, Charles," she says.

"Yes. A present from Cesca."

"Nice," she comments, noting how striking it is with his wavy white hair. Now all three wear black. Charles takes his clothes off the towel rack and leaves to change.

After they have gone off to start the fire, Gina leans over the tub and stares at the pig. It doesn't know she's staring, of course, but she feels like she does when looking at a blind person. They don't know you're looking so you can just look straight at them and it makes you feel guilty, being so blunt like that. But maybe the boar knows she's looking. The spirit, they say it stays around for a while. She touches its fur and shivers at the bristly coarse fur, which is used for brushes. Maybe she's painted with bristles from one of its relatives. She loses track of time, leaning against the cool porcelain, watching the boar on its bed of ice.

Charles comes in with a long pole, and a length of rope.

"Oh, isn't it too soon?" she asks, startled.

Charles says it is, the rocks will take longer to heat, but they're taking it down now; he needs to use the blow torch to burn off the fur. The butcher should have taken care of that, he tells her, probably a translation problem between the German and the Italian butchers. He flips the boar over onto its back and rests the pole on top of the tub, then ties two legs to each end of the pole.

"Okay, Danny, take this end," he orders as the boys come in. Danny grimaces, but takes his end of the pole as one who has no choice but to do this unpleasant, though intriguing duty. Charles and Chris take the other end and they all leave with the boar suspended on the pole, going through the kitchen and out the side door, apparently taking the long route to avoid dripping onto the carpets. Gina washes her hands and looks for a sponge and mop.

CR

Gina is sitting in the living room when the doorbell rings. Reluctantly she heads to the door, not really wanting anyone to know of the horrible event taking place.

"Oh, Rosa, come in. I'm glad it's you."

"What is that awful smell?"

"Charles is burning the fur off a wild boar with a blow torch. Down at the beach," she answers with a grimace.

Rosa shakes her head.

"Well, never a dull moment. It's not boring. Boaring," Gina laughs to herself.

"Are you all right? Gina, I'm a little worried about you."

Gina insists she's fine, and says the luau's going to be tonight, rather than tomorrow and that they'll probably be eating in the middle of the night. It has to steam quite a long time. Hours. She plans to stay on the beach and then get everyone out of bed when it's time to eat. She'll make leis while she's waiting. "Will you come, even if it's in the middle of the night?"

Rosa says she wouldn't miss it for anything. Rather shyly, she asks Gina if she is going to ask Rinaldo, and she readily agrees. Anyway, he got all the grape cuttings they're using, and is out rounding up flowers today. "I didn't know you liked him Rosa. I mean like that."

Rosa responds rather primly that she only meant that he's a very nice gentleman. And of course they have known each other for years. His wife, Cinzia, and Rosa were quite good friends. Rosa sighs, a faraway look of remembrance in her eyes. As to the fruit, Rosa has oranges, bananas and grapes to bring over, but she couldn't get pineapples anywhere.

"Didn't you say Mario and Giovanni are coming back tonight?"

"Well, yes. I think so." She's not sure if she told them Charles would be back today, and is hoping they'll call before driving in. Of course Charles knows Mario well. But Giovanni?

"You want some coffee, Rosa?" Gina asks.

"No thanks. I'm sorry. The smell is too bad," Rosa replies.

Gina agrees it's quite unappetizing at the moment. Before Rosa leaves, Gina asks her to take Mario's journal and put it under the seat of his car. Rosa agrees, although she feels she is taking part in something slightly wicked. At the door, she asks Gina what time she thinks she'll be calling.

Gina mentally calculates the cooking hours and tells her about 3:00 a.m.

Rosa laughs and says she hasn't been up at that hour since her children were born. Rosa leaves with Mario's journal. Gina is happy to see her excited about the night ahead, and looking forward to the luau and the promise of a little adventure in her routine life. Gina could use a lot less in her own.

They'll come up from the beach hungry, so she sets the dining room table and puts out plates of cheese, rolls and apples. Not too much as they should be slightly starved, if the luau is to have the proper effect. She tosses the dirty clothes from the suitcases in the wash and settles down with a glass of wine. Out on the patio she watches the hunters prepare their ready-made catch. The seared boar has already been lowered into the pit and they're throwing grape cuttings on top. The wet gunny sacks hang over the lawn chair. They work almost ceremoniously, with Charles directing the show. He is spreading the wet sacks, and there's Danny coming with an extra shovel from the shed. She watches them work as they fill in the pit with dirt. They level it off to seal in the steam. Charles crosses himself and the boys after him. They wade into the water to wash off dirt and grime. Even the boys walk slowly, almost solemnly, their energy drained by the work.

Chris is the first to get up to the house.

"Really gross, Mom. Do we really have to eat it?"

"Ask me later. You might change your mind when it smells better."

Charles comes in followed by Danny, who walks over to his mother. "He pulled its teeth, its tusks, with a pliers," he says shaking his head. Heading to the bedroom for clean clothes, he calls out that they'll have some story to tell when they get back to school. She hears the boys laughing in the bedroom. Charles stands with a hand awkwardly behind his back as he figures out the approximate time they'll eat, which coincides with Gina's estimate. He seems no longer exhausted yet avoids looking at Gina when he leaves to change.

The boys come back wearing dry shorts. At the table, no one except Charles has an appetite. Both the boys ask to be excused. They're too tired, or they ate too much at lunch.

When the boys leave, Gina and Charles sip wine, and he talks about Vienna, though half-heartedly, and he agrees with Gina, that they should all turn in early, then get up and dig up the boar about 3:00 o'clock. Yes, invite Rosa and Rinaldo. There will be plenty for all. She decides to wait to tell him about Mario and Giovanni. Perhaps they won't even return. Still, she knows Charles will be happy to hear of Mario's upcoming wedding.

The late sun casts shadows over the table and she thinks about the pig. The poor thing. Are they really going to eat it in the middle of the night, under the Mediterranean moon?

"What's on your mind, Gina?"

"Oh, the boar. And the flower leis I still have to make," she answers. "Rinaldo's bringing flowers for the leis. Soon, I hope."

"Good," he says through a yawn. "I'll set the alarm." He pats Gina on the shoulder and leaves for bed.

Gina goes to the boys' room and is taking the puzzles and books off the lower bunk as they come in. She likes seeing them in their summer pajamas. Goodnight kisses. She wants to tell them a story since she hasn't done that since they've been gone, and doesn't want them to fall asleep thinking about the boar buried in the earth. When they're in bed she asks if the bunks are okay or are they a little lumpy? They're fine, Chris tells her, and they both agree, they're pretty comfortable.

Gina sits on the bed where Giovanni had slept, at the edge next to Danny and it seems all right to her too. She tells them she's going to wake them in the middle of the night for the luau. They're much too sleepy for a story.

ॐ

She hums to herself while she works on the flower leis. It's exciting and relaxing being on the beach while everyone else is asleep, a tub of flowers waiting to be strung beside her. She threads the needle through the base of each flower, expertly now that she's on her third lei, using small gold sunflowers and white flowers she doesn't recognize. For the current lei she's using five sunflowers, then one white, alternating the colors in pattern. If she finishes in time she can put them in the refrigerator and sleep for a while.

She's wearing the first two leis she's made, and is feeling tired, but happy. She counts: the boys, 1,2, Charles 3, herself 4, Mario and Giovanni 5 and 6, Rosa 7, Rinaldo 8 and an extra for the boar.

Continuing, and feeling peaceful, using purple blossoms now, mostly corn flowers, and a red carnation here and there, each lei a little different, except that hers and Giovanni's are all gold, but they are all beautiful and thick. She has so many flowers she can afford to be generous. Finally she has one more to go and makes the last one for Mario, of all red flowers. She uses carnations, zinnias, and geraniums. With the remaining blossoms she makes two hair wreathes, one for her and one for Rosa, choosing white for Rosa's which will be nice in her dark hair. For her own she uses gold to match her lei. She takes the flower leis from the lawn chair and puts a couple more around her neck, and the rest on her arm.

The night is still clear and warm, the stars bright and the sea as calm as her heart. She walks carefully up the path in the dark like a flower maiden who has walked out of the sea. After setting the leis in the refrigerator, she gets out two tablecloths, a stack of plates and napkins. She looks in on the boys, all sleeping soundly.

In the bathroom, Gina sees the white tusks Charles pulled from the boar lying on the sink top. Apparently, this was something he had to do, and which seems inexplicable to Gina, even if he is a dentist. It seems like a hunter's rite; something a caveman would do.

She leaves her clothes on, so tired, and climbs into bed next to Charles, looking at his white hair. Just a few years ago it was as black as Mario's. "Night," she murmurs into the pillow, and glancing at the green dots on the clock, sees that it's quarter to 2:00. She falls asleep, smelling of flowers.

ʘ

"Hey, time to get up." Gina opens her eyes. It's Mario, sitting beside her. Charles isn't there, and it's very dark. She looks at Mario, a light from the other room behind him makes him look like a painting. He's sitting so still, but he's wearing the Hawaiian shirt and the red lei. Her gold one and hair wreath hang loosely from his wrist.

"He sent me up to get you," he says.

She sits up and rubs her eyes, looks at him for an explanation.

"He was in the kitchen when we came. I told him I came to invite you two and the boys to the wedding. Then I introduced Giovanni as my friend, said he was going to sing at the wedding. Well, what else could I say?"

Gina gets up and slips a gold silk top over her T-shirt. She tells him that his car is at Rosa's house, and his journal is under the car seat, and that she didn't read it, or just a little, she says. He puts the gold flower lei around her neck and leans near, as if for a kiss, but then backs off. They're far away from each other now and still too close. She leaves to comb her hair and to arrange the flower wreathe. The night has begun.

Mario is waiting for her, and as she touches the lei resting against his chest, asks how he knew the red one was for him.

"I've been to see your fortune teller," he says, laughing, and somehow, she knows Giovanni's wearing the other gold lei, without her having chosen it for him and she hears the music from the beach below.

"Let's go," Mario says, his hand on her shoulder, getting her started. They leave and head down the path to the Italian luau.

No one notices them coming down in the dark, they're all around a huge bonfire. It's still warm, and the boys are in shorts, and everyone is wearing leis, the fire light reflects off skin, flowers, with the theatrical set of the night sea behind. Two tables have been set up, covered with red tablecloths, bowls of fruit on one, and the boar in the center of the second. Someone has scattered the extra flowers over both tables, and a tub is filled with ice, beer and pop. Gina and Mario walk into the scene—the music, the boys clapping and dancing, a sort of childish free form break dancing. Rosa and Giovanni are singing *Honolulu Baby*. Rosa knows the song from an old Laurel and Hardy movie and is clapping her hands and dancing a modified hula while Giovanni plays the guitar like a ukulele. Giovanni and Rosa sing on as Giovanni circles around Gina, dancing playfully, welcoming her, so alive and beautiful in his Hawaiian shirt and flowers, his golden curls like fire. Charles and Rinaldo take turns at a dancing duet with Rosa, and Rinaldo comes up with a plate for Gina—orange slices and grapes and a huge charred rib.

Everyone settles down around the fire, refilling their plates. The boys are eating ravenously, their faces smeared from the greasy meat, eyes glowing in the beautiful savage scene. Rosa and Rinaldo stand before the fire and harmonize on a popular Neopolitan song, while Giovanni accompanies on guitar. Charles goes to the boar to carve more meat with a large carving knife, and looking over at Gina, he smiles.

Gina sighs, takes a drink of her beer, and continues eating. Everyone is happy, as if with smiles from a secret they all share, except Mario. He sits chewing on a bone on the other side of the fire, his eyes steady, staring at the fire. Giovanni plays the guitar and everyone quiets down to listen to the haunting melody fill the night and the beach. His music comes from his heart, of beauty and sorrow, and Gina loves listening, and watching his fingering on the guitar, his down-turned eyes. When the music ends, everyone applauds. Chris wants him to play *On the Banks of the O-hi-o*, so they can sing along. As Giovanni begins they all join in, singing of the Ohio River, here next to the Mediterranean, with Rinaldo and Rosa humming along, and Gina sees that Mario has walked off down the beach. She sees his dark form walk slowly toward the cove.

She knows she can't go after him, there would be nothing to say; there would only be the night around them, above them. All those times she wanted to hear him say the unspoken things and there were never any words. Why hadn't she known it was the silence that counted, the silence that spoke. She feels Giovanni looking at her and turns toward him.

Giovanni looks at her until she has to turn her head away. He gets up and lights a cigarette and starts down the beach toward Mario, a beer in hand. Chris has lain down on the sand near the fire, half curled up, fighting sleep. Charles and Rinaldo start wrapping large chunks of the boar in foil and Danny starts burning paper plates.

The luau comes to an end by itself, as Danny sits picking out chords absently on Giovanni's guitar, humming a stray phrase now and then, his own young tune in a soft clear voice. Rosa and Rinaldo fold a tablecloth together, and Gina gets up and looks down the beach. She walks over to Charles, feeling old. She folds the last tablecloth by herself. Rosa comes over and puts her hand on Gina's shoulder, tells her it was a wonderful night, a wonderful luau.

Quietly, she tells her that Mario and Giovanni are spending the night, what's left of it, at her house.

"Coming?" Charles asks Gina, ready to head up the hill.

"In a while. I'll see the boys up." She says goodnight to Rosa and Rinaldo and wakes up Chris and starts him up the hill with the others. Though he's very groggy, he says, "Kind of sad that it was so good, Mom."

"I know what you mean. That's the way it is sometimes." Just a quick wash up of greasy hands and smeared faces and they're in bed. Charles is already dead to the world. She walks back down to the beach. No sign of Giovanni or Mario. She picks up a stray red flower from the sand and sits beside the dying fire, next to Giovanni's guitar, looking across the sea and wondering if she can stay awake to watch the sun rise. She lies down, waiting, playing with the smooth petals of the flower, keeping an eye on the stars, lazily picking out constellations. She falls asleep.

Later, she wakes, rests on one elbow, and notices a lightening of the sky. She isn't sure if she's been asleep, or for how long, when she sees two long legs stretched out beside her, and sits up. It's Giovanni asleep beside her. He's taken off his Hawaiian shirt and scrunched it up under his head for a pillow. He wears just the gold lei around his neck and khaki shorts, no shoes. She notices the green around his eyes, the black and blue now turned to a pale almost yellow green. Other than his wounds, he doesn't seem quite real, but instead a story book prince fast asleep on the sand. She gets up quietly, leaving him to his dreams.

By the time she reaches the house, she is weary with the night, and with total exhaustion, falls asleep next to Charles, who doesn't stir.

15. Last of the Mohicans

Sunday Morning: The boys take their bowls of Cheerios out to the patio and their morning chatter fills the house with their energy. They quiet down as they pass their father talking on the phone, a conditioned reflex. Danny slides the glass door shut and tells Chris he's a dope, eating all the raisins in bed last night before the luau; there aren't any left and he hates cereal without raisins. "Hey, there's Giovanni," Danny says, looking down toward the beach. He sets his cereal on the table and dashes off down the hill to the beach.

"Did you sleep down here?" he asks when he gets to him, breathless.

"Yes. You're Danny, right?" Giovanni asks, standing up and stretching.

"Officially, Raphael Daniel del Tredicci," he answers, grinning. "Just Danny. You want some Cheerios?"

"Sure, sounds good," he answers, wondering what they're doing with Cheerios in Italy, and trying to remember a show he used to watch, Cheerios sponsored it, some western rerun, maybe "The Lone Ranger."

"After you," he says, and Danny leads the way, concerned that his cereal is getting soggy. Giovanni grabs his crumpled shirt and shakes out the sand, slipping into it as they start toward the hill. Watching Danny's sturdy young legs run up the stairs, he senses Gina's intensity in the boy. When they reach the top, Danny tells Giovanni that they're out of raisins. Giovanni just smiles, unaccustomed to being around children. He's enchanted with Danny's youth.

Giovanni and the boys are finishing their cereal when Charles steps out to the patio with his breakfast on a plate, and coffee. The boys exchange glances, eyeing their father's breakfast: a large cold boar rib, and toast.

"Well, I see our singer's here. Good morning, Giovanni," he says, sitting down.

"Morning Charles," Giovanni responds as they shake hands. "The boys invited me out on the boat today. I'm a little early."

"He slept on the beach," Chris says, and Danny pokes him under the table.

"Yes," Giovanni laughs, a little embarrassed. "Too many beers last night. I fell asleep on the beach." Charles looks at him, curious, puzzled, and asks where Mario is. Giovanni tells him he decided to start back to St. Moritz last night.

"I thought he came with you," Charles says.

"Yes, but he had a rented car in town. I drove him in."

"Men who drive Ferraris generally don't sleep on the beach," Charles says, taking a bite of the rib, thinking of how sullen Mario was last night, and noting Giovanni's good looks, the green of his healing black and blue eyes. He chews silently.

"Would you like some?" he asks, referring to the meat. Not waiting for an answer, he tells Danny to get coffee for Giovanni. The boys leave with their empty cereal bowls.

"I can't chew," Giovanni says. "I have a loose tooth and had to eat on the other side last night. It's worse today." He runs his tongue over the tooth, thinking Gina was right, Charles has amazing teeth, marvelous carnivorous teeth; he could probably eat through bone.

Danny brings the coffee. Charles purses his lips, says he'll have a look at the tooth when they're done. Charles finishes his breakfast and asks about Giovanni's tooth while they have coffee, inquiring into Giovanni's dental history. Giovanni is not at all happy as Charles asks a battery of questions, hardly giving him time to catch his breath between questions. Is he married? What does he do? Where does he live? How long has he lived in Venice? Is a he a strong swimmer? The only dental question is how often does he floss? He avoids asking about Gina, or anything more about Mario. Giovanni is a good sport and answers the questions matter-of-factly, apparently under some sort of dental spell. Giovanni determines that Charles's animal spirit would be that of a polar bear, white and dashing, though possible dumb, or just as possibly too smart. His questions, the dental ones, the most innocuous, seem sly.

Charles's large mouth seems to be covering up something, perhaps fangs. Finally, Charles says "Let's go into the den and have a look." Giovanni follows along, quite concerned about his loose tooth.

Gina is in the den, and is startled by their entrance. "Oh, good morning," she says. "I was just getting one of these notebooks." She stands and moves aside, hugging a black-covered book to her chest. Charles smiles, not really looking at Gina; he's ready to have a look in Giovanni's mouth. As Gina leaves the room, she and Giovanni exchange sidelong noncommittal glances. She goes back to the bedroom and climbs onto the bed, propping herself up on the pillows. She leans back and begins to write—Sunday: I had a strange dream last night. I was on a large couch reading and Charles was there, but Mario was there too and he was pretending to read. I could tell because he never turned a page but was always on the same page, just pretending. He looked like himself. Then he left and came back and when I looked at him, he looked different, but I couldn't tell what had changed. Then I saw that he had shaved off his beard, though he still had the moustache. I said *When did you decide to shave off your beard, Mario?* and he said *Oh, five minutes ago.* Then I can't remember what happened next, except Charles was gone and Mario was gone, but then Mario came back into the room in a wheelchair.

She stares at the paper and can't write further, puts the cover back on the pen, wondering what the dream meant, the part she doesn't want to write, the wheelchair, the empty shirt sleeves, the pants legs pinned in like that, empty, and the room in that place. He said he had been there, the hospice place, with a name like an actual place, though it wasn't. Love, New Mexico. That's what he said. She could look in an atlas; see if there is such a place. And how could he have stood up with no legs?

She rests her face in her hands, the dream like a weight within her. She slides the notebook under the mattress, and concentrates, mentally forcing the dream away, first down into her feet where the dream drops like lead, and her toes feel like brass. She wiggles her toes and they lighten, and the unwanted dream goes away, and she's left with a soggy feeling in her feet, as if they are large and wet, the veins collapsed inside like leftover spaghetti at the bottom of a garbage bag.

She stands and tests her balance and starts a slow limber dance, her feet floppy, her body pliant. She dances around the room and turns into a shadow of herself, and the hardwood floor is like a trampoline for her lightness. She bounces about, doing a version of a dance class routine.

She thinks of presents, a wedding present, what to buy, then ends the dance and walks out of the bedroom, walking carefully along an imaginary line like a ballerina in a comedy. Seeing Charles on the patio, she raises her arms and dances toward the door, kicking one leg back playfully, then the other. She pirouettes out through the open sliding door.

"Remember when I used to dance for you, Charles?" She does a little toe ballet, as well as she can, in tennis shoes. "I haven't played tennis since we've been here. Aren't there some courts anywhere?" she asks, coming up behind him, talking to his back. He's filing the root end of one of the boar tusks, and seems happy and smiles up at her, ignoring her question. Giovanni doesn't ignore her questions; he always listens, even if he doesn't always have an answer.

Below, she sees Giovanni and the boys out in the old wooden boat. They're using a tarp for a sail, and they're all wearing red bandannas, and she imagines their looting plans, their pirate tales: Captain Giovanni and his crew, sailing their mighty old wooden row boat in search of treasures, adventure. She watches for a time to the sound of Charles's tusk filing and the laughter and cries in the distance from the sea. Without turning around, she asks Charles if he's ever heard of Love, New Mexico.

"You're in a good mood this morning, Gina," he responds, fairly sure that something has been going on with Giovanni while he was in Vienna, and also sure of his assessment of him, that Giovanni will never leave Italy.

"Yes," she sighs and leaves for the kitchen to fix an omelet. "Want some eggs?" she asks on her way.

"No thank you, I had breakfast. I'll take another coffee, though," he responds, before glancing down to the beach. He holds up the boar tusk. It just needs a little polishing.

After Charles has his coffee, he tells Gina he needs to go into town and asks if she wants to come, but she'd rather stay with the boys, and she needs to wash her hair.

"What do you think we should get for Mario and Anita?" she asks, not yet having any idea herself.

"Why don't you give them one of your paintings," he suggests, but she doesn't think she has anything appropriate, and she's burned so many. They'd probably like something more representational, which she doesn't do much anymore.

She painted someone's pet cocker spaniel once, just to see if she could do it and her friend had loved it and hadn't noticed the crazed look she had given one of the spaniel's eyes. That dog had never liked her.

She has always liked those personal touches in old paintings, the alert, questioning pair of eyes in a corner, often a self-portrait of the artist himself. And then there are the sprightly little cherubs with mischievous bright eyes and rosy arms and legs, with the liveliness of real children. Those she likes. They seem to claim no kinship to adult angels who are too heavenly; grown-up angels who look like they have never lived on earth but were simply born of marble mothers and granite fathers, born into lives of stone. Of course, there are exceptions, still. ...

Yes, a statue might be just the thing, and Gina suggests an angel. What could be more Italian, and it would remind them of their wedding. They could use it in the garden, and it should be easy enough to arrange shipping. "Marble, a marble sculpture, something of quality," she says.

"Good idea, Gina."

"All right. The wedding is on Thursday. Giovanni could help me shop—he's knows a lot about sculpture. He owns a marble quarry near here, did he tell you that?"

"Yes."

"How's his tooth?"

Charles says it's loose and might reset itself, if he's careful, but he'd like to put a pin in it. He offered to do it, but Giovanni was against it and said he would just let it heal naturally. *"He might lose it,"* Charles says, laughing his deep manly laugh, like a boat motor turned on somewhere in his throat. Gina thinks he's being mean but doesn't say so.

The phone rings and Charles answers. It's Anita, looking for Mario. Charles tells her that Mario left last night so he must be on his way. He hangs up.

"It was Anita. Charming voice she has. Have you met her?" he asks.

"No, but I've seen her hair. I mean I've seen her. She has red hair." Charles looks at Gina and tells her that hair is trivial, while thinking of how odd it is that Mario hadn't arrived in St. Moritz by now.

Gina sits twisting a strand of her own hair, thinking of Mario and Anita and the wedding coming up. Anita, the pediatrician with red hair. Will they be happy? What is happiness, anyway?

"Do you want to keep writing for the greeting card company when we get home?" She sighs. "I don't know. I'm not sure. I don't think I do."

"You could go to school, now that Chris'll be in Kindergarten and you'll have time. Think about it," and he goes over to her, kisses the top of her head.

What to do? Well, it's certainly true that she's into collages now, not college. She can hardly stay out of the studio when she's by herself. No, she won't go back to the card company. Definitely not. Since Italy, since Giovanni, she's feeling like a real artist. Maybe that's Giovanni's gift to her.

She gets her bathing suit from the dresser and stops to look at herself in the mirror. I'm perfectly normal looking, she says to herself, at least from the outside. She takes off her clothes and observes herself objectively. She has good lines, good skin and flowing hair, the oval shapes of her eyes below rounded brows are fine, the curve of her breasts above a waist just right, the simplicity of shoulders and neck, as one part merges into another like tree branches. People should look at themselves more, and at each other, she decides. She slips into her bathing suit and goes to the kitchen and fills a thermos with lemonade.

At the beach she waves to her pirates in the sea and with a good grip on the rope strap of the lemonade container, she starts swimming out toward the boat, doing the side stroke so she can glide along with the lemonade. Swimming is hard, as she has to work extra with her right arm, but finally makes it to the edge of the boat. She hollers out that she's a stranded mermaid, sputtering sea water and looking up at the boys and Giovanni. She feigns drowning and cries, "Save me." Giovanni pulls her into the heavy boat.

೦೩

BACK ON LAND—The boat is docked at the beach and four red bandannas are tied to one oar. After pirating, they had a fine lunch of pasta primavera, garlic bread and salad. Charles is still in town.

Gina and Giovanni sit directly opposite each other on the sand, a sketch pad on each of their laps, intent on drawing one another. They have been at it for at least half an hour, when Danny rushes up to them with his own sketch book, and colored pencils. He says that Chris is next door with the neighbor girl and they're just going around and around on their bikes in front of her house. Her mom's sitting out there on the steps. "He tried to take off his training wheels, but they wouldn't come off," he says.

"Nice," Danny says, looking over their drawings. "I'm going to draw too. I love drawing," and he plunks down beside them, nearer to Giovanni so he can draw his mother, but then decides to draw the boat's oar. Danny tells them about a wonderful drawing of a rabbit he saw at a museum in Vienna. He wants to draw like that, he tells them. He wants to draw people and animals and everything. "Yes, I'm going to be an artist," he says before losing himself in his drawing. Time passes. They notice nothing outside of the subject of their drawings, so intent on their work, and warmed by the Italian sun. Life is good.

When Danny finishes he shows them his drawing. He's pleased with how it turned out, but is ready for some more biking. Watching him rush up the path, Giovanni says Danny needs better colored pencils. He's really good, he tells Gina, who already knows of his talent.

They move up to the house and Gina makes a pot of tea. Out on the patio, they discuss the wedding present. Giovanni insists they go to Venice for a statue. He knows an elderly couple with a collection of antiques stored in an old boarded up family warehouse, and they like him. He's sure they would sell to him, and for a good price. Gina can't make up her mind about whether to go along.

"It's not just to Venice we're talking about," Giovanni says. "Are you going to come with me, or are you going to stay with Charles?" He waits for an answer.

"I'm not asking you again. I need to know." He looks at her, still waiting.

"I don't know. How could I?" she says.

Giovanni gets up and goes over to her, looking down at her as she sits staring into her teacup, much like on the day they met, at the café.

"Damn it, Gina," he says, kissing the top of her head, before walking off and out the door. He is driving off at full speed by the time she gets to the door, her mind working slowly, a shock flooding through her as the red car goes over the hill.

"Giovanni. I can't do this," she says to the door. Then, thinking she could chase him, catch him in the van, she rushes over and opens the door to the empty garage, and remembers: Charles took the van into town.

She walks around the garage, stomping her feet. The cement floor is dirty and oily and cold on her bare feet. She steps on the head of a nail, picks it up and looks for a hammer and finds one on the work shelf. She takes the nail and holds it upright on her foot and smashes down on the nail with all her might. She looks down with hatred at her foot. The nail is nowhere in sight, she didn't hit it right, it veered off and ripped through the skin with the blow, making a tear, which is bleeding profusely, and sputtering. She must have hit a vein. It feels numb and wet and warm. Standing still and looking at her foot, she feels detached from the gurgling pain; she might just as well be the light bulb above the garage workshop, her foot simply wounded marble. Finally, she gets out the hose and washes off some of the blood, using the red bandanna Giovanni put around her neck, as a tourniquet, yet it keeps bleeding.

In the house she hops along the wall to the bathroom and cleans the wound properly in the tub. She puts a piece of dental gauze directly on the wound and quickly winds white bandage tape around her foot, using up what's left on the roll. Next, she rinses out the wet bandanna, and drapes it over the tub to dry and hops off to the dressing room. Ignoring the throbbing of her foot, she slides on her dark blue knee socks and wiggles her wounded foot into a navy tennis shoe.

"Oh darn you, Mario," she says to the empty afternoon. "I mean Giovanni," and flustered, her voice raised, angered at her mistake, the names, on the verge of hysteria. He's left his cigarettes and lighter. She takes out a cigarette and rolls it between her fingers, then takes the one he started from the ashtray, it went out, and she relights it, recalling his mouth, the way he would sit sometimes, running his finger back and forth across his lower lip. The cigarette, some of his breath may still be there. She smokes seriously, intentionally drawing him in and blowing him away. If he goes up in smoke, there'll be nothing left. She watches the smoke vanish in the breeze.

"Osmosified," she says, wondering if there is such a word. Now Giovanni and Mario can be the wind, or birds, she says to herself, and hears a songbird out at the feeder, and she puts her head down to rest on the table, her eyes as dry as keen knives.

A short time later, when Charles returns from town, she's still on the patio, shredding Giovanni's cigarettes, building a haystack of tobacco on her saucer. She has two more cigarettes to go when Charles comes out to the patio with two beers. He sets one down for her and she says hi without looking up, intent on piling up the shredded tobacco, carefully layering it. She's developed a technique so it doesn't blow away in the breeze. She rolls the papers up into little crumpled balls, like cracked eggs, and drops them into her coffee cup. Charles purses his lips and watches her demolish the last two cigarettes. When she's finished she leans back in her chair, scrutinizing the haystack, then grins up at Charles and takes a sip of her beer.

"What are you going to do with that?" he asks.

"Sell it. To the Museum of Modern Art," she answers. "It's called the *Last of the Mohicans.*" Charles smiles condescendingly. He doesn't mention Giovanni, had noticed the Ferrari was gone when he drove in. Finishing his beer, he tells her he's going to clean up. She needs the van keys, she says; she has an errand to take care of and tells him the boys are over at the Maestrelli's, next to Rinaldo's place, that they took their bikes over to play. Charles drops the keys on the table, and as soon as she hears the water running in the bathroom she gets up, guzzles the last of her beer and hobbles off to the van and takes off. She drives down the road into the countryside, following as far she can remember, retracing their route.

Arriving at a small town, she stops for gas. She has plenty of euros in her purse but isn't sure if her passport is there. The attendant fills the van and she asks for a map, using her handy guidebook to look up the phrase. He doesn't understand. She has to point to the phrase in the book and he nods his head and says something in Italian and goes to the station and returns with a map. She's grateful for his kindness.

Studying the map, she marks the route with a yellow felt-tipped pen. Driving on, she makes good time until she has to stop by the side of the road, where she opens the car door and dangles her legs, and loosens the laces of her shoe. Why hadn't she hit her left foot, it hurts so now, the pressure against the pedal when she drives, and it's getting hard to ignore. She's grateful to find an aspirin packet tucked away in the pouch of her purse. Having no water, she takes two pills dry and swallows hard, tasting the powdery aspirin against her throat. She turns on the radio to drown out the pain and drives on, and despite the pain, it's a beautiful day. The country is green and she loves the hills and vineyards, the fields of grain, mile after mile, song after song. As she drives north, the earth moves and the car moves across the curve of the earth, and an early evening sunset begins to soften the countryside, turning the fields a soft golden rose.

Continuing, the beginning of shadows appear, and she drives into the brightness of the sunset, into orange, and into the red and purple of the sky, until the farmhouses and trees become black silhouettes as she nears Venice. She's sure there are many more sunsets and sunrises here in Italy than anywhere else in the world.

After parking the van in an outer parking lot beside the train station, she has only to wait a few minutes for the train to the city. It's dark and pleasant on the train ride in, the routine she now knows well. At the Venice station, she waits in the dark for the next boat, then boards carefully, and takes a seat, relaxing as it pulls out smoothly and heads down the canal toward the museum near Giovanni's studio. She watches the night lights reflected in the water as the boat moves along the canal, and of all the rivers and roads in the world, she knows this is the river she has to follow, even if it is a canal and not a real river. Getting out at the *vaporetti* stop near the studio, she listens to the boat motor going away down the canal, sounding final, and certain of itself. Orienting herself, she walks, as best she can, the half block to the studio, and slowly climbs the stairs, feeling the wetness of blood in her shoe. At the top she rests a moment before knocking, her mind empty, only following itself. She raps at the door, weary, and almost at peace.

The door opens and she sees a woman, very tall and pale, with an explosive mane of red hair standing in the doorway. She spots Giovanni's gold lei on a wicker chair behind the woman who says something to her but Gina doesn't understand. She sees white marble statues standing about like ghosts, and chunks of gleaming raw marble scattered like tombs on the studio floor.

"I have the wrong building," she says, making her voice steady, avoiding the red-headed woman's eyes, and she starts down the stairs, forcing herself to walk normally, though the pain of the wound shoots up her leg. Natasha watches her leave, then shuts the door.

Gina waits in the dark for the next boat to take her to the down-and-out hotel she stayed at before. It's turned cold, and shivering, she climbs into the boat when it arrives. Mechanically, she hands her ticket to the driver. Unaware of the ride or the lights on the water, she arrives at the hotel and walks in through the revolving door and registers. The clerk in the purple uniform hands over the keys to her old room, and she takes the rickety elevator up to the third floor. She makes her way along the worn gaudy carpet of the dim hallway to room 307. Inside, she locks the door, turns out the light, and sits on the edge of the bed to take off her shoes. She ignores the swollen bloody sock and climbs into bed without undressing. Clinging to the soft white pillow and listening to water running somewhere in another room, she is asleep within seconds.

Later in the night, she wakes in the dark hotel room. Only a crack of light from the hallway is visible, but her eyes adjust. Gina stares at the moon pale wall. A dream flickers and slips away.

She needs to get somewhere. Somewhere. Out in the hallway she moves slowly, her legs feeling both heavy and light, like fat balloons, and she favors her left leg, and leans against the wall, slipping down and down. The rug is colorful, how nice that they've turned on the lights again. The radiator is cool on her hand as she goes down, slowly, semi-conscious—part of her feels hot, some misplacement, it's so easy, the soft bright rug, so many colors, sparkling and soft, her foot hot as fire. She passes out on the carpet of the third floor hallway.

CR

MIDNIGHT IN THE SOUTH—"Hello, Rosa. It's Charles. Did I wake you? Oh, I'm terribly sorry, but I'm trying to locate Gina. She left on an errand this afternoon and isn't back. Have you talked to her today? No?"

It's not like her. She lets me know where she is, or at least sends an email. He's very worried, yet does not want to say too much, unsure how well Rosa knows Gina.

Rosa tells Charles that she's probably fine, she'll be driving in soon, or she'll call, but she's worried now too. They decide to do nothing, just to wait and see what develops. Charles suspects Gina is probably with Giovanni. Rosa wonders which one she's with.

Rosa tells Charles to go to bed; there's no use worrying—that won't do any good. They say goodnight and both go to bed, lying awake under their respective roofs, under the same moon, unable to sleep, letting their imaginations play out the possibilities. Rosa's mind soon wanders to Rinaldo, and the luau. He's coming to dinner tomorrow night, and she goes over the menu and tomorrow's shopping, and her concern for Gina slips away with thoughts of sweet basil.

Charles, in the shadows of his room, imagines Gina asleep in Giovanni's strong young arms. Back home, he would sometimes hear her walking about at night, opening cupboards, down in the kitchen. He didn't pay much attention, just went back to sleep.

◌ℛ

In the morning, Charles is up early and makes coffee in the silence of the kitchen. The boys are still asleep. He'll tell them she had some shopping to do in Venice, which he reasons is probably true. With the boar tusks in his pocket, he's ready to file and think, over coffee. He goes to the garage for a file, and turning on the workshop light, spots a dark red puddle on the cement floor and has to steady himself with a hand on the work bench. The boar, simply blood from the boar, but then recalls that the meat truck was in the drive, never in the garage. He stops to examine the blood, running his fingers through the dark liquid, his heart beating wildly.

He ignores his own rapid pulse, leaving himself open for explanation, an explanation that will surely come in a moment; after all, he is Charles, logical calm Charles. People count on him. A small noise startles him and he looks around the empty garage, expectantly. Who is he expecting? Mario or Giovanni, with their blackened eyes and wounds? Of course there's no one. There are always explanations, reasons for things. The world is a logical place, yet he can't stop the flood of questions. Just who is Giovanni? And why is he in Italy, an American with a name like that. Charles wipes the blood off his fingers with an old rag. His hands are shaking. Murder? The word, the idea, flutters momentarily through his mind. Mario? Did he lie here bleeding? No, no, of course not. Then that violent painting of Gina's that he saw in the studio yesterday. And Gina's cold strange eyes while she played with the cigarettes. And what about her good humor, in spite of the wedding on Thursday, or *was* it good?

A whirling of images, like violent clouds, keeps him frozen in place. For how long, he's unsure, but as he leaves the garage, he needs to steady himself momentarily against the doorway before entering the kitchen. Yes, coffee, settle down. His mind is blank while he waits for the coffee. Heading to the patio for some fresh air, he sits down and drinks the coffee to calm himself. The veins in his forehead stand out like snakes and he's forgotten the file in the garage.

The boys get up and he makes pancakes. After they eat they want to go over to the Maestrelli's again. They tell him about the fort they're building on the hill behind their house, and Charles is relieved to see them go off happily on their bikes to play.

He'll figure it out. The mailman delivers the mail just as the boys ride off. Only a few bills, an ad from a Denver architect, a letter for Gina from a girlfriend back home. He takes the mail to his desk. The phone bill shows calls made this past Friday. There's a call to San Diego and one to St. Moritz , and then one to St. Moritz from last Tuesday. Mario must have made the calls but he puzzles over this, recalling how Mario had acted like he had arrived for the first time the night of the luau.

Then a call on Friday to Venice, and one to the Congo, and another to Monaco. Giovanni made those, there's no doubt in his mind. When he examined Giovanni's tooth, he told Charles about how he was planning to sell some of his assets, some African mines. He was liquidating. A certainty is settling in his mind, and Charles stares at the word Congo, the shapes of the letters, ominous, like pools of blood, red bull's-eyes, red as Ferraris. He recalls a movie he saw about arms trafficking—shady characters in trench coats meeting in bars at night in Third World countries, and exchanges of foreign currency under streetlights in the night fog.

Charles grinds his teeth, gets up and goes to the kitchen for a rib. He walks down to the beach, gnawing on the bone like a lollipop, chewing and sucking out the marrow. He doesn't walk far, but stands looking down toward the cove, the wind of the afternoon in his face. The waves of the sea snap out of their raggedy surface while the ever-present seagulls squawk.

Back in the house, he sits down with the phone bill in front of him and calls the number in St. Moritz. Anita is called to the phone, and he asks her about the wedding, the exact time and place, accommodations, conversing matter-of-factly with Anita, and no, she says Mario hasn't yet arrived.

After hanging up Charles stares at the numbers on the phone. The phone rings, and at this close range, startles him. He answers. It's Rosa, and no, he's heard nothing. Rosa's calm studied words fail to hide her concern for Gina, and their sensible conversation ends with both hanging up into a cliff of panic.

Charles calls his friend James, Gina's father, and arranges for the boys to spend the week and a half remaining before school starts, with their grandparents in Minneapolis. Then he calls the airport to make reservations.

 CR

EARLY AFTERNOON OF THE NEXT DAY—Charles is driving back to the beach house after seeing the boys off from the Rome airport. With his old efficiency and precision, he's arranged to have the boys met by friends at each stopover until their grandfather picks them up in Chicago. So odd, that it was only just last night that it really sunk in, that his old pal James, actually a few years younger than himself, is the grandfather of his sons. Of course he had always known that, after all it was simply a fact, but he had always let that fact slough off until last night. Somehow it had always been too close to be noticed in any significant way these last busy years. Then last night and now, it hangs there like a heavy new fact, freshly excavated from a moth-balled corner of his mind. It unnerves him.

He thinks of her youth, oh, his sweet Gina, with her bright innocent eyes, and her hair shining in the sun. A twitch, like a bug beneath the surface, jitters near his eyes. He ignores it, and a sensation, an awareness of the surface of his skin, nerve endings pouring heat across his face. She moved into his big house when she was so young and Cesca was there. It was a happy time and seemed normal when they fell in love, even though it surprised a lot of people. They married when she turned eighteen. His hands are tight against the steering wheel of the rented van as he drives at a steady, safe speed, toward the coast. He drives for miles, suspended in thought, and he nears the beach house with no recollection of the time spent on the road, as he pulls into the drive, stopping the car.

Sitting in the car like an automaton, the motion and posture of driving holding him captive, the after-effect of the drive accumulated inside him like an invisible motor that needs to slow down and stop before he can move. After a few minutes he gets out of the car and goes inside, more or less braced for whatever he'll find inside. Inside is the emptiness of a house that has been noisy with the sounds of happy children and he walks through the stillness, from room to room, looking for Gina, who isn't there. No one. No messages.

He sighs and heads to the kitchen where he fills a plate with food: more meat, a hefty wedge of gorgonzola, some cherry tomatoes, and a large hard roll spread thick with butter. And Scotch on the rocks. On the patio, a few strands of tobacco dangle from the wrought iron of the table and flutter like hair. Charles flicks them away. He eats.

It goes on, the not knowing, and being on the edge of anything for two days. Eating and drinking relaxes him some, but it's a taut relaxation. He stretches out his stiff legs. He wants it to be over, just wants to go home with Gina. Sucking on an ice cube, he hears a car drive in. He hurries to the door.

It's Rosa and Rinaldo. He invites them in and out to the patio. Rosa looks sheepish; both look concerned. He gets more glasses and ice and fixes drinks, refreshing his own from the bottle on the table. Speaking in Italian, Rinaldo says they want to help, if they can, and when Charles responds in Italian, that yes, he would appreciate their help, their support, Rosa visibly breathes a sigh of relief and, fortified with her drink, she begins to tell Charles certain facts she thinks he should be aware of.

She starts with the fight, and how last Thursday she had talked to Gina on the phone and she had sounded extremely confused, so she drove over to see what was going on. She saw a car in the driveway and heard music inside, but no one answered the door and so she let herself in. Gina was sitting on the floor holding that old brass duck, beside herself and incoherent. Gina said she knocked out Giovanni and Mario. They were both lying there on the floor.

Charles leans back, thinking, and feels this little Italian lady is politely screwing a corkscrew into his brain, and he feels a pain tighten in his chest. But he simply nods his head, thinking, swallowing. His mouth seems to be filling with saliva at an unusual rate and he has to keep swallowing, while retaining a minimal amount of sophistication. He asks Rosa if she knows who started the fight and she tells him that Gina said Giovanni hit Mario first.

"I see," Charles says, lapsing back into English, and motions for her to go on. She tells how she got the doctor and then when she came over the next day, Giovanni and Mario had gone off somewhere together, to some quarry, and Gina seemed fine, acted like everything was just fine and normal, like things like that happened every day. Rinaldo breaks in at this point and tells Rosa she should tell him about the luau.

Rosa nods and goes on, recalling the night of the luau, before Gina came down to the beach, and before Mario went up to get her. Mario was standing alone down next to the water, just standing there staring. He had two leis around his neck, a gold one and the red one, and she had to say his name twice when she came near him, before he heard her. She thought he looked like some sort of devil prince, with those flower leis, but she doesn't tell Charles this. He turned to look at her, she says, but he seemed far away. She told Mario that his car was parked in her driveway, and she gave him the keys. He seemed very tired. She told him that he and Giovanni could stay at her house after the luau, she had plenty of room. All he said was thanks, and then he kind of shuffled his feet in the sand and turned toward the sea again. He wanted to be left alone, and so she left him there, Rosa says, sitting back in her chair. They all sit quietly, thinking, and sipping their drinks.

As the level of the Scotch goes down, the imaginations of the threesome rises. Rinaldo embellishes his kidnapping theory. He thinks Giovanni is a professional kidnapper and is holding Gina somewhere in Venice and says Charles should prepare himself for the ransom call which should come at any minute. This Charles dismisses as nuts. Charles listens politely, listening for new facts, anything that might help.

He tries to make sense of it all. He has no intention of telling them about the blood in the garage. Mario's car was gone when Rosa went home from the luau. Why did Giovanni say Mario had a rented car in town? Giovanni could have returned Mario's car during the night while Gina followed in the Ferrari and driven back together in the Ferrari after dropping off Mario's car. Charles wonders if Rosa knows more than she's telling. There doesn't seem to be any motive for Mario's murder, but Charles has this feeling that Mario is dead. Is it because he actually wishes him dead?

Rosa has her own ideas. She insists Giovanni is a nice boy, and Mario is the one to be wary of. Every now and then Rosa stands up and looks around. She thinks Mario is stalking the house. She is going to spend the night at her daughter Leanna's house, with Mario on the loose, she thinks anything is possible. She thinks Rinaldo should bring Charles one of the guns from his gun collection.

They continue to talk and drink. Small details, trivial facts, swell into monstrous possibilities. When Rinaldo starts talking about his grandfather's war, Charles politely suggests they call it a day, and he walks them to the car.

After Rosa and Rinaldo leave, Charles walks through the house, pacing back and forth. He stops at the coffee table and picks up the brass duck, looking at it for some clue but its smooth eyeless head is dumb as a gold brick. It's clean. What if she had actually killed one of them last Thursday? Had she wanted to? What has happened to her? Is he responsible? Should he have left her home alone?

The police. Why hasn't he called the police? His logic is failing him, yet he doesn't want to call the police. The pain in his chest tightens. He sits down trying to control his breathing. Gina used to try to get him to try marijuana, but he couldn't. He just couldn't let himself, and doesn't know why he thinks of that now, except he'd try it if she walked in e door, if she would only walk in. Of course she no longer uses drugs. That struggle has long been over. So many things Charles never learned. He never learned to smoke. He never played the banjo she gave him for his birthday. He canceled the lessons. He had an automatic built-in *no* for anything new. But they could begin again. Start fresh.

He gets up to retrieve the phone bill from the den, then gets the key to his bottom desk drawer. He unlocks the drawer and sets the gun on the desktop. He sits down, looking at it. He used to joke about a good cure he had for an abscess, but there's nothing funny about it now, nothing amusing about its cold black shape. He needs it next to him to make the call, that's all. Suddenly he laughs out loud, wipes his eyes with the palm of his hand, and pulls over the phone.

He places a call to the number in Venice. He'll find out. The raspy voice of an old man answers. No, Giovanni's not there, he might be at the studio, he's told, and Charles asks for the number. After a minute of silence, the old man gives him the studio number and asks him to tell Giovanni that Pascal is fine. Charles is puzzled, but says he'll tell him, and asks who he's talking to. "Luigi," the man says, sounding equally puzzled. Charles thanks him, says good night and hangs up.

He calls the studio number. It rings twice, and he recognizes Giovanni's voice when he picks up. He asks if Gina is there, no he should have asked if he knows where she is, where is she? Does he know? Words rush out, incoherent. Giovanni has to question Charles to understand. How long has she been gone? Charles tells him, then silence. Charles hears him talking to someone—a women's voice, not Gina's, a voice with a heavy strange accent in the background. He listens as Giovanni describes Gina, hears anger rising in Giovanni's voice.

"Charles," he says, returning to the phone. "She was here. But I didn't know. I'll try and find her. I'll call you back." Charles takes a studied deep breath and then asks Giovanni if he has his number. He does. Giovanni asks how he got the studio number.

"Luigi," Charles says. "Who's Pascal?" he asks.

"That's my monkey."

"Find her, Giovanni," he says, his voice breaking with emotion. Charles hangs up and wipes the sweat from his brow.

16. Dr. Giovanni

Giovanni sits in a chair pulled up next to the hospital bed, watching Gina, waiting for her to wake. Her face is flushed like sunburn, and moist strands of hair cling to her cheeks and forehead. Asleep, she looks like an abandoned doll, and he starts to hum softly, a tune from nowhere, a lullaby, and he rocks gently back and forth to his own music, calling to her in her dreams, until she begins to stir. He moves closer, onto the edge of the bed slowly, continuing the quiet song, and guided by nothing, by her mouth, her breath, some part of him leaves his physical self and climbs above her like a cloud, his ghost, his invisible self, circling her, while his body remains carefully seated at the edge of the bed. She wakes.

"Hello," he says. She's quiet, looking up at him, letting him come into focus. He doesn't say more, just waits.

"I called Charles," she says.

"So did I," Giovanni responds.

"Do you have any cigarettes?" she asks finally. He smiles and goes to close the door of the room, comes back and opens the window. He picks up a small metal tray and comes back to the bed and lights twin cigarettes in his mouth and hands her one.

"You came after me, didn't you," he says, sitting down on the chair near the bed. Gina listens, there's not a trace of smugness in his words. She sucks on her cigarette, glancing up at him, thinking of that woman, that red-headed woman, wondering why they keep turning up with that hair, like a plague. Then fully awake, she starts to laugh, somewhat bitterly.

"I pounded a nail into my foot. Did they tell you?"

"They told me." He exhales smoke toward her. "Gina, I just want to pick you up and shake the daylights out of you."

Before Gina has time to respond, the door opens and the doctor comes in.

"No smoking," he says in Italian, shaking a finger at them. Toward Giovanni he asks questioningly, "Dr. del Tredicci?"

"Yes, pleased to meet you," Giovanni responds immediately in Italian, a whimsical look on his face; he assumes an attitude, a stance Gina has never seen before. They correspond in Italian, ignoring Gina. The doctor unwraps the bandages on her foot and Giovanni leans in to watch, and she sees him looking at her foot, curious, seeing the wound with a kind of awe, at the colors, the look and wonder of it, as she herself might look.

When the doctor finishes dressing the wound, Giovanni stands back, assuming his new mock professional stance, and they talk again. The doctor leans near Gina and very kindly says *ciao*, patting her shoulder and smiling. Then he says something to Giovanni that she interprets as *take care of her and don't let her do anything so stupid again*. When the doctor leaves, Giovanni closes the door and lights another cigarette and brings Gina her clothes. He helps her slip on her blouse and skirt.

"Why does everyone think I need to be taken care of?" she asks, adjusting her skirt.

"It's pretty obvious. Still I just want to shake you up," he adds. As she laces the shoe on her good foot she glances up from the lace and asks who the woman in his studio was.

"Natasha."

"I hate her," Gina says, pulling the bow of the shoe lace tighter than necessary.

"Okay, you can hate her. But it's all over between Natasha and me. I ended it before we went to your beach house." He sits with a hand casually resting on each knee, absently patting his knee caps as if to comfort them.

"She's going back to Russia," he continues, and moves over onto the edge of the bed, looking down at Gina, her hair cascading like a waterfall toward her shoes. She's staring into the empty shoe. "Some of her Russian colleagues came down for a visit. Now she's going home for the cure. She drinks. She was drunk when they came to see her." Giovanni laughs, a sad kind of laugh. "She probably was when you went to the studio too."

Gina picks up the tennis shoe by its tongue, letting it dangle in front of her.

"She had vodka bottles stacked up in a pyramid and insisted on playing the old national anthem on them with a spoon. I hope she can be helped. She's a very talented sculptor." He looks at Gina. She can't figure out how to put the shoe on. He gets down on the floor and lifts the wounded foot, removes the lace and slips the shoe carefully onto her foot, then leans his head against her knees.

"You know I have to stay with Charles and the boys. But here I am in Venice, chasing after you. What's going to become of us?" He moves up to the bed and sits next to Gina and begins to sing. Watching him, his eyes and his music are like a sweet happy waltz that he invites her into. She thinks of Mario when they danced on the patio, how awkward and how good that was. She thinks of how the boys dance with her too sometimes, after dinner, her young men, when they're in a silly, happy mood and dance to the radio in the kitchen. And she thinks of Charles's gentle ways, when they would waltz so formally and their eyes would meet, and whatever it is, she looks at it now in Giovanni's eyes, and hears it in the music.

"I like it like this," she says, when he finishes his song.

"Me too," he says. "Let's get married, Gina, just the two of us." Gina laughs, and it seems like the second half of a laugh, a high surprised note. She repeats, "just the two of us," cocking her head in readiness of the other half of something.

"I don't give up," he says, and tells her she needs to stay off her feet and he lifts her legs onto the bed and lays his head on her stomach, running his fingers along the waistband of her skirt, stopping on a button that he turns around like a little wheel as he breathes onto her stomach, feeling its rise and fall.

The door opens and a nurse enters the room, her dark eyes open wide. They look up at her. Giovanni gets up and introduces himself as Dr. del Tredicci and says that everything's fine, just fine, and she's ready to leave. He shakes her hand, talks her to the door and out the door. Gina gets up and gathers her meager belongings.

"Let's go," she says, and limps out the door and down the hall where she checks out and leaves the hospital on Giovanni's arm.

They cross the bridge to the *vaporetti* stop, waiting as it comes down the canal. Climbing in they sit near the back, though there's plenty of room, most of the passengers get out at the hospital stop. As the boat pulls out, Gina watches the water swirling behind the motor where the ripples drift out, and she enjoys the warmth of the sun, after the hospital, leaving some of the confusion and darkness behind.

"I love the water. I don't even care where we're going," she says. As they move along the canal, everything is bright and fresh. They pass in and out of the sun, slices of sun measured by the shade of buildings, passing old palaces, building after building with terraces, windows circled with wrought-iron trim, short wide doors, each rectangular portico with its own mystery, its own past. The city seems old and permanent, steadfast and clever.

"Venice," Giovanni says with a sigh. He's at home here where everything is possible in a city like this, built out of nothing, where you can almost touch the past, the ages, the lives lived, and now like faded figures of a ghostly fresco, absorbed into the ancient bricks staring out at them. He turns to Gina and takes her hand. Before she is aware of what he's doing, he has slipped the wedding ring off her finger and tossed it into the shimmering water of the canal. Water rings circle out from where it sank and they both watch until the surface is smooth again. Stunned, she turns back as they pass the spot where it disappeared into the water.

Giovanni begins a quiet song, the same song as he woke her with at the hospital, followed by a popular Italian ballad. As they move along the Grand Canal, a passing gondolier joins in with Giovanni and they harmonize until the gondolier has turned a corner. The motor of their boat purrs them along and Gina taps Giovanni's knee and tells him she wants to go to their island. "That's where we're headed," he answers. "The ferry is just around the bend. "We'll get married there," he says.

"You're crazier than I used to be," she tells him.

"But we can," he responds. "We can have a legal wedding later, a nice official and meaningless ceremony. We'll fly to St. Thomas. The real thing is now," and he begins to sing again. A few passengers from the boat heading in the other direction join in on the verse, until the boats move away from each other and the song gets fainter as they near their stop, and Giovanni stops singing to listen as the sound floats off without him. "This sure is a singing place," Gina comments. "It's like being in a musical. Or a dream."

"Life is but a dream," Giovanni sings, as they pull onto shore and he helps Gina out. They walk slowly toward the ferry, and on land again, he asks how her foot is doing and she tells him it's not too bad. She tries not to limp; she doesn't want anyone to feel sorry for her.

As the ferry pulls out, they're quiet, each within their own thoughts. When they are well out into the open water, he tells Gina that he will buy a large beautiful house, with studios, and rooms for the boys. Their conversation as they cross the water to the island becomes a kind of shorthand, a word or two, a dangling phrase. For the last quarter of a mile to the island they are both as silent as the sea. Just before they dock she says, "two big studios," and tries to picture such a scene, knowing it's just a dream and hoping it is a good dream for Giovanni too.

On the island they walk toward the old Byzantine ruins, and Gina's tennis shoe, the laceless one on her wounded foot, keeps slipping off. When they get to the old place, she sits down to rest and contemplate the mosaic face, leaning close, brushing away some grass at the top of the head where a recent rain has left puddles. Then she spots some letters. "Giovanni, look at this." Coming around to examine the newly exposed words, he says it's Latin, and pauses, trying to work out the translation. "It says *Console Me*," he tells her, and stands up. Giovanni wanders around picking wildflowers from the scruffy grass growing around the stairs and out of the cracks near the ancient mosaic floor. Finally he has a neat bouquet of small blue and white flowers which he offers to Gina, tipping an imaginary hat, and asks if she would like to marry him, since it's such a nice day, and he has these flowers he doesn't know what to do with. She stands up and says yes, she'd love to, but it's just for today.

He takes her arm and they climb the few stairs of the ruins that lead to nowhere. At the top, Giovanni gives Gina the flowers. She reaches into her purse for a present and retrieves a piece of driftwood. "For you. So we can drift together," she says, handing him the wood.

"Okay," Giovanni says. "Into the same dream; in life and in death." They kiss, standing at the top of the stairs, and then make their way to the rocks next to the sea. Giovanni digs around between some of the rocks and pulls out a bottle of wine. Surprised that it's still there, he laughs, and holds it up like a prized fish.

He opens the wine with the corkscrew of his knife, and they drink from the bottle in celebration of their union, and watch the breaking of the waves as they roll in from the Adriatic, each like a measure of happiness, splashing over the rocks in a timeless song of the sea.

CR

EARLY EVENING, ON THE RETURN FERRY—Leaning shoulder to shoulder in the boat, Gina holds her bouquet of wildflowers and asks how old Natasha is. He says she's about ten years older than Gina, and four years older than he is, and assures her again that they had broken up before he went to the beach house.

"I was driving like you, really fast, even with my bad foot. I was so anxious to get to Venice to see you. And then, when Natasha opened the studio door. I was shocked. I felt deceived and had to slink off to that gray hotel."

Giovanni pulls one of the flowers out of her hand and holds it between his fingers like a cigarette. "I wanted you to decide what to do yourself. I didn't want to decide for you, though I might have. If you hadn't come, I would have kidnapped you at Mario's wedding."

He grabs her by the hair. "I would have stolen you. Livia was the one who told me to wait." He lets go of her hair. She runs her finger down his arm, touching his moonstone ring for a mere second.

"Oh, here," he says, getting a small box from his jacket pocket. She opens it and finds a diamond. "It's just the diamond. You can have it set on a ring, replace the one I threw in the canal. This one's brighter." She admires the diamond, thinking Charles will never notice the difference, but she'll always know. She thanks Giovanni.

"This is a magic boat," she says, looking at the sea rather than at Giovanni. She says that the sun on the water looks like melted gold, like it could be scooped up. She looks up and sees a quick grimace cross Giovanni's face. She looks questioningly at him.

"Headache," he says. "It's nothing. It comes and goes." They both think of the fight and say nothing. Gina moves closer to Giovanni and they cross the rest of the water sitting together like children.

♋

WEDNESDAY AFTERNOON— Dear Diary: Giovanni is asleep and I'm sitting on the studio floor writing in an old lined notebook with all the pages torn out except these last few. I'm writing by candlelight and the moonlight is shining on the wall, bounced off the canal and scattered into bits of whirling light over the animals and flowers and people in the big tapestry.

Alas, tomorrow will soon be here. My poor little candlelight fire. If I were Livia I could find something in the flame. I'm too worried about tomorrow and the drive to St. Moritz. Charles will be there. Giovanni told him he would pick me up from the hospital in the morning. I wonder if he believes that. And I don't know why I invited Natasha along. Even Giovanni was surprised at that. I just felt sorry for her. She is so formal and strange and also very strong. Anyway, she only has a week left. She doesn't want to go back to Russia. She wants to go to America, even though she's never been there. I can't sleep, even after Giovanni put sheets on all of her statues, the shapes seemed worse when he covered them and it got dark. They're too still. They're ghosts. I have my back to them now.

I'll be with Giovanni in the Ferrari, and Natasha will ride up with Luigi and Pascal in the Fiat, and Giovanni's friend, I can't remember his name, it's a tongue twister, is bringing the angel sculpture in his truck. It's bigger than the little cherub Charles and I had envisioned. Maybe I could have a Bloody Mary for breakfast.

No, I'm done with bloody scenes. I really am. And neither of us has been smoking. I don't know why I'm writing this down. I'm tired.

Gina tears out the pages and crumples them up into a ball and tosses them under the bed, blows out the candle and climbs in next to Giovanni. She kisses his shoulder and he moves slightly. She stares at his back, trying to wake him. He does wake and turns two sleepy brown eyes toward her and she immediately relaxes. "I still think of Mario sometimes," she tells him in a whisper. "I know," he says drowsily, glad that she can tell him. He draws her next to him, and near each other the warmth of arm next to arm, and weariness, ends the night and they drift into simultaneous sleep.

THE NEXT MORNING—Gina wakes up to the sun on the bedcovers. She turns over and dreamily surveys the studio, the tapestry on the wall, all the flowers and birds and animals in subtle time-softened colors. She's looking at a bear peering out from a rounded rose bush as Giovanni comes over with a breakfast tray.

"Cornetti and coffee," he says, setting the tray down on the table. He hands her a large yellow cup on a saucer. "Thanks, Giovanni. Delicious," she says, pointing out the bear in the tapestry. "Bruno," he says. "He's staring at you because you look good enough to eat." Giovanni growls lasciviously under his breath and leers at her over the top of his coffee cup as he takes a drink. She laughs, spilling coffee onto the saucer and mopping it up with her napkin.

"Well, I'm ready for this day. Probably because I know I'm never really ready for anything. Somehow that makes me ready for anything. Sounds a little illogical I suppose. But since I can't do anything to get ready, I don't have to bother getting ready. I'm being repetitious. But you know what I mean."

He nods, yes, and takes a big bite of his cornetti, offering her a bite. "Wedding cake," he says with his mouth full. She takes a voracious bite. "Mmmm," she mumbles.

They eat their breakfast like happy animals, feeding each other, wiping away crumbs, rolling back on the comforter, becoming one.

Resting, Gina looks at the ceiling while Giovanni looks at Gina. She turns to him, pushing her hair out of her eyes, telling Giovanni he is so quiet, like he's lived for centuries. "When you look at me like that, like the face on the island mosaic. What are you thinking?"

"I'm not thinking, just feeling," he says, and there's a link between them like two morning stars hanging in the sky before dawn.

17. On the Road

In the car Giovanni drives like a race car driver, effortlessly, his speeding undetectable in its precision, the movement along the back road toward St. Mortiz steady and certain, as the wind blows his hair like waves of a stormy sea. Gina is relaxed, her night fears blown away with the wind. She's forgotten the pain in her foot and settles back, becoming part of the ride, the movement, and she and Giovanni move over the earth like reckless angels.

She thinks the ride is unlike buses, where you're neither here nor there, as on a Greyhound coach, sitting beside people with paper bags, bumping along. Nor is it like trains, with their mechanical chugging; or planes, where you feel no movement, but are simply tricked by the clever airlines into watching a movie in a big easy chair thousands of feet above the earth.

Riding now with Giovanni, she is aware of finally having chosen something for herself, even if for a brief moment of her life. As they round the bend of a lake, she feels inconsequential and happy, a thrill floods over her; she leans back and sighs with the joy of the edge. He smiles over at her, knowing they are best like this, riding, speeding, flying. Gina starts to laugh, her eyes flashing at nothing, at everything, her head back.

"I'm so happy," she says, too quietly for Giovanni to hear in the wind. "I think I'm most alive when I'm almost dead. How can that be?"

"What?" he asks back.

"Why is it so good?" she hollers through the wind to him. He doesn't answer but she knows he heard because he smiles one of those once-in-a-lifetime smiles that never require another question, and Gina feels her heart spin like a whirling top. He slips a CD of Chopin into place, and they drive on toward St. Moritz with Chopin's No. 1 Piano Concerto following them in the wind.

ST. MORITZ, IN FRONT OF THE HOTEL—Giovanni flips through the cards in his billfold looking for the slip of paper where he wrote the name and address of the hotel. While he hunts, Luigi and Natasha and Pascal round the corner in the Fiat. Gina spots them at the same time Pascal sees Giovanni. Pascal starts bouncing up and down on Natasha's lap, clapping his hands together, making a series of nonstop Cheshire cat grins. He whoops and bounces and grins his toothy grin all along the half block until they reach the Ferrari, which takes a considerable time, at Luigi's pace. Giovanni has found the name of the hotel and the address. It has a similar name to the hotel further down the street, and he confirms to Gina that they're parked in front of the right hotel. Luigi brings the car to a dead stop in the center of the street next to Giovanni. He rolls down his window and proudly tells Giovanni that they made it. Natasha waves and leans over to ask if this is the right hotel and he tells them yes. He's tempted to ask how long they've been on the road, but doesn't. Pascal climbs all over Luigi, trying to climb out the window to get to Giovanni, and he presses his lips up to the window and lets his lips slowly spread against the smooth glass, and the sensation of his lips on the glass momentarily stills his bouncing.

Someone starts honking a horn and Giovanni tells Luigi that he's double parked going in the wrong direction. He looks puzzled and worried but doesn't understand. Giovanni yells over to him to back up, that he's blocking traffic. Luigi backs up with a sudden jolt. Giovanni pulls the Ferrari out and motions to Luigi to pull into the space by the curb, but he just sits there smiling and nodding and Pascal starts bouncing up and down again, frantic that Giovanni will go away. Natasha grabs the wheel and points to the parking place, explaining what he's supposed to do, and after another jerk, Luigi slowly and ceremoniously pulls into the parking spot. The man who was honking drives on, giving Giovanni the fist and a few choice words as he drives by.

"Don't translate," Gina says. He shakes his head and wonders however did Luigi get them up here. Natasha looks like she's been through an ordeal, no doubt, with Luigi and Pascal. She'll hit the vodka tonight for sure.

Giovanni parks up the street. He helps Gina out, and points out a clothing shop next to the hotel. She smooths her wrinkled skirt and tucks in her blouse, pulls at a knee sock that has half fallen down above the bloody tennis shoe. "Yes, I'd better shop," she says. Giovanni will settle Luigi and Natasha and Pascal at the hotel, and then come back to the clothing store.

Gina limps into the small, exclusive looking clothing store. The saleslady speaks to her in Italian, her tone implying that Gina must want to use the ladies' room, or she's lost; that she couldn't possibly want to buy anything here. Gina pulls out her billfold and a wad of euros so the woman understands that she is a legitimate customer. The sight of large denominations changes the saleslady back into a saleslady, who looks Gina over for size, studying her like an inanimate object. She holds up a dress from the rack, a dark rust-colored linen. Gina likes it. She needs other things, underwear, stockings, some sandals with straps that won't hit her at the wound. Velcro.

The saleslady finds everything she needs quickly, anxious to get her out of the refugee clothing and into some proper attire, before any other customers come into the shop. When Gina comes out of the dressing room, the saleslady claps her hands together, delighted with Gina. The ragamuffin died behind the dressing room door and a princess emerged. With a new dress and her hair combed, she is a new woman.

A bell rings as Giovanni comes into the shop, and he whistles appreciatively at Gina, comes over and kisses her. Gina pays for her purchases and the clerk asks if she wants her old things put in a bag, motioning toward the dressing room. She shakes her head, no thanks. As they leave the store, Giovanni tells Gina he likes her dress, says the rust color is nice with her amber necklace.

Gina finds she can walk quite normally in her new sandals, as long as she walks slowly, and as they stroll toward the hotel she asks if Charles has checked in yet.

"Yes. I asked at the desk, he's here," he tells her and she tenses up. He takes her hand.

"And Mario?" she asks.

"Not here yet."

"That's odd, isn't it?"

"Very."

Gina knows she has to talk to Charles. She hasn't even sent him an email since the hospital. She'll ask him to come to the hotel's coffee shop, wants to talk to him in a public place. Giovanni knows this will be the talk where he could lose her. He hands her his cell phone.

Soon she's faced with the dreaded meeting. As she and Giovanni enter the hotel lobby, she sees Charles, at a table by himself, over coffee. He sees her and stands up, all smiles, obviously moved and glad to see her. Instantly, her throat tightens. She fights back tears. "Go on, Gina," Giovanni says.

Giovanni's elevator door closes as he watches Charles take Gina in his arms, patting her back with his huge hands, like a long-lost friend. He feels himself trembling as the elevator moves up, and he walks to his room, passes it and walks down the hall and knocks on Luigi's door.

Pascal leaps through the air into his arms as soon as Luigi opens the door. He walks around the room with Pascal in his arms and Pascal makes his funny excited faces for Giovanni, and they sit down on the bed. Pascal smiles and puts a long arm around Giovanni and keeps patting him on the back, peering over, looking sincerely into his eyes. Giovanni starts to laugh, thankful that he can laugh right now, thank heavens for monkeys. Luigi's been talking since he came into the room, about the fancy hotel, the view of the mountains, about hiding Pascal in the trunk at customs like Giovanni told him, about how pretty Natasha is, how nice it is to drive. Luigi's happy, in his own world. Giovanni loves the old man. He lies back on the bed and Pascal gets down and runs to the drapes, quickly climbing to the top. Luigi beams, tells Giovanni he's been doing that all the time lately, he's so healthy again, and he'll come down even without peaches, because he's just real happy, like me, Luigi says "We like it in the country."

Giovanni tells Luigi they are a good pair, and he gets up to leave, and waves to Pascal, giving him his sign that means he'll see him soon. Pascal waves back from the window top.

THE COFFEE SHOP—Gina sits alone, tapping the key card Charles gave her against the placemat. She'll head up to his room as soon as she finishes her cocoa. They didn't talk much, but mostly sat waiting to hear what each other would say. Words came slowly. They discussed Chris's upcoming birthday next month, and what the boys were busy with, at her parents now, until school starts. Charles had been ready to finalize two tickets from Rome to home, the day after the wedding but she said she needed two more weeks at the beach house and that he should go ahead without her. That was when he tapped her ringless finger and she told him it disappeared at the hospital. He became so quiet that they just sat listening to each other breathe. She noted dark circles under his eyes and how haggard he was up close and wondered if she looked the same. Then he just smiled and left the room key card for her, and left her to herself.

She can't take her eyes from the woman in the back corner. She had noticed her when she first came in, at the table nearest the kitchen, her back bent under some tragic weight. She seems like someone from Rosa's newspaper photographs of those people fleeing their troubled homelands and huddled together in one of those dilapidated boats. She gets out Giovanni's cell to take a picture, if she can do so without the woman noticing. She pretends to look to the right of the woman and clicks several photos. The woman stands up slowly and walks straight toward Gina. Gina brazenly takes a close up of the woman. The woman says nothing, but points at Gina, her finger like a gun, then leaves the coffee shop and the hotel. She shouldn't have, but she had to take those pictures. She needs that face for a collage. That woman's sorrow is real sorrow, real loss, and Gina knows that her own woes are of her own making.

"Hi," she says when Giovanni answers her call. "Why don't you come down. They have a nice menu."

"Okay, be right there."

Giovanni joins Gina at her table. She's ordered a bowl of soup for him.

"How's your tooth?" she asks.

"It's still loose. Well?"

"Well, I'm going back with Charles. He's leaving right after the wedding and I'm staying on for two weeks at the beach house. That's all I could do."

Giovanni sips the soup. He's finished half the bowl by the time he speaks.

"I won't give up. I don't give up."

"I'm going to my room," she says, getting up. "I'm tired. My head hurts."

She moves one foot in front of the other with concentration to get herself through the lobby and onto the elevator. Walking toward Charles's room, she meets the porter, who is walking down the hall with a handful of white envelopes. When she slides the key card into his door, the porter hands her one of the envelopes before continuing down the hallway.

Inside the room, Charles is standing beside the door as if he had been waiting for her. They open the envelope and read the card together. *The wedding has been postponed until tomorrow afternoon.* They look at each other with surprise, but Gina sighs, another day, she needs another day.

"Is there a tub?" she asks. "Yes," Charles answers, pulling her near him, stroking her hair, noting cold sweat on her forehead. Resting her head wearily on his shoulder she tells him she'll take a bath, and then rest for a while. He says he'll go out to have a look around but first runs the water for her and sits at the edge of the bed and watches her undress. She asks him to get shampoo while he's out, closing the bathroom door behind her, ready for her bath.

In the tub Gina leans back, picturing Giovanni, his Botticelli curls. She thinks of the wildflowers he gave her at their pretend wedding, his kindness, and last night's loving ruckus.

Outside, Charles walks down the street, looking up into the mountains above the city. It's a beautiful location. He walks to a small park facing the lake and sits down on a bench in the sun.

❦

Meanwhile, Giovanni is standing outside of an old church, one block further along the town's main square. The doors are propped open and he smells coffee. Looking inside he sees Anita at the front and recognizes her from the photo Mario so proudly showed him. There are a dozen or so people in the church. An older woman sits at the organ leafing through music. Mario is nowhere in sight, and suddenly he wants to see Mario. He walks down the center aisle of the church and approaches Anita, introducing himself as Mario's friend, the singer.

"Is this the rehearsal?" he asks. "My guitar is in my car, just down the street. Where's Mario?"

Anita shakes her head. "He isn't here. I just don't understand," she says, trying to maintain a semblance of poise, but with considerable difficulty. "Where could he be?" she asks, shaking her head.

"I don't know; but he'll be here," he says reassuringly. "Are you rehearsing?" he asks again.

"Well, we're supposed to be. How could he do this to me," she says angrily, staring toward the open door.

"Let's just get everyone together and run through it," Giovanni suggests, and says he'll be back in ten minutes, and leaves abruptly, leaving her to watch him go down the aisle and out the door.

Outside the church, Giovanni steps inside the first store he comes to and asks to use the phone. Gina still has his cell. He gets Livia's number from the operator and she puts the call through. There's no answer after a dozen rings. She must not have an answering machine. He writes down the number on a card and hangs up and walks to his car. He gets the guitar and walks slowly back toward the church, walking around the block humming. He needs to keep busy with something, just put Gina on the back

177

burner. Mario too. Entering the church, he closes the large doors behind him.

The afternoon passes, the wedding party, minus Mario, rehearses, and Gina sleeps. Luigi naps and Pascal occupies himself playing on a shower curtain rod before curling up in the bathtub with his blanket, exhausted from the excitement of traveling in a car.

Charles sits in the park, soaking in the sun and the scenery. He is startled by a loud greeting from a woman, waving and calling to him from across the park. It's Natasha, whom he met when he was checking in. She ambles over, in a half run, half walk and sits down, laughing and out of breath.

"That monkey," she says, and goes on to tell Charles about having to ride all the way from Venice in a car with a monkey and someone who can barely drive. She rambles on and on about her life. Charles lets her go on without much interruption, hearing about her sculpture that's been packed up and is on its way to her studio in St. Petersburg. She is supposed to go to a detox clinic, though she has already quit drinking. She insists on this several times, and Charles cannot smell alcohol on her breath, but simply notices how wound up she is. She wants to go to America. She's all excited about America. She worked as a gymnastic coach for a full year in Russia and is sure she could do that in America until she establishes herself as a sculptor. She tells all, including how Giovanni was her lover for several months, but he ended that, and she's okay with that. Her final words after the long and explosive confession: "To cut to the chase, I need a green card. Can you help me? I need a sponsor."

Charles says he'll consider her problem. Maybe he can find someone to help.

For now, he asks her to help him choose some shampoo for his wife, from the shop next to the hotel. 'She doesn't like hotel shampoo,'" he says, getting up from the bench. Natasha is eager to help, stating that shampoo is very important.

CR

EARLY EVENING—Gina sits on the bed drying her hair, wearing Charles's black robe. Charles is in a chair turned toward the bed, watching Gina like she's in a movie, her pale breasts half exposed in the loose robe. He moves near her on the bed and watches her pick hairs out of her hairbrush. She holds a fluff of light hair from the brush out to him. "Doesn't it look like letters and words, but you can't read it?" she comments, holding a tangle of hair up toward the lamp. He takes the fluff of hair from her and looks at it seriously, turning it in his fingers, peering at it and squinting *"It reads: It's time to go home,"* he says.

Meanwhile, Giovanni is in the lobby, ready to try Livia again. This time, she answers, and sounds happy and surprised to hear from him. He tells her he didn't think she was ever surprised at anything. She laughs. He can hear a lot of voices in the background and asks if she's having a party. "Yes, I have company. But Giovanni, where is Gina?" she says, all in English

"So you speak English. Why did you let us think you didn't?" he says, more hurt than angry.

"I provide what my customers need. Did it work? Where's Gina?"

"She's with Charles. But I haven't given up. I believe we'll be together. It's our destiny." There's silence on Livia's end of the line.

"Livia, are you there?" After another pause, she asks him if he remembers that night when she asked if he preferred a short happy life to a long life of not quite such intensity.

"Yes, of course," he answers.

"Well, then remember what I told you. That great joy comes to few, and there are risks. Love each other as though each day is the only day you have."

"I couldn't love her more," he says. They're both quiet again, until Giovanni asks about Mario, tells her he's not here, and the wedding is tomorrow. He asks her to come up with her friends, he wants Mario to be happy, but where is Mario?

Livia says not to worry. Mario will be there, and yes, she and her friends will drive up in time to get there tomorrow night. They'll come to sing and dance.

But where is he, Giovanni asks again, and she tells him she doesn't know, but in a tone that makes him wonder if he's there with her and her Roma friends. Something keeps him from asking.

"All right, Livia, I'll see you tomorrow," he says, and hangs up. Giovanni walks outside for some fresh air and strolls down to the lake. He sits down to contemplate his life, sitting on the same bench where earlier Anita told her life story to Charles. As the sun sets over the lake it cools off considerably. Giovanni walks back to the hotel. He sees Charles in a booth in the restaurant talking to Natasha. They seem unaware of anyone around them and he's glad to leave without being spotted.

From his room, Giovanni uses Luigi's old-fashioned clunky cell phone to call Gina. She answers with his phone.

"Gina, Charles is downstairs in the bar with Natasha."

"That's weird."

"They're in the bar talking to each other. What are you doing?"

"I'm watching a Carol Burnett rerun in Italian. Tim Conway is scratching his head and sticking his head through a picture frame. No, it's in French."

"I'm going down there," Giovanni says, hanging up.

He takes the elevator down, buys a package of cigarettes, taking note of Charles and Natasha still in a corner booth. Seems innocent enough. Still, peculiar. He heads to the elevator again, getting on with an elegant white-haired woman in a trim navy suit.

"Hello," she says. "Do you speak English?"

"Yes, I'm Giovanni," he introduces himself with a nod. "And I am Mrs. O'Reilly, Mario's mother," she announces in a way that suggests she is a very important person, but currently defensive about it. They shake hands, and Giovanni tells her he and Mario are friends, and he is going to sing at the wedding tomorrow. She raises her eyebrows and primly tells him good evening as she steps off onto the third floor.

Giovanni knocks on Gina's door. She answers the door laughing, says she loves Ethel in Italian, and Fred too. She's watching *I Love Lucy* now.

"Do you know who I just met on the elevator?"

"Who? Is Mario back?" She suddenly loses interest in the TV show.

"Mrs. O'Reilly, his mother. She's quite formal. Doesn't look anything like Mario."

Gina had met her, a time or two. Once at a shopping center, and again at a Christmas party. She has a regal bearing and treats everyone but Mario in a condescending manner. She's hard to like.

"Remember that photo I took of you and Mario in front of my painting? I was trying to find it on your cell phone." She grabs the camera from the desktop and fiddles with its buttons.

"Look, Giovanni," she pulls up a photo she took in the café downstairs of the woman she was so sure was a refugee, the woman who pointed at her so dramatically, so accusingly.

"How do I move back to the previous picture? I don't want to mess this up," she says.

Giovanni and Gina are peering at the cell camera when Charles steps inside.

"Well, look who's here," Charles says. "Stay right there, Giovanni; I have something with you in mind." Charles rummages in the closet. Stepping directly in front of Giovanni, he holds up the gun.

"Now get out. And don't you ever come near Gina again."

Giovanni backs away, leaves with his cell phone, both hands in the air. Charles slams the door, locking both locks. Gina climbs in bed and stares at the TV. Charles sits on the bed and removes the bullets from the gun. He gets ready for bed and joins Gina. They both sit in silence staring at the TV, listening to the laugh track. Gina nearly jumps off the bed at a knock on their door. It's room service with individual pizzas, salad, and orange soda. They eat and watch TV in bed, listening to each other chew the crusty pizza. There is nothing to say.

CR

THE NEXT MORNING, IN THE NORTH OF ITALY—Mario is in the forest high above the lake and city where the wedding is to take place. He hikes upward, a water bottle fastened to his belt. He doesn't know where he is, whether he's on an actual trail or just a deer trail. He's humming to himself, walking steadily, making his way. The sun streams through the trees, onto the rich colored moss and grasses, spotlighting wildflowers, kinds he's never seen before, and occasionally berries, unfamiliar, catch his eye, and he stops to look them over.

He has the gentle, intense concentration of one who has long been away from nature on his own. Delicate toadstools and mushrooms grow along the way. Most are light brown; others a startling bright white. At one point, deep in the forest, he picks a bright orange toadstool, turns it slowly in his fingers, admiring the exotic pale gills of its underside, and breathes in the fleshy moist aroma as he touches its orange top to his nose. He sets the toadstool down in the center of a minuscule mossy meadow, bright and smooth as a golf course green. His mind is empty, receptive. He stops to rest on a log, unhooks the plastic water bottle, and takes a drink of spring water, thankful for the cold, pure liquid, thankful for springs, for the thickness of pine needles under his boots. He licks the overspill from his lips and wipes his beard with his sleeve. Sitting quietly, he listens to the birds, hidden in trees rustling high above him, and looks up toward their tips and breathes in the scent of pine, pulling it deep into his lungs.

He walks on, like a happy sleepwalker. The trees have become familiar, the pines like men, warty-faced friends with green beards. The pale smooth-barked trees seem female, with loins reaching high into the rustling leaves. He pauses near a large pine, looking up as it rises into the sky. He touches its trunk, running his finger over its sappy blisters and picking off a chunk of thickened gold gum, which he sniffs, and rolls in his fingers for the pleasure of its touch. Turning to the smooth tree beside him, he smears two spots with the sap, like eyes, onto its soft eggshell smooth bark. It feels like a ceremony.

A sudden snapping of branches startles him. A deer is watching him with its large forest eyes, its upright ears barely twitching. They observe each other, the moment caught outside of time, until the deer bounds off noisily into the trees and vanishes into the dark shadows of the forest.

As Mario continues, the terrain becomes rockier, and more exposed to the sky. He leaves the forest and crosses onto open expanses of large flat rock. Ground pine grows out of crevices of huge slabs of granite. The moss edging the rocks is spongy from recent rains, bright green and dense, with red-topped lichen growing in clusters. A grayish, pale green tufted moss sprouts here and there, like the raggedy hairs from an old man's ears. Patches of iridescent orange and lime fungi mottle the larger expanses of dark rock. He stares at the patches of lichen and they become locations, like countries on a map. A red ant scurries over a patch that looks like France, crossing the entire country in seconds. It hurries over the open grey expanse of rock to a gaudy orange pumpkin-shaped country. Mario laughs to himself and leaves the ant to its small adventures, and like a giant, he walks on, crossing the rocky area; each step taking him over entire continents, until he finds himself climbing a steep stretch of rock beside a cliff.

The rocks level off to a gentle slope and he continues upward. He's become aware of a pain in his hip and its ache increases as he climbs the rocks, which seem endless, like the large flat back of the earth. He walks step after step. Ahead the rocks level off again and he continues to the point he can't see beyond. The sky becomes closer and larger. As he climbs the last stretch to the summit, he's limping. On the top, it's cool and there is a pleasant breeze. The wind against his sweaty face sweeps over him as he stands looking at the lake below. He's at the top of a cliff overlooking the blue water of the lake, and he knows he is where the earth ends and the sky begins.

He sits down and takes a drink, feeling both tired and happy, and an inexplicable thrill races through him, like invisible lightning, from something, he doesn't know what, except that it must be the opposite of a storm. He wants to laugh or cry, but his hands, like someone else's hands, reach for his pipe. He lights the pipe, fondly running a finger along its crack, not remembering that it split against the wall when Giovanni slugged him. With the pipe under control, he takes a piece of paper from his pocket, and the stub of a pencil. The name, L. K. Zingaro, and a telephone number are written in Livia's peculiar hand at the top of the sheet. Mario turns the paper over and starts to write:

I am a pine tree

And my beard is green

 I am a man

on a mountain top.

He folds the paper carefully and slips it back into his pocket and stands up.

Below, he sees a boat move along the lake. It moves out of sight as he puffs on his pipe, content with the Indian chief contentment of a poet who has just written his first poem, and is making his own clouds, and wondering at himself and the world and what it means to be alive.

଎

EARLY FRIDAY MORNING—Charles and Gina walk down the street in the morning light. There is little traffic on the street and no one on their block. They both look uneasily up and down the street, commenting casually about the scenery. It's a sleepy peaceful morning and the clear blue sky above promises a perfect day for a wedding.

They step inside a small café just around the corner from their hotel, with the intention of avoiding certain of the wedding guests. They're already in the door when they see Natasha. To Gina's surprise, Charles jovially waves to her and she invites them to join her. Making herself somewhat comfortable at Natasha's table, Gina feels resigned. What is going on anyway?

Charles is going to help Natasha come to America. He has made calls to friends, of whom he has many. Natasha is excited about her prospects, and confident that she will indeed be able to find a job coaching gymnastics, even if her past coaching experience was limited to the one year when she was twenty years old. She is certain she would be able to find clients to keep her busy as a sculptor and finally make the move to work as a full-time sculptor.

Natasha nods at Gina, who finds her confidence unnerving.

"Colorado has very good marble," Natasha says. She has a plan to create a beautiful white sculpture with wings, for Charles's new clinic. "Like a great white flying tooth faerie, to repay his kindness," she says.

Gina tells her she hopes it all works out. She holds herself slightly back, leaning into the cushion behind her. This Natasha is too confident, too pushy.

They all order orange juice, coffee and biscotti.

A bell rings as the door to the café swings open wide. Gina has her nose in the menu, even though they've all ordered. Charles and Natasha look up and she hears him say good morning. Startled, Gina looks up into those eyes. Mario hands her a piece of crumpled paper. He keeps an arm oddly wrapped around his chest, and stands waiting, looking at her; everyone is talking, asking where he's been, what happened, is he okay?

Gina reads the note. It's a poem. A sort of haiku. She smiles reading his note, knowing he'll be okay.

Well, she sees he hasn't shaved off his beard like in her dream. It's not green but he has some grass in his hair and his clothing is all rumpled. He opens his jacket and hands her a very small black kitten.

Of a sudden, Mario has left, and she is petting a small kitten in her lap. It's chewing on her napkin. She holds the kitten close and it nuzzles up against her. She can't hear what anyone is saying, the sounds all blend together. She and the kitten are in a world by themselves. She gets up from the table and leaves with the kitten. Tables and chairs are a blur as she walks past, the door seems to tilt at a crazy angle. Outside she leans against a building holding the sweet tiny cat.

Charles comes up behind her, sees her leaning against the clock shop next to the car, just as Mario turns a corner down the street. As he stands beside Gina he wonders what the hell happened to Mario. He looked like he'd been sleeping in the woods, and his eyes were strange, like an animal. At least he's alive.

"Oh, he wet," Gina says. "Right on my good dress," and she feels the warm wetness soak through to her stomach. She holds the kitten out from her and sets him down on the cobblestones. He tries to climb her ankles and nips at her shoe.

"A black panther," Charles says, bending down to look him over. "Come on, let's cross the street. We'll get a basket. You'll have to name him."

"Lucifer," Gina says. No, she reconsiders. The nickname would be Lucy whether it's a boy or a girl. When they cross the street, the store they want hasn't opened. Charles suggests she go on up and take care of her dress while he gets the basket, a dish, and a litter box.

"And a blanket, Charles. Blue if they have it." He nods to her and watches her leave with the kitten.

CR

While Charles is shopping Giovanni walks down the street toward the church. He sees Mario sitting on the steps. Coming up to him, Mario looks up, just looks without moving. Giovanni isn't sure what to say, and Mario doesn't look like he expects him to say anything, but rather expects him to join him on the steps and sit there with him like a statue, listening to the silence of the early morning. Something about Mario makes Giovanni breathe easier, and he knows Mario's all right without having to ask. He sits down and lights a cigarette.

Mario tells how he got a boat ride back from some fisherman. "Did they have the wedding without me?" he asks, and laughs. He's only one day late, but he's here; he couldn't call because his phone was out of range, he explains, and asks Giovanni if Anita is still here, and has he seen her. And is she going to kill him or marry him? Giovanni assures him the wedding was postponed to 4:00 o'clock this afternoon.

"Are you sure about this, Mario?" he asks, looking at him bluntly.

"No. But I have to do this; I need a life I can understand. I'll be happy with Anita. Here I'm just lost. I've been on the verge of, oh, I don't know. Something good," he shakes his head. "Maybe shrinks just aren't very good gypsies," he says, and takes out his pipe. Giovanni watches him light up, noticing the crack in the pipe. A sharp pain rips through Giovanni's head, just above his brow, and he leans forward, resting his face in his hands until it passes.

Mario gets his pipe going, then reaches into his jacket pocket and pulls out some papers. Some people on the dock had a box of kittens, that's where he got the black kitten for Gina, he explains. He forgot to give her the papers, the pedigree and such. "Don't know if any of it is authentic." He looks down at his shoes.

Giovanni pulls out his camera and brings up the latest picture, snapped when his hands were in the air and Charles was holding a gun on him, and Gina, looking stricken was standing beside him.

"What do you think of this?"

Mario laughs, astonished. "Unbelievable. Guess you're lucky to be alive, Giovanni."

"Aren't we both. Well, I wanted to show someone. Before I deleted it," he says. "There now; it's gone."

"He wouldn't have used it. Never," Mario says, sure of himself.

Giovanni is not so sure.

"God help us all," Mario says, getting up abruptly. Putting a hand on Giovanni's shoulder, he says he'll see him at the wedding and asks him to tell Anita he'll be there, he's got to get cleaned up. Giovanni stands watching him walk down the street, puzzled at his slight limp. Mario gets in a car and drives off.

The day proceeds with preparations for the wedding like the frenetic backstage activity before opening night of an unfinished play. Stagehands move in with props. Natasha supervises the transport of the angel to the church, directing the movement of the truck, the men and the ropes, until the angel is hoisted up on a dolly to stand at the front of the church, its delicate white wings perched in readiness of Act One.

Gina lingers at the back of the church and Lucifer rests in a basket at the end of a pew. When the angel crew leaves, she walks to the front of the church to have a look. It's not the cherub she was thinking of, this giant white angel, but it is very beautiful, and she cannot take her eyes away from its face. The gold light coming through the stained-glass streams over the figure and over the backdrop of wooden church beams. She looks at the angel for a long time, at the translucence of its marble flesh, its benevolent smile. She doesn't notice when Giovanni comes up beside her, doesn't know how long he's been standing there when she sees his face in profile.

Before they have time to say a word, a group of noisy women enter from a side door of the church with armfuls of flowers, fluffy white and pink bouquets, explosions of baby's breath, coral bells, and cascading bleeding hearts and ferns. The organist announces her appearance with a sudden chord cluster that takes Gina out of her reverie. Giovanni has disappeared. Gina leaves the church, picking up the basket with the cat on her way out. Giovanni is nowhere in sight.

Giovanni has made a beeline to the hotel. A refreshing shower is what he needs. Afterwards, he gets out of his shower and into his tux. An old hand at tuxedos, he's ready to go with guitar in hand, anxious to get back to the church on time and before Charles and Gina arrive.

CR

On her way back to the hotel Gina sees Natasha and Charles. He's holding a coil of rope, left behind by the men who moved the statue into the church. Gina waves and keeps going. Luigi and the monkey are on the corner looking in a store window. When she arrives at the hotel, Mrs. O'Reilly is at the front desk, fluttering and fussing over something. Gina takes the elevator, wondering why she hasn't just left in the Ferrari with Giovanni. But that dream is just that, a dream.

She runs water for a bath and Lucifer falls asleep. Climbing into the tub and sliding under the hot water, her ears are under the surface and she can hear herself breathing. She likes these sounds of being alive, and closes her eyes and holds her nose and slips farther down. Bye bye bye bye, *ciao*, she says, listening to the watery bubbling words, saying them separately, distinctly, like fish bubbles, until she has to come up for air. She closes one eye, then the other, looking at the pink tip of her nose. She thinks of the boar, when she watched it in the tub. She finishes her bath and lifts the water drain; she finds herself in tears. Her mother used to tell her not to make faces or her face would stay that way. She forces her face into a neutral position.

Stepping out of the tub, she examines her dress for the wedding, hanging in readiness on the back of the door and wipes away a last tear as the water gurgles down the drain. Well, that's that, she says, drying off and slipping into the dress for the wedding. She dries her hair.

When Charles returns to their room with his freshly pressed rental tux he finds Gina sitting in a chair in a frozen position, mechanically petting the kitten.

"I'd rather stay with Lucifer," she says. "I really don't want to go to the wedding."

He ignores her comment and she watches him undress and re-dress into his tuxedo. Like Giovanni, Charles is completely at home in a tuxedo. He finishes his tie before he answers the knock on the door. It's Luigi, who says he and Pascal are all ready. Luigi is dressed in his dark Sunday suit, with a red tie, and he is holding Pascal's hand. Pascal smiles politely, all dressed up in a red suit with gold trim, making him look like a circus performer.

They hear someone running down the hall and Charles peers out. It's the hotel clerk who says they're waiting for everyone and they're supposed to hurry up. Gina tries to settle the kitten back into his basket but he's wide awake now, tugging at his blanket. He chews on her fingers with his sharp little teeth and gives her hand a lick. She plunks him gently into the basket and rinses her hands before they leave.

CB

THE WEDDING—There is a good crowd in the small church and the organist is playing regular organ music while everyone settles into place. It smells like flowers. To Gina, it smells like a funeral. Anita comes down the aisle accompanied by her father, a distinguished looking gentleman. Mario enters from the side. The angel watches over the proceedings, and the vows are exchanged. The priest speaks with a beautiful Italian accent and pronounces Anita and Mario a married couple. When Giovanni sings, there are tears from the mothers, while others dab at their eyes with a tissue, including Gina. She has decided that a wedding is everyone's wedding, not just the two people getting married. And the same is true at a funeral; it is everyone's death and so the tears flow for one and all. In any case, she's glad it's over and she is truly happy for Anita and Mario.

At the reception, they eat cake. It's a beautiful white cake with lemon filling. When Charles takes a bathroom break, Giovanni appears out of nowhere, and taps Gina on the shoulder. He smiles.

"People are disappearing," Gina says. "They just disappear, before you even know them. We know all these facts about a person, lots of details, but we don't even know them."

"It's how you feel that matters," Giovanni says, standing close to Gina, almost whispering. She touches his sleeve and asks if Charles paid for his share of the angel. Giovanni laughs, startled by her question, and tells her that he did, says all of her men are very fair. Then she asks if Mario seems happy. "Yes, I think so," he answers. "I care about him too you know," he says, realizing how true this is, especially lately, after their visit to see Livia, and their mutual feelings for Gina.

CR

Early evening at the lake the wedding dance has begun:

The sun is setting and the sky is a burnt orange fury over the mountains, spilling its coppery fire onto the lake like some vain master artist showing off. Members of the wedding party, now complete with Roma, are feasting, drinking and dancing. Tambourines jingle and jangle as lights bounce off the lake. Nimble hands clap out steady rhythms in the air and skirts twirl above legs. Banjoes strum and voices rise like the crimson streaks across the sky, and the wine flows like wine.

Mrs. O'Reilly is smiling. Unaccustomed to drinking, a prohibitionist at heart, except this once; she's on her third glass of wine. Luigi dances with Anita's aunt, doing a stiff sort of polka that resembles jumping up and down in one spot to the music. Livia's friends mingle, dancing with everyone, their contagious enthusiasm stirring up hidden rustlings in ordinary hearts and coaxing joyous dancing out of the most conservative legs.

Livia is dressed in red, wearing bright necklaces and scarves like her younger twirling sisters. She directs the show, motioning to one musician or another, sending one person off to dance with another. She starts up a dance line, all hands joining, and the beginners quickly learn the steps, absorbing confidence from the wine and the Roma's easy movements. When the folk-dance ends there is a natural pause, an ease, and glasses are refilled with sangria and people stop to catch their breath.

Zenora, the youngest and prettiest of the Romas comes to the center court to dance. She dances by herself, to a tambourine. She begins slowly, provocatively, until she has everyone's attention. She twirls, and snaps her castanets, clicking her heels in intricate coquettish steps. Her neck is arched, and she tosses her long black hair in dramatic snaps, and all the while her dark eyes flash like a true enchantress. When she finishes everyone applauds. Livia beckons to Giovanni. She wants him to sing a *conzone* for the bride and groom, slow she tells him, because of Mario's limping. She hands him a guitar case but he says he has his own. No, she says, use this one. He opens the case. It's a beautiful classical guitar with intricate inlaid wood patterns of gold and red swirls and its stem is the carved head of a woman.

He takes the guitar out of its case. Livia watches as he starts tuning the strings, and she looks at his hands, his fingers. "I know," Giovanni says. "I don't have the calluses for it now. I can't play very long." She takes a flat round jar out of her pocket and hands it to him, telling him to rub it on his fingers. It's a wet powdery substance, like slightly moist corn starch, which vanishes as he rubs it into his hands.

"Ground roots," Livia says

He leaves Livia on the sideline and walks over to Mario and Anita and tells them he wants to play something for them, something slow, so they can dance if they like. Mario looks tired and admits he has a sore hip. He has been dancing but the pain is pretty bad. Anita is his doctor now and they will sit this one out and just listen.

Giovanni climbs up on the stone ledge by the lakeshore, above the circular stone terrace where Anita and Mario are sitting. He plays an old Spanish melody, a beautiful song he's sure everyone will like. It begins quietly, the magic of the music drifts through the crowd, and one by one they come over to listen, until everyone has come and formed an audience. Giovanni plays for the bride and groom, and the last rays of the sun leave the day and night falls with Giovanni as its accompanist.

After the applause, even by Charles, the party disperses into segments of small groups talking and drinking, and the tambourines begin again. Giovanni pulls Pascal up onto the ledge with him. Further down, Gina climbs the stairs that lead up to the ledge and walks along the ledge to Giovanni. She has a bottle of wine and settles down by Giovanni and Pascal. She refills his glass and her own. Pascal sits calmly, resigned and tired. They sit silently sipping wine. She sees Charles turn away from her to talk to Natasha, who's talking to Anita. Charles joins the two redheads. Mario is talking to his Mother. He's smoking his pipe.

"I feel invisible, sitting up here watching everything," Gina says.

"Gina, let's leave tonight," Giovanni says.

"You know I can't," she says sadly as she stares out over the dark lake.

"I meant it when I said I don't give up," he says, and slides down from the ledge. He helps Pascal climb down and lets him run off to Luigi. Gina hands down the guitar and the wine glasses and as he helps her down, he realizes she's had too much to drink. He takes her arm but she doesn't want to move.

"I'll stay here a while," she says. He leaves to return the guitar to Livia. A few of the Roma have started singing a Bohemian melody, slow and soft in a minor key. Gina stands in a stupor staring out at nothing. Mario walks over to where she's now leaning against the rock wall.

"One last dance," he says, putting his arms on her shoulders. "I can't," she says. "I hurt my foot."

"I know," Mario answers. "I hurt my hip." And his eyes are smiling. They start to dance to the music, though they barely move, only to get nearer one another, until they're simply standing there in each other's arms. "It's not so bad, with enough wine," Gina says. "Me too," Mario says absently, resting his mouth on her hair, they seem to be holding each other up.

Giovanni returns and moves them apart, a hand on the shoulder of each. Giovanni's not really angry; he keeps his hands resting on their shoulders, looking at them, both helpless and a bit drunk and basically innocent, he decides. Then suddenly, he slaps Mario on the back. "You might've made a good gypsy, Mario," he tells him. "*Arrivederci*," he says, and walks off to his car and drives off into the night like a streak of lightning.

Mario and Gina are unaware that Charles and Anita are headed their way, soon to whisk them off to the next phases of their lives. Gina is soon in bed, trying to keep her eyes open, thanking Charles, though she's not sure for what. For getting her to bed, for letting her say her goodbyes to Mario and Giovanni, or just for being Charles. Before she falls asleep, she sits up abruptly, like a dying person with one last comment to make. "Why were you named Charles?" she asks. All the other brothers have Italian names.

"I looked like a Charles. My mother said I had a big English head, and my father agreed that I should have the name of a king." Charles hums as he carefully hangs up his tuxedo on its hanger, ready to be returned in the morning. Half talking to himself, he tells Gina that Natasha will never make it to America, too Russian. Russian to the core. She'll also never give up her vodka, that's his prediction.

"Very pretty though," Gina says, before she falls asleep.

"Great hair," Charles says, "but you're prettier; you're the beauty." Gina sleeps through his compliment.

CB

Back at the beach house.

Reluctantly, Charles had agreed to fly home without Gina, after arranging her flight for the following week. She simply refused to leave, insisting on a need to finish the collages and see to their packing. He gave in.

She's wearing her ring, set like the old one, but with the sparkling diamond from Giovanni.

She and Rosa have taken up where they left off, shopping together on a daily basis, for tomatoes and other fresh fall vegetables at the outdoor market. Today Gina picked up the rest of the photocopies from the town photo shop, emailed as attachments by Giovanni. Yesterday she picked up the enlargements from the architectural firm that lets her use their blueprint machine. She has been eating well but getting little sleep. Nighttime seems to be her best time to work in the studio. She has a routine down and wishes for more time but is prepared to leave soon and has already picked up the largest size tubular packs from the architect who's been helping her. All of her collages can be rolled neatly and mailed in town before she leaves.

The collages are all of the boat people. There are seven in all and the last two feature the woman from the hotel coffee shop, the one who pointed accusingly at Gina. The portrait is strong and scares Gina. Already she has painted the face many times, in sienna tones, and the last collage is a circle of boat people on a carousel. No animals, just boats on a carousel, crowded boats. She has added seagulls and herons to two of the other collages. One is night, with a golden moon and countless stars.

Before each evening's work, she calls Charles and they talk. Each of the boys has something to say before they leave for school. The timing of the call works out just right. Chris is now a vegetarian, Mondays through Thursdays. Danny is on the fence. They're all excited about the rabbit family living under the bushes in the front yard. Always something new to tell.

After finishing her collage work each evening, she calls Giovanni, who doesn't mind being woken at odd hours. Often, he's still up working on his fresco project in Florence. He tells her she would love fresco work. She can paint and she can draw, so she would be a natural. He wants her to co-teach with him in the coming winter. She lets herself dream, all the while preparing to fly home. Her artist self, her dream self, her spirit self, knows she belongs with Giovanni. He tells her he mailed a set of good quality colored pencils to Danny. Thirty-six colors, plus gold and copper.

CR

One more day. Giovanni is coming for one last day. She has finished all of the collages, though they haven't been rolled up for packing. She wants him to see them first. And she'll surprise him with the large yellow oil she did for him, inspired by the field of wheat they saw on their first drive in the country.

This morning she arranged flowers for the table on the deck, and now has three cookbooks open on the kitchen counter. She's cooking her best recipes and the aromas are already inviting, although she has an hour or so before she expects Giovanni to drive in. Even though it's fall, she's playing Stravinsky's *Rite of Spring*, turned up high. The house is loud and full of energy and excitement. She's happy and bursting with joy.

The music fills her with hope, and she dances around in the kitchen, taking off her apron and testing the artichoke dip. But something stops her in her tracks. She shudders of a sudden. What can it be? Something is wrong. But no, it's just the music, so loud and expectant. No. Something is wrong. She steps outside to the deck and looks out over the sea, something inside of her crying out no, no, no.

That's when she hears the siren. Trembling, she walks to the front and looks up the hill. Nothing. The siren has stopped at the top of the hill.

Rinaldo comes to the door and tells Gina. Not long afterwards Rosa comes to the house. She doesn't remember anything beyond that. Giovanni is dead. Giovanni is dead. They told her. The Ferrari went over the cliff, at the crest where it curves, where Rinaldo's goats sometimes get out, like they did today. He was going too fast.

Rosa has been helpful. Making calls, to his sister in California, the local authorities, even to Charles. She made the call to Natasha herself. Everyone is stunned. By the time it turned dark, Rosa had moved in for the night. They were both picking at the meal Gina had prepared for Giovanni's return. She was glad Rosa was staying the night and doesn't know what she might have been capable of, had she been alone. Still, after Rosa was asleep, she headed down to the beach and made a fire. She kept feeding the fire all night, just sitting there communing with the fire, the sea and the stars above. It was a clear night. She wanted some of the starlight from this place to stay in the diamond of her ring.

In the morning she went through the motions of living. She packed her collages and Rosa took them to the post office for mailing. She cleaned the house which was already clean. She sat on the rug that used to have the blood from Giovanni and Mario's fight, and cried. Charles called. He would be there by early evening.

At lunch, she ate tomatoes with basil and cheese with Rosa. Rosa kept talking about the kitten, which she had given to her after the wedding. Rosa calls it Luca now and says it sits in the deep window ledge with the geraniums and watches her cook. It climbs up the curtains to get to the window ledge. She says Rinaldo likes Luca too, and he brought the kitten a fish head. Gina starts to cry again, quietly, mopping the tears, eating bites of tomato.

She takes a nap in the afternoon and when she awakes takes her sketchbook to the beach. She sits on the beach drawing nothing.

"Oh, you're here already?" Charles sits down on the log beside her, takes her hand and says he's sorry, so sorry.

"You got your ring back," Charles says. "It's shined up. Seems brighter now."

She can't even talk. Just shakes her head, and he holds her. The sun is warm. They start up the path, past the rosemary, for the last time. He suggests a drive into town for gelato. He's thinking pistachio, he tells her.

"And you?" he asks.

After a long pause, "chocolate."

He takes her hand. "It'll be all right. We'll be fine," he says

She knows it's true. Oh this eternal world of love, madness and ice cream. Her heart is wide open. It's time to go home.

Part Three

Gold

TEN YEARS LATER—Dan is packing for his first year at Colorado College; Chris and Gina are in the kitchen making pizza; and Gabriel is playing the guitar in his room. Charles is at work, now abbreviated to three mornings a week, giving him more free time for research and golf.

Dan adds a few favorite T-shirts and that's about it. From the back of the drawer, he takes out that old package that has been there forever.

At Gabriel's door, he listens to his brother humming along with the guitar.

"Hey Gabe, something for you." Gabriel sets the guitar aside, and Dan hands him the package.

"What's this?"

"Well, I'd better explain." He sits on the bed, figuring out how to start. Start right in, that's what his dad always says. "Okay. This came in the mail to me, like ten years ago, from Italy. It's from your dad. When we stayed there once, before you were born, I was watching Mom and Giovanni sketching down on the beach. They were so still, just drawing for a long time. Anyway, I ran and got my drawing book and colored pencils and went down and joined them, so we all sat drawing stuff. I did some shells, and an old oar. Your dad liked my drawing and wanted to look at my colored pencils. Guess he didn't think much of them because he sent this box of fancy German colored pencils. They came in the mail two weeks after he died in the car crash. I put them in the back of my sock drawer and just left them there. Till now anyway. I think you should have them."

Gabriel slides the metal box of colored pencils out of the old wrapper, and peels off the plastic, still intact.

"This came too." Dan hands him an envelope, saying it was in the package, with their mother's name on it but it wasn't sealed so he had opened it. "A photo"—he hands it over. "I never gave it to mom."

Gabriel studies the photo. On the back it reads 'Gina and Giovanni, on the island.' They are sitting on some old steps by a partially exposed mosaic floor.

"He looks like me," Gabe says.

"You look like him," Dan corrects. "Well, I'd better finish packing. See you when the pizza's done."

Gabriel studies the photo. After a time, he adds it to his bulletin board, pinning it next to his favorite galaxy. Then he climbs on his bed with the pencil set and grabs his outer space notebook. What color to start with? He chooses gold.

Acknowledgments

Thank you to my friends and family who have encouraged me with my writing over the years, reading early drafts of stories and poems, and long unruly manuscripts.

Thanks to Tom Driscoll for his know-how, patience, and enthusiasm. And to Wendy Weir, for her gently chiding suggestions and editing, and to Marcia Ragonetti, for much fun working on Italian ways and opera, and to Mary Harrison McConnell, detective with the sharpest eye. Particular thanks to dear friends Jessica Wicken, Pat Krohn, Susan Brienza, and Todd Upton, for reading and support over the years. With a final thanks to the inimitable departed Donald Keats, for telling me in an early draft that there are no cars in Venice. Finally, thank you to Dr. Abbas Khajeaian for the use of a line from the poem SEA, which appears in his collection, *Desiring, Pomegranate*.

About the author

Konnie Ellis is a writer and artist. She is the author of *The Ice Dancer*, *The Dharma of Duluth*, and *The Poet's Daughter*. Her stories have appeared in various magazines and journals, including Lake Superior Magazine; Sojourner; Skylark; Weber Studies – Voices and Visions of the American West; and Lost Lake Folk Opera. She is the recipient of a Norcroft grant, and lives in Duluth, Minnesota with her husband, Robert Ellis, a pianist and composer. Konnie is a graduate of the University of Minnesota, Duluth, and loves living in Minnesota after many years away in Colorado.

www.ingramcontent.com/pod-product-compliance
Lightning Source LLC
Chambersburg PA
CBHW020842260626
47169CB00003B/1095